Welcome to
HOLSOM®
POPULATION: WEIRD

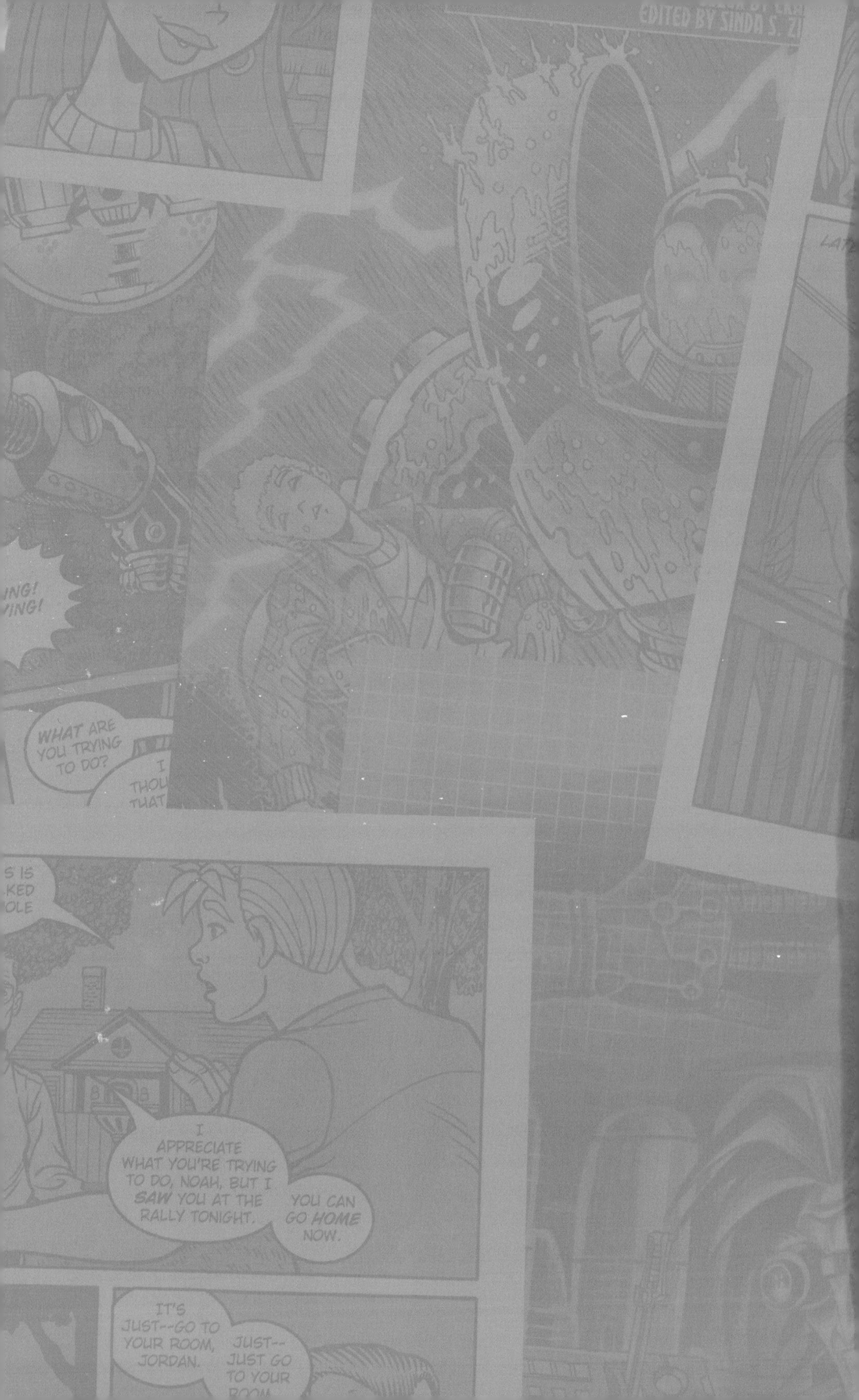
EDITED BY SINDA S.
WHAT ARE YOU TRYING TO DO?
I APPRECIATE WHAT YOU'RE TRYING TO DO, NOAH, BUT I SAW YOU AT THE RALLY TONIGHT.
YOU CAN GO HOME NOW.
IT'S JUST--GO TO YOUR ROOM, JORDAN.
JUST-- JUST GO TO YOUR

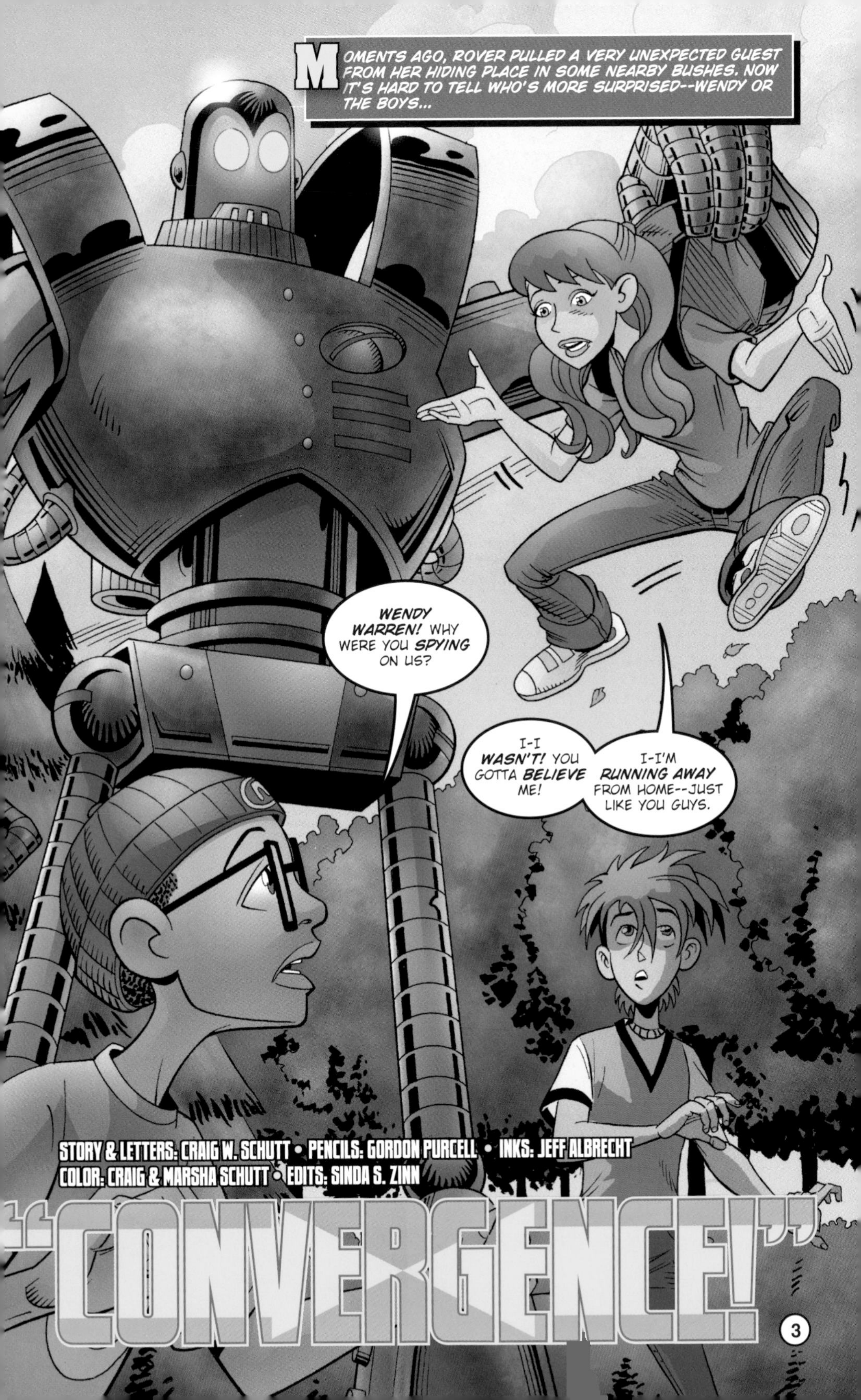
MOMENTS AGO, ROVER PULLED A VERY UNEXPECTED GUEST FROM HER HIDING PLACE IN SOME NEARBY BUSHES. NOW IT'S HARD TO TELL WHO'S MORE SURPRISED--WENDY OR THE BOYS...
WENDY WARREN! WHY WERE YOU SPYING ON US?
I-I WASN'T! YOU GOTTA BELIEVE ME!
I-I'M RUNNING AWAY FROM HOME--JUST LIKE YOU GUYS.
STORY & LETTERS: CRAIG W. SCHUTT • PENCILS: GORDON PURCELL • INKS: JEFF ALBRECHT
COLOR: CRAIG & MARSHA SCHUTT • EDITS: SINDA S. ZINN
"CONVERGENCE!"

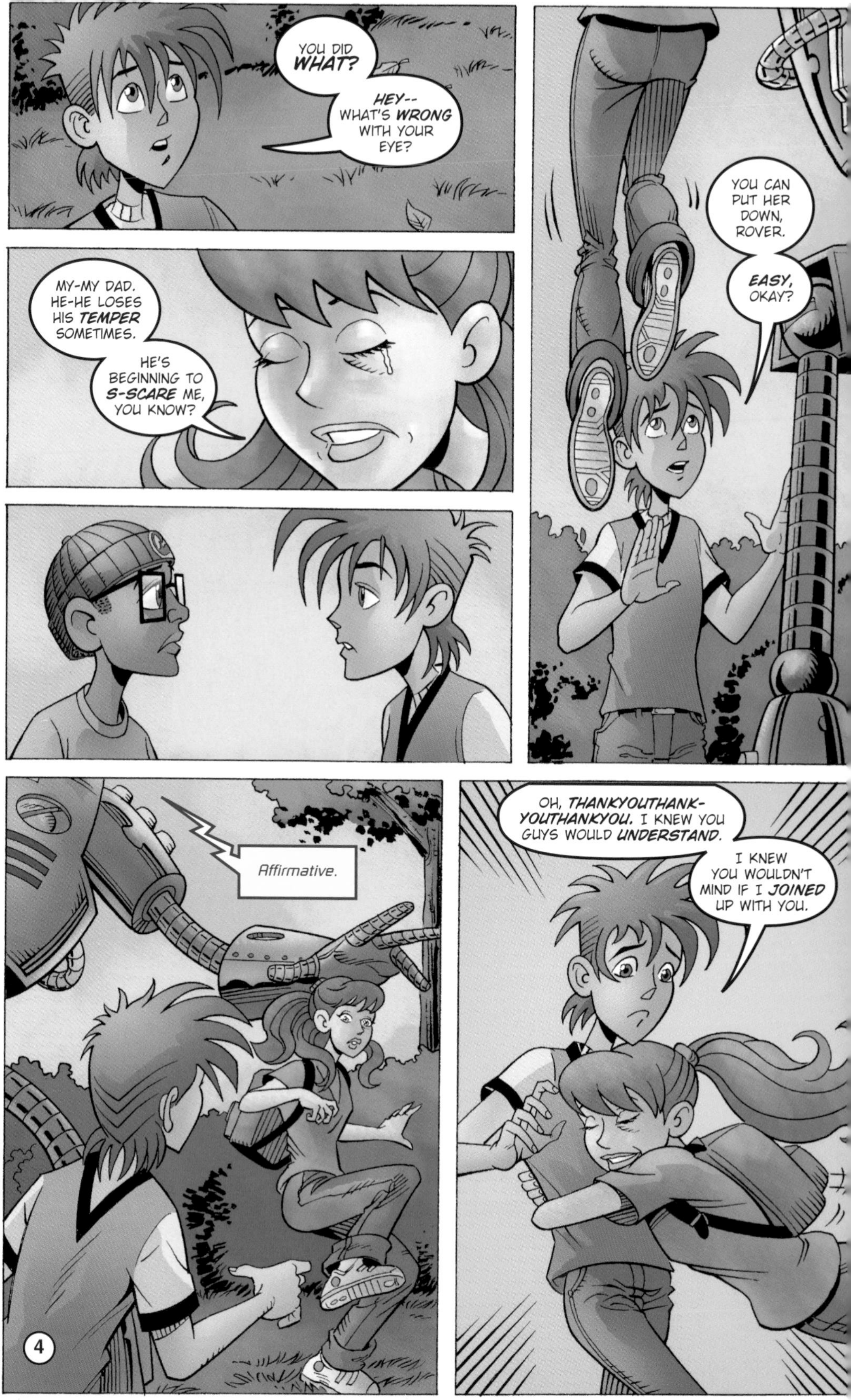
YOU DID WHAT?
HEY-- WHAT'S WRONG WITH YOUR EYE?
MY-MY DAD. HE-HE LOSES HIS TEMPER SOMETIMES.
HE'S BEGINNING TO S-SCARE ME, YOU KNOW?
YOU CAN PUT HER DOWN, ROVER.
EASY, OKAY?
Affirmative.
OH, THANKYOUTHANK-YOUTHANKYOU. I KNEW YOU GUYS WOULD UNDERSTAND.
I KNEW YOU WOULDN'T MIND IF I JOINED UP WITH YOU.

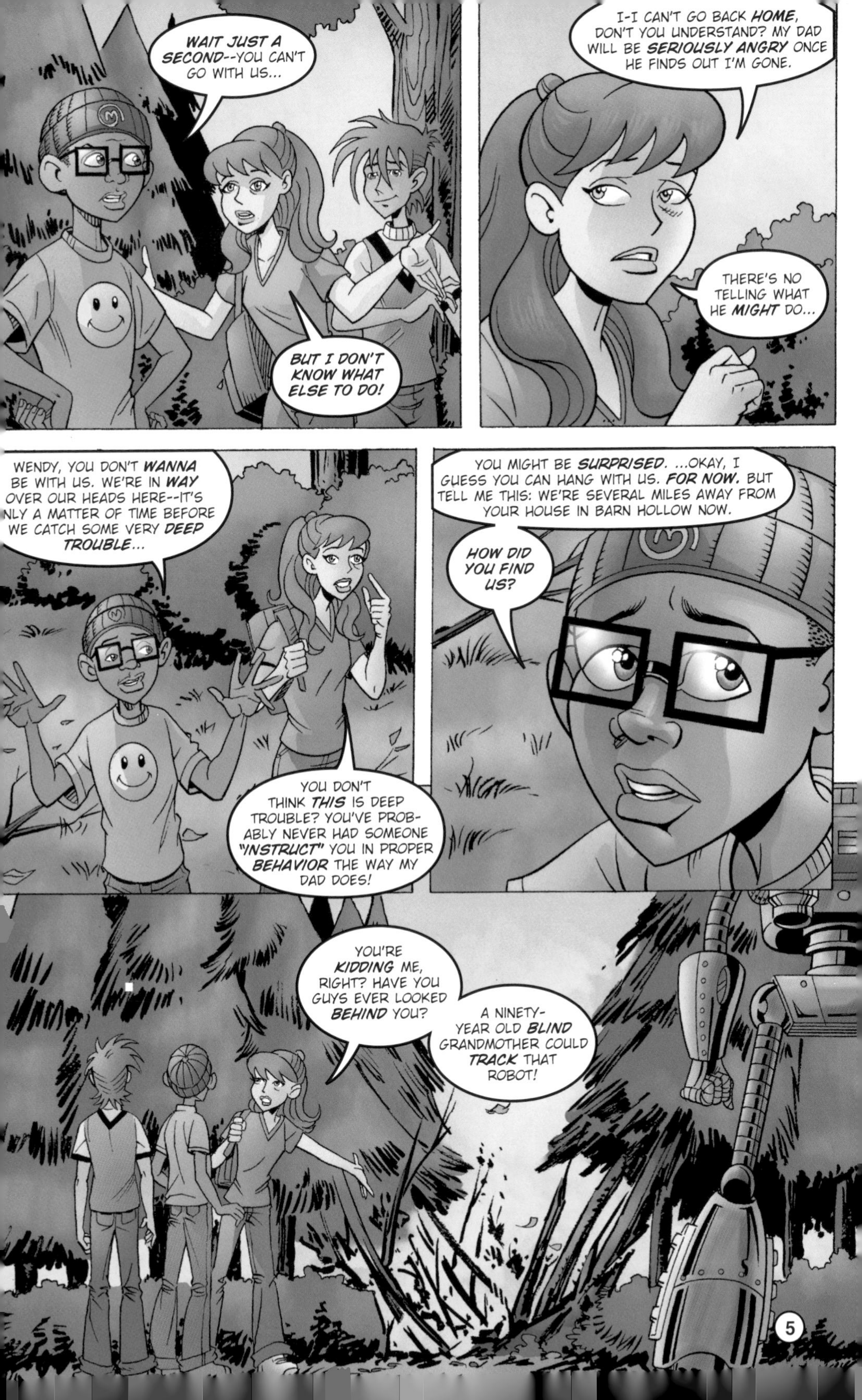
WAIT JUST A SECOND--YOU CAN'T GO WITH US...
BUT I DON'T KNOW WHAT ELSE TO DO!
I-I CAN'T GO BACK HOME, DON'T YOU UNDERSTAND? MY DAD WILL BE SERIOUSLY ANGRY ONCE HE FINDS OUT I'M GONE.
THERE'S NO TELLING WHAT HE MIGHT DO...
WENDY, YOU DON'T WANNA BE WITH US. WE'RE IN WAY OVER OUR HEADS HERE--IT'S NLY A MATTER OF TIME BEFORE WE CATCH SOME VERY DEEP TROUBLE...
YOU DON'T THINK THIS IS DEEP TROUBLE? YOU'VE PROBABLY NEVER HAD SOMEONE "INSTRUCT" YOU IN PROPER BEHAVIOR THE WAY MY DAD DOES!
YOU MIGHT BE SURPRISED. ...OKAY, I GUESS YOU CAN HANG WITH US. FOR NOW. BUT TELL ME THIS: WE'RE SEVERAL MILES AWAY FROM YOUR HOUSE IN BARN HOLLOW NOW.
HOW DID YOU FIND US?
YOU'RE KIDDING ME, RIGHT? HAVE YOU GUYS EVER LOOKED BEHIND YOU?
A NINETY-YEAR OLD BLIND GRANDMOTHER COULD TRACK THAT ROBOT!

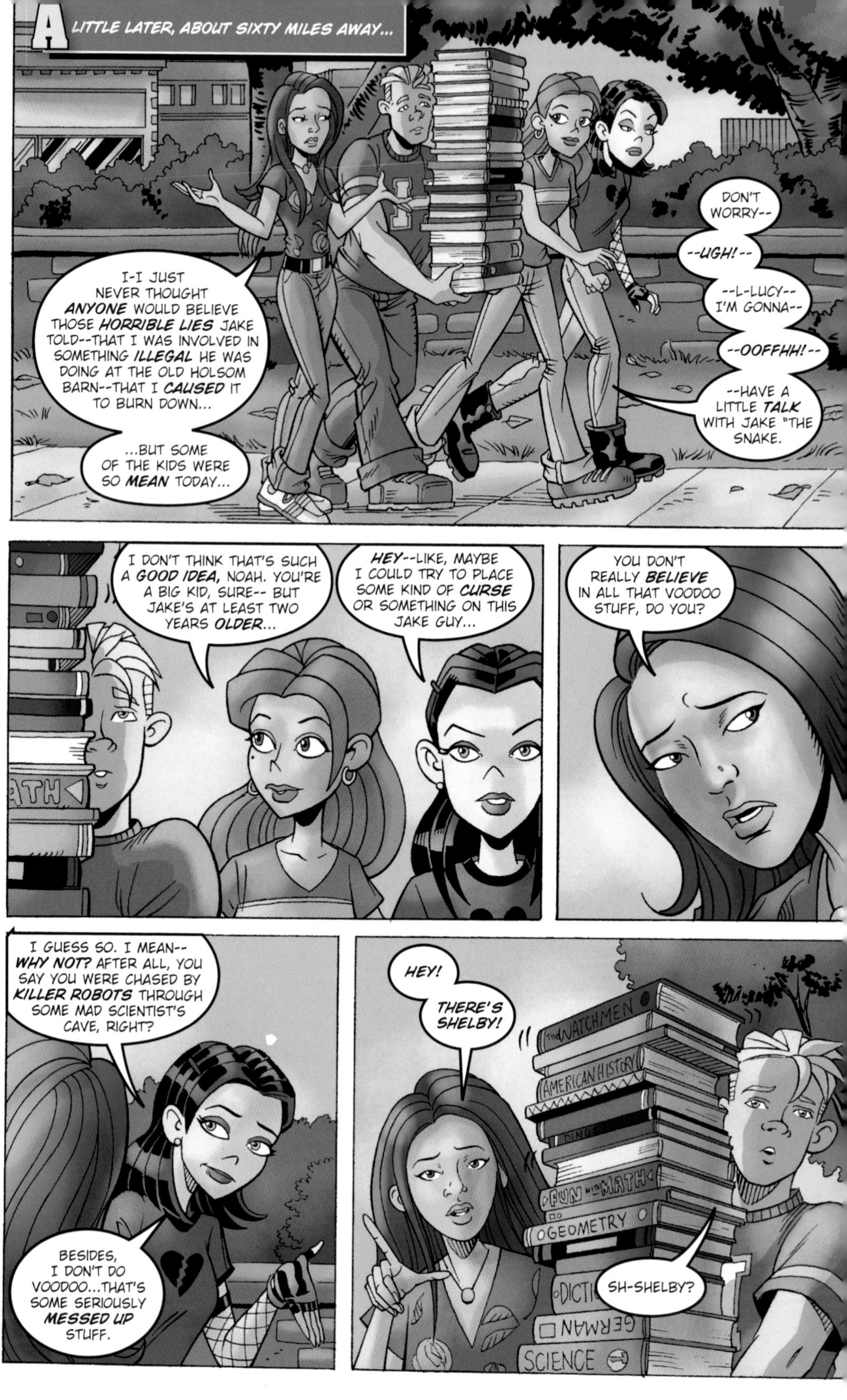
A LITTLE LATER, ABOUT SIXTY MILES AWAY...
I-I JUST NEVER THOUGHT ANYONE WOULD BELIEVE THOSE HORRIBLE LIES JAKE TOLD--THAT I WAS INVOLVED IN SOMETHING ILLEGAL HE WAS DOING AT THE OLD HOLSOM BARN--THAT I CAUSED IT TO BURN DOWN...
...BUT SOME OF THE KIDS WERE SO MEAN TODAY...
DON'T WORRY--
--UGH!--
--L-LUCY-- I'M GONNA--
--OOFFHH!--
--HAVE A LITTLE TALK WITH JAKE "THE SNAKE.
I DON'T THINK THAT'S SUCH A GOOD IDEA, NOAH. YOU'RE A BIG KID, SURE-- BUT JAKE'S AT LEAST TWO YEARS OLDER...
HEY--LIKE, MAYBE I COULD TRY TO PLACE SOME KIND OF CURSE OR SOMETHING ON THIS JAKE GUY...
YOU DON'T REALLY BELIEVE IN ALL THAT VOODOO STUFF, DO YOU?
I GUESS SO. I MEAN-- WHY NOT? AFTER ALL, YOU SAY YOU WERE CHASED BY KILLER ROBOTS THROUGH SOME MAD SCIENTIST'S CAVE, RIGHT?
BESIDES, I DON'T DO VOODOO...THAT'S SOME SERIOUSLY MESSED UP STUFF.
HEY!
THERE'S SHELBY!
SH-SHELBY?

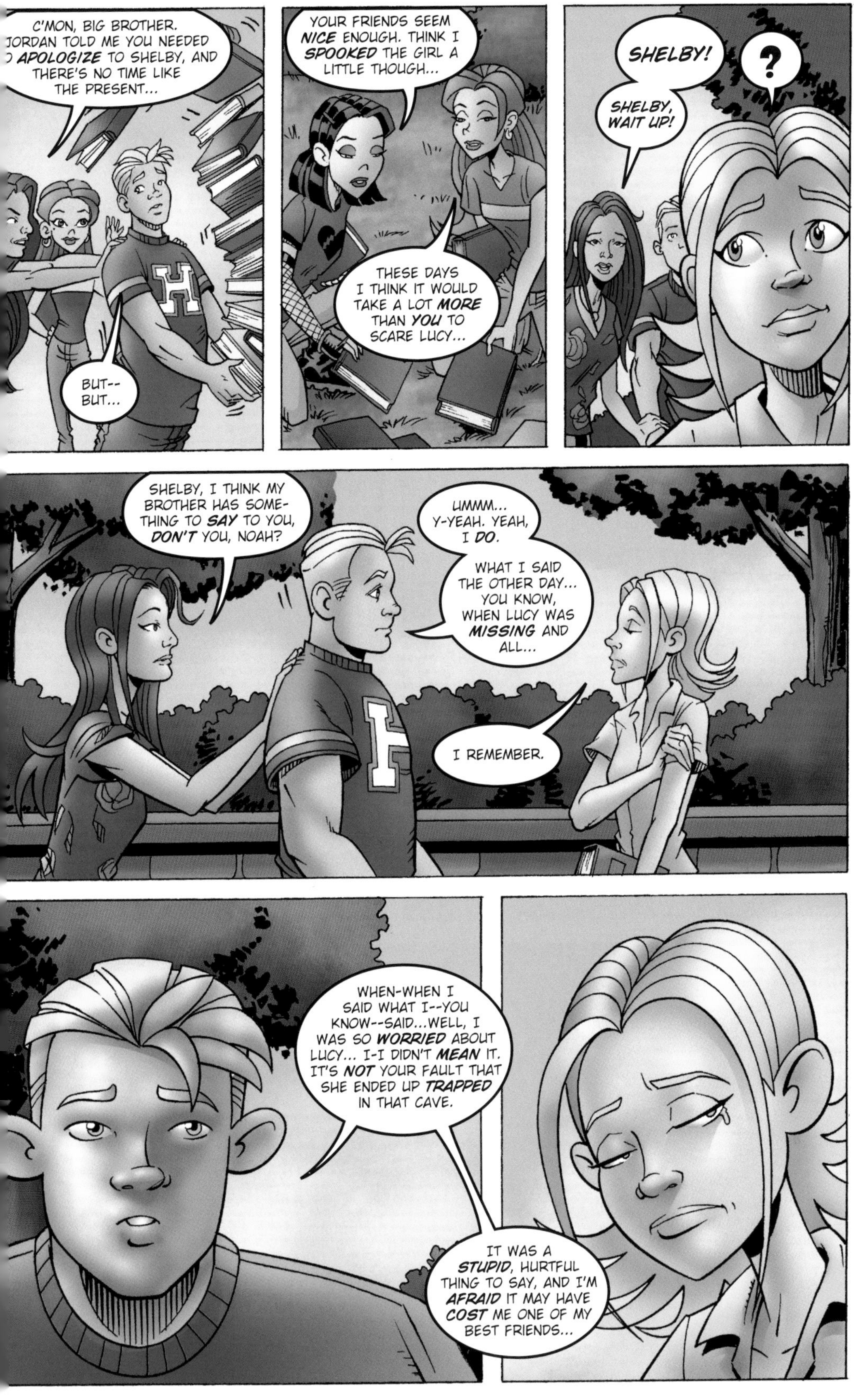
C'MON, BIG BROTHER. JORDAN TOLD ME YOU NEEDED TO APOLOGIZE TO SHELBY, AND THERE'S NO TIME LIKE THE PRESENT...
BUT-- BUT...
YOUR FRIENDS SEEM NICE ENOUGH. THINK I SPOOKED THE GIRL A LITTLE THOUGH...
THESE DAYS I THINK IT WOULD TAKE A LOT MORE THAN YOU TO SCARE LUCY...
SHELBY!
SHELBY, WAIT UP!
?
SHELBY, I THINK MY BROTHER HAS SOMETHING TO SAY TO YOU, DON'T YOU, NOAH?
UMMM... Y-YEAH. YEAH, I DO.
WHAT I SAID THE OTHER DAY... YOU KNOW, WHEN LUCY WAS MISSING AND ALL...
I REMEMBER.
WHEN-WHEN I SAID WHAT I--YOU KNOW--SAID...WELL, I WAS SO WORRIED ABOUT LUCY... I-I DIDN'T MEAN IT. IT'S NOT YOUR FAULT THAT SHE ENDED UP TRAPPED IN THAT CAVE.
IT WAS A STUPID, HURTFUL THING TO SAY, AND I'M AFRAID IT MAY HAVE COST ME ONE OF MY BEST FRIENDS...

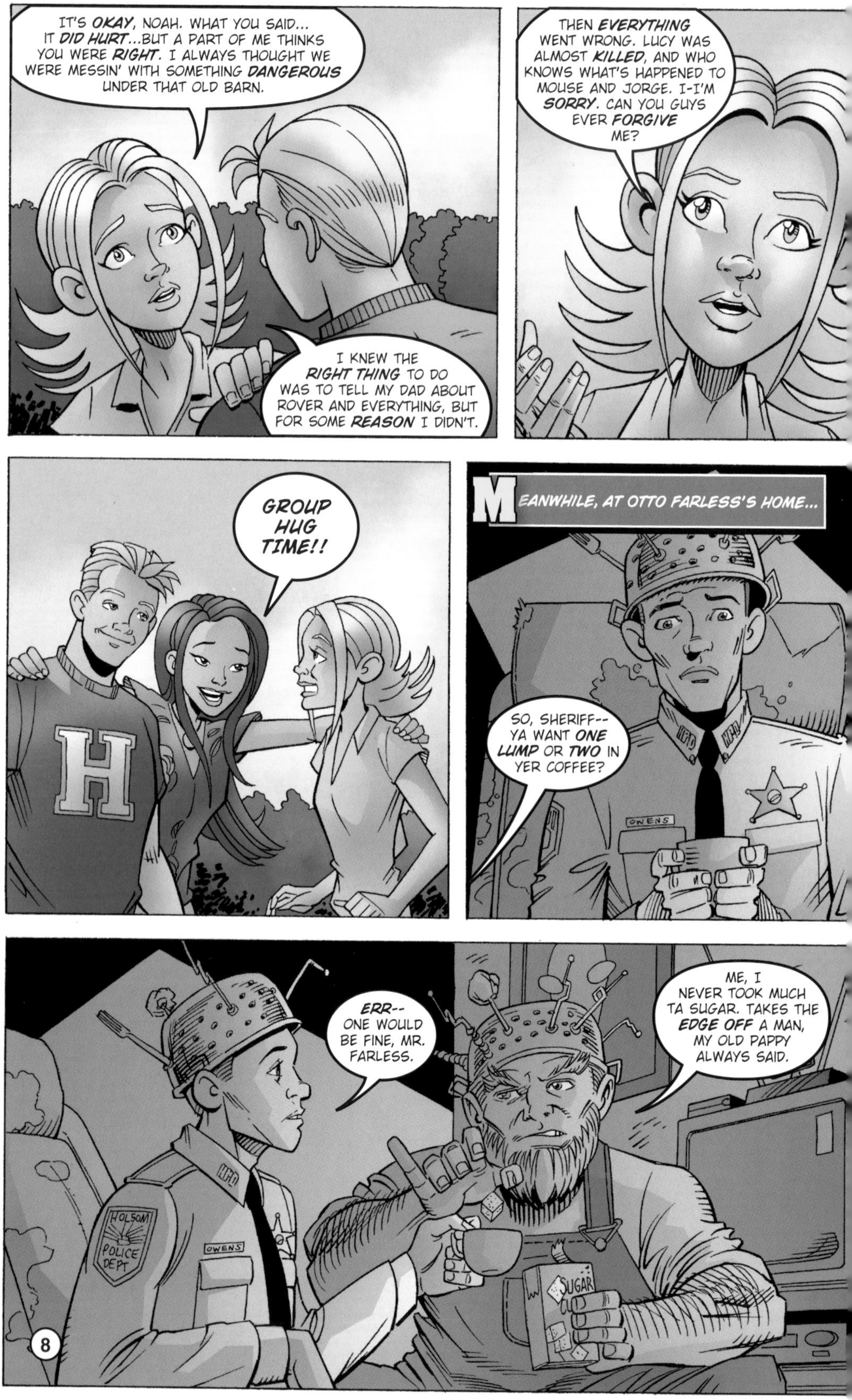
IT'S OKAY, NOAH. WHAT YOU SAID... IT DID HURT...BUT A PART OF ME THINKS YOU WERE RIGHT. I ALWAYS THOUGHT WE WERE MESSIN' WITH SOMETHING DANGEROUS UNDER THAT OLD BARN.
I KNEW THE RIGHT THING TO DO WAS TO TELL MY DAD ABOUT ROVER AND EVERYTHING, BUT FOR SOME REASON I DIDN'T.
THEN EVERYTHING WENT WRONG. LUCY WAS ALMOST KILLED, AND WHO KNOWS WHAT'S HAPPENED TO MOUSE AND JORGE. I-I'M SORRY. CAN YOU GUYS EVER FORGIVE ME?
GROUP HUG TIME!!
MEANWHILE, AT OTTO FARLESS'S HOME...
SO, SHERIFF-- YA WANT ONE LUMP OR TWO IN YER COFFEE?
OWENS
ERR-- ONE WOULD BE FINE, MR. FARLESS.
ME, I NEVER TOOK MUCH TA SUGAR. TAKES THE EDGE OFF A MAN, MY OLD PAPPY ALWAYS SAID.
HOLSOM POLICE DEPT
OWENS
SUGAR

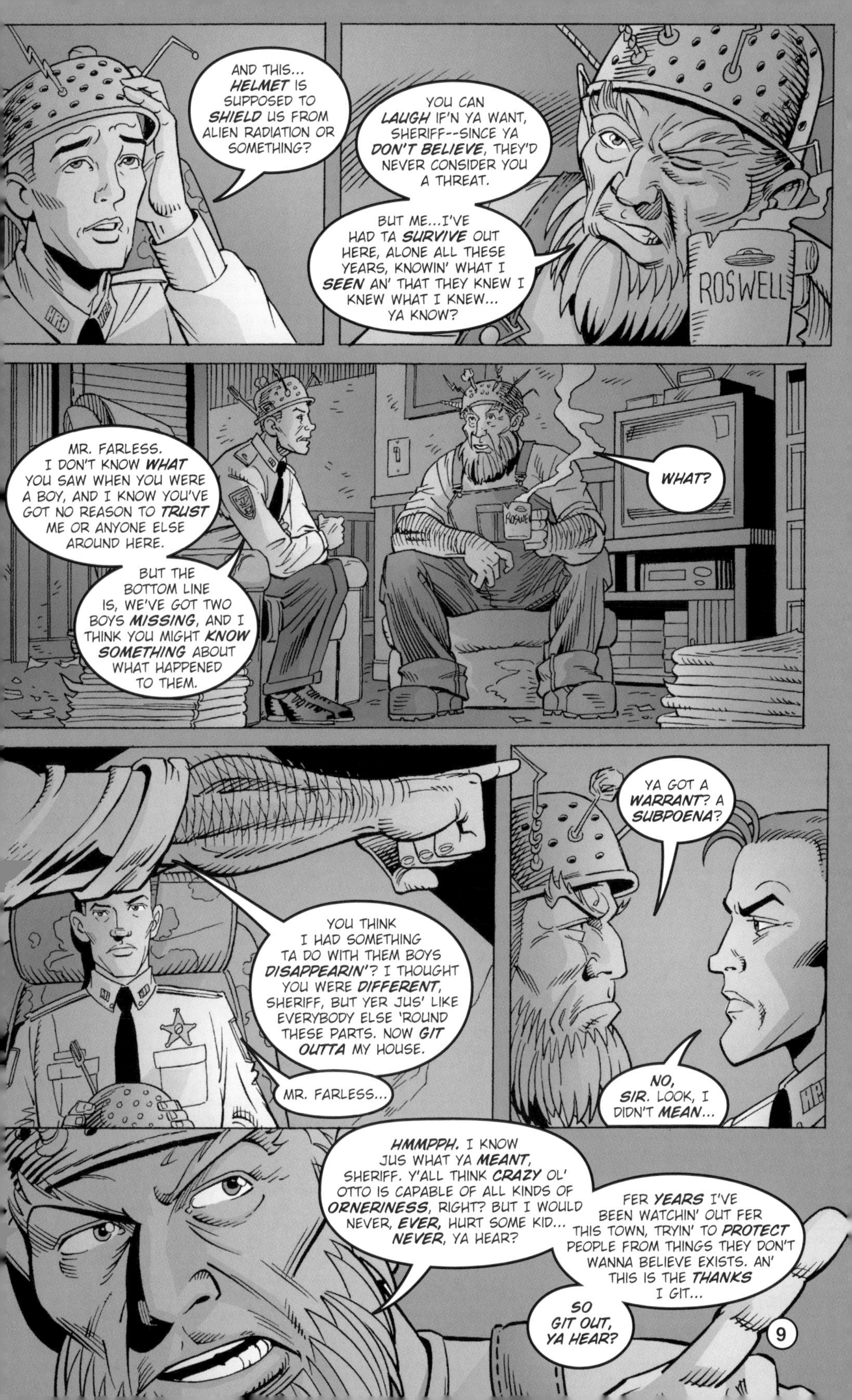
AND THIS... HELMET IS SUPPOSED TO SHIELD US FROM ALIEN RADIATION OR SOMETHING?
YOU CAN LAUGH IF'N YA WANT, SHERIFF--SINCE YA DON'T BELIEVE, THEY'D NEVER CONSIDER YOU A THREAT.
BUT ME...I'VE HAD TA SURVIVE OUT HERE, ALONE ALL THESE YEARS, KNOWIN' WHAT I SEEN AN' THAT THEY KNEW I KNEW WHAT I KNEW... YA KNOW?
ROSWELL
MR. FARLESS. I DON'T KNOW WHAT YOU SAW WHEN YOU WERE A BOY, AND I KNOW YOU'VE GOT NO REASON TO TRUST ME OR ANYONE ELSE AROUND HERE.
BUT THE BOTTOM LINE IS, WE'VE GOT TWO BOYS MISSING, AND I THINK YOU MIGHT KNOW SOMETHING ABOUT WHAT HAPPENED TO THEM.
WHAT?
YOU THINK I HAD SOMETHING TA DO WITH THEM BOYS DISAPPEARIN'? I THOUGHT YOU WERE DIFFERENT, SHERIFF, BUT YER JUS' LIKE EVERYBODY ELSE 'ROUND THESE PARTS. NOW GIT OUTTA MY HOUSE.
MR. FARLESS...
YA GOT A WARRANT? A SUBPOENA?
NO, SIR. LOOK, I DIDN'T MEAN...
HMMPPH. I KNOW JUS WHAT YA MEANT, SHERIFF. Y'ALL THINK CRAZY OL' OTTO IS CAPABLE OF ALL KINDS OF ORNERINESS, RIGHT? BUT I WOULD NEVER, EVER, HURT SOME KID... NEVER, YA HEAR?
FER YEARS I'VE BEEN WATCHIN' OUT FER THIS TOWN, TRYIN' TO PROTECT PEOPLE FROM THINGS THEY DON'T WANNA BELIEVE EXISTS. AN' THIS IS THE THANKS I GIT...
SO GIT OUT, YA HEAR?

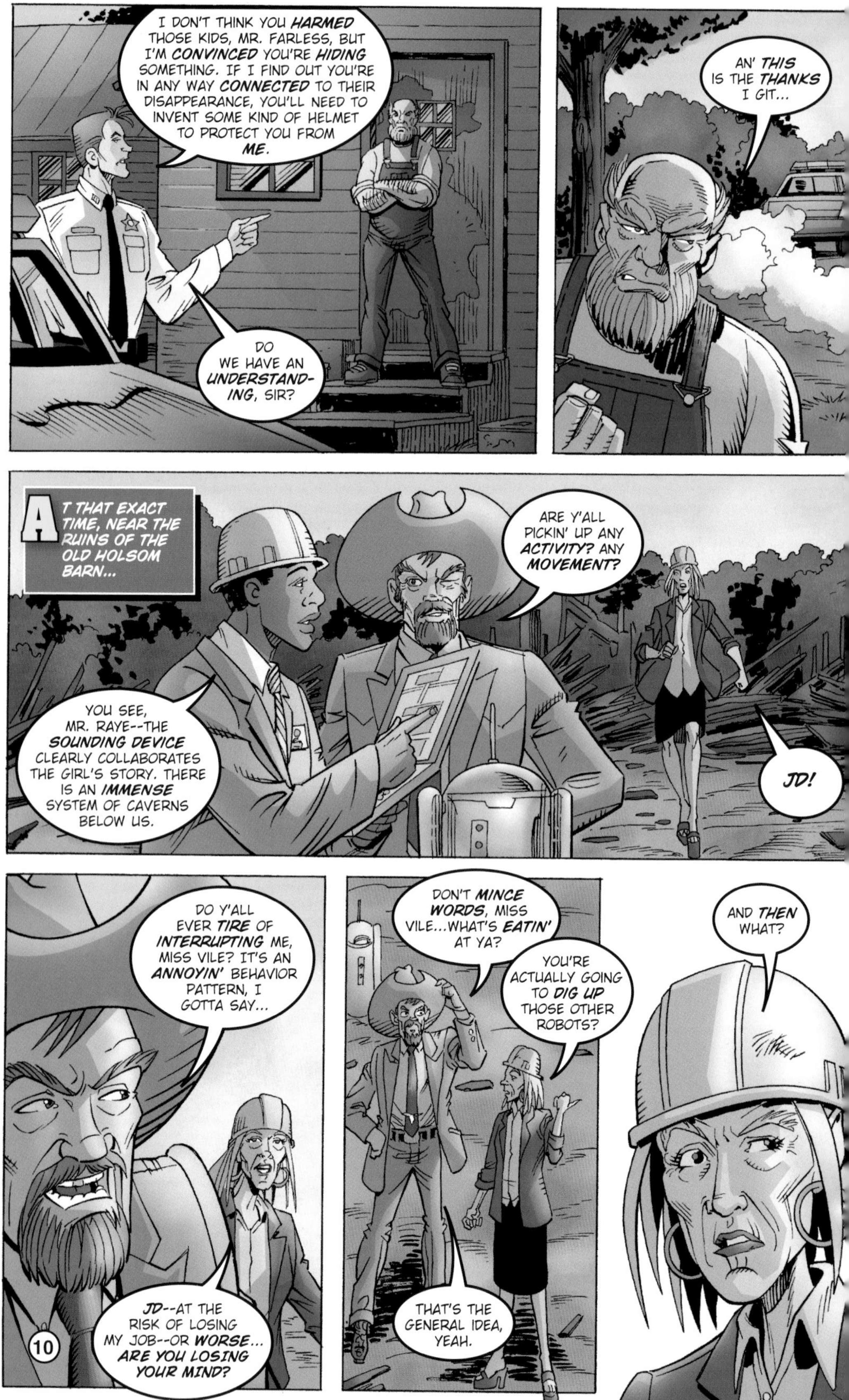
I DON'T THINK YOU HARMED THOSE KIDS, MR. FARLESS, BUT I'M CONVINCED YOU'RE HIDING SOMETHING. IF I FIND OUT YOU'RE IN ANY WAY CONNECTED TO THEIR DISAPPEARANCE, YOU'LL NEED TO INVENT SOME KIND OF HELMET TO PROTECT YOU FROM ME.
DO WE HAVE AN UNDERSTAND-ING, SIR?
AN' THIS IS THE THANKS I GIT...
AT THAT EXACT TIME, NEAR THE RUINS OF THE OLD HOLSOM BARN...
ARE Y'ALL PICKIN' UP ANY ACTIVITY? ANY MOVEMENT?
YOU SEE, MR. RAYE--THE SOUNDING DEVICE CLEARLY COLLABORATES THE GIRL'S STORY. THERE IS AN IMMENSE SYSTEM OF CAVERNS BELOW US.
JD!
DO Y'ALL EVER TIRE OF INTERRUPTING ME, MISS VILE? IT'S AN ANNOYIN' BEHAVIOR PATTERN, I GOTTA SAY...
JD--AT THE RISK OF LOSING MY JOB--OR WORSE... ARE YOU LOSING YOUR MIND?
DON'T MINCE WORDS, MISS VILE...WHAT'S EATIN' AT YA?
YOU'RE ACTUALLY GOING TO DIG UP THOSE OTHER ROBOTS?
THAT'S THE GENERAL IDEA, YEAH.
AND THEN WHAT?

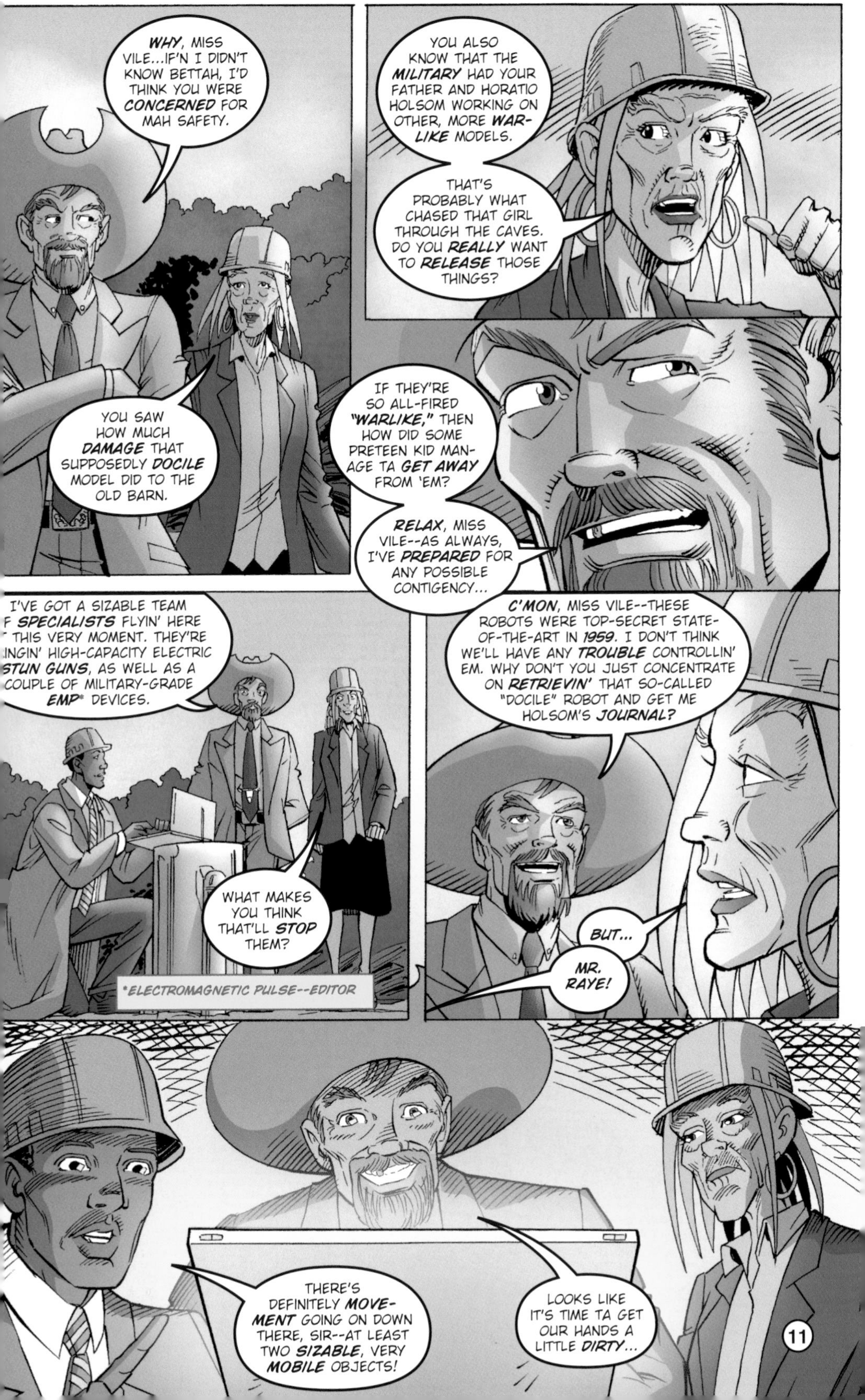
WHY, MISS VILE...IF'N I DIDN'T KNOW BETTAH, I'D THINK YOU WERE CONCERNED FOR MAH SAFETY.
YOU SAW HOW MUCH DAMAGE THAT SUPPOSEDLY DOCILE MODEL DID TO THE OLD BARN.
YOU ALSO KNOW THAT THE MILITARY HAD YOUR FATHER AND HORATIO HOLSOM WORKING ON OTHER, MORE WAR-LIKE MODELS.
THAT'S PROBABLY WHAT CHASED THAT GIRL THROUGH THE CAVES. DO YOU REALLY WANT TO RELEASE THOSE THINGS?
IF THEY'RE SO ALL-FIRED "WARLIKE," THEN HOW DID SOME PRETEEN KID MAN-AGE TA GET AWAY FROM 'EM?
RELAX, MISS VILE--AS ALWAYS, I'VE PREPARED FOR ANY POSSIBLE CONTIGENCY...
I'VE GOT A SIZABLE TEAM F SPECIALISTS FLYIN' HERE THIS VERY MOMENT. THEY'RE INGIN' HIGH-CAPACITY ELECTRIC STUN GUNS, AS WELL AS A COUPLE OF MILITARY-GRADE EMP* DEVICES.
WHAT MAKES YOU THINK THAT'LL STOP THEM?
*ELECTROMAGNETIC PULSE--EDITOR
C'MON, MISS VILE--THESE ROBOTS WERE TOP-SECRET STATE-OF-THE-ART IN 1959. I DON'T THINK WE'LL HAVE ANY TROUBLE CONTROLLIN' EM. WHY DON'T YOU JUST CONCENTRATE ON RETRIEVIN' THAT SO-CALLED "DOCILE" ROBOT AND GET ME HOLSOM'S JOURNAL?
BUT...
MR. RAYE!
THERE'S DEFINITELY MOVE-MENT GOING ON DOWN THERE, SIR--AT LEAST TWO SIZABLE, VERY MOBILE OBJECTS!
LOOKS LIKE IT'S TIME TA GET OUR HANDS A LITTLE DIRTY...

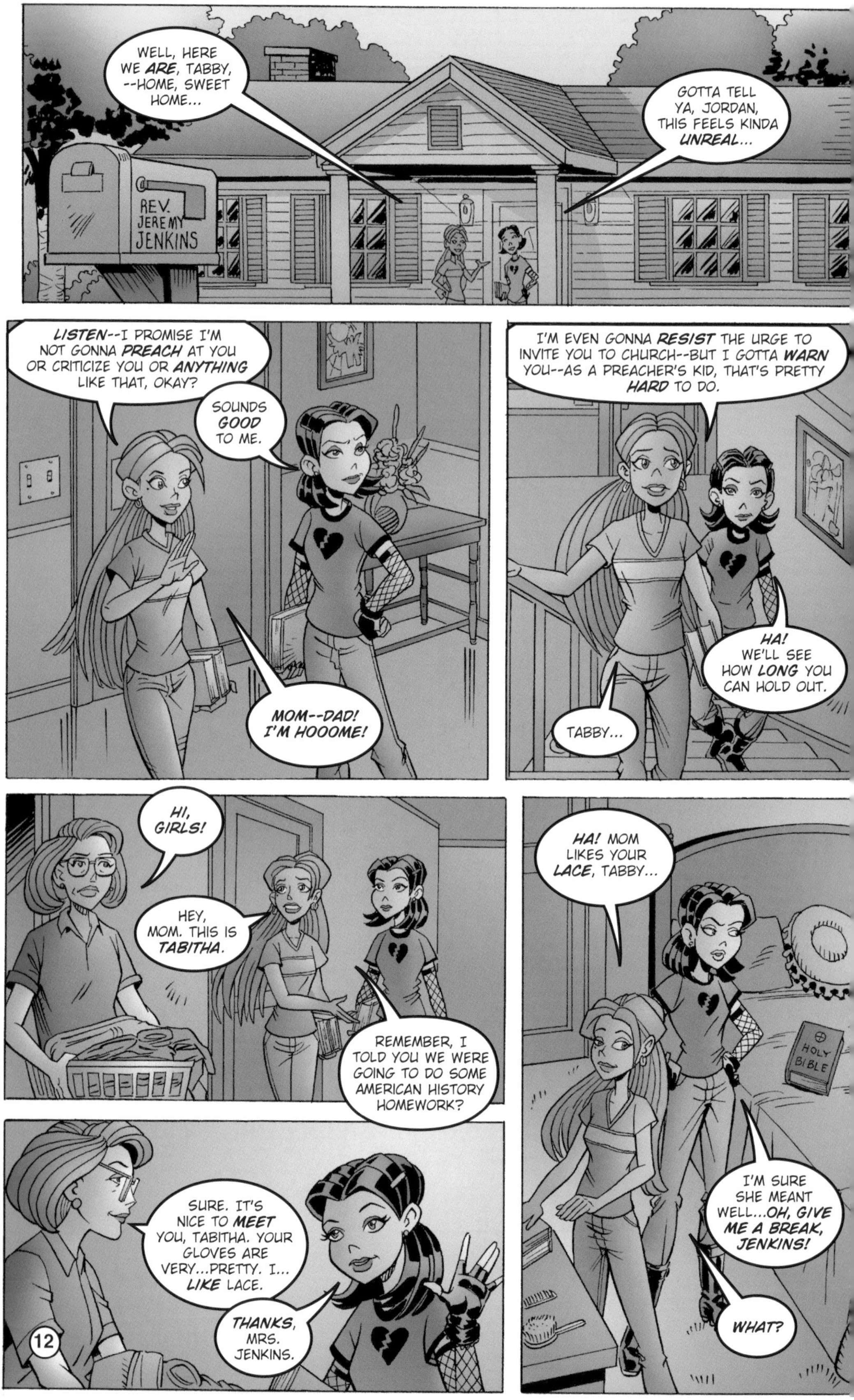
WELL, HERE WE ARE, TABBY, --HOME, SWEET HOME...
GOTTA TELL YA, JORDAN, THIS FEELS KINDA UNREAL...
REV. JEREMY JENKINS
LISTEN--I PROMISE I'M NOT GONNA PREACH AT YOU OR CRITICIZE YOU OR ANYTHING LIKE THAT, OKAY?
SOUNDS GOOD TO ME.
MOM--DAD! I'M HOOOME!
I'M EVEN GONNA RESIST THE URGE TO INVITE YOU TO CHURCH--BUT I GOTTA WARN YOU--AS A PREACHER'S KID, THAT'S PRETTY HARD TO DO.
HA! WE'LL SEE HOW LONG YOU CAN HOLD OUT.
TABBY...
HI, GIRLS!
HEY, MOM. THIS IS TABITHA.
REMEMBER, I TOLD YOU WE WERE GOING TO DO SOME AMERICAN HISTORY HOMEWORK?
SURE. IT'S NICE TO MEET YOU, TABITHA. YOUR GLOVES ARE VERY...PRETTY. I... LIKE LACE.
THANKS, MRS. JENKINS.
HA! MOM LIKES YOUR LACE, TABBY...
HOLY BIBLE
I'M SURE SHE MEANT WELL...OH, GIVE ME A BREAK, JENKINS!
WHAT?

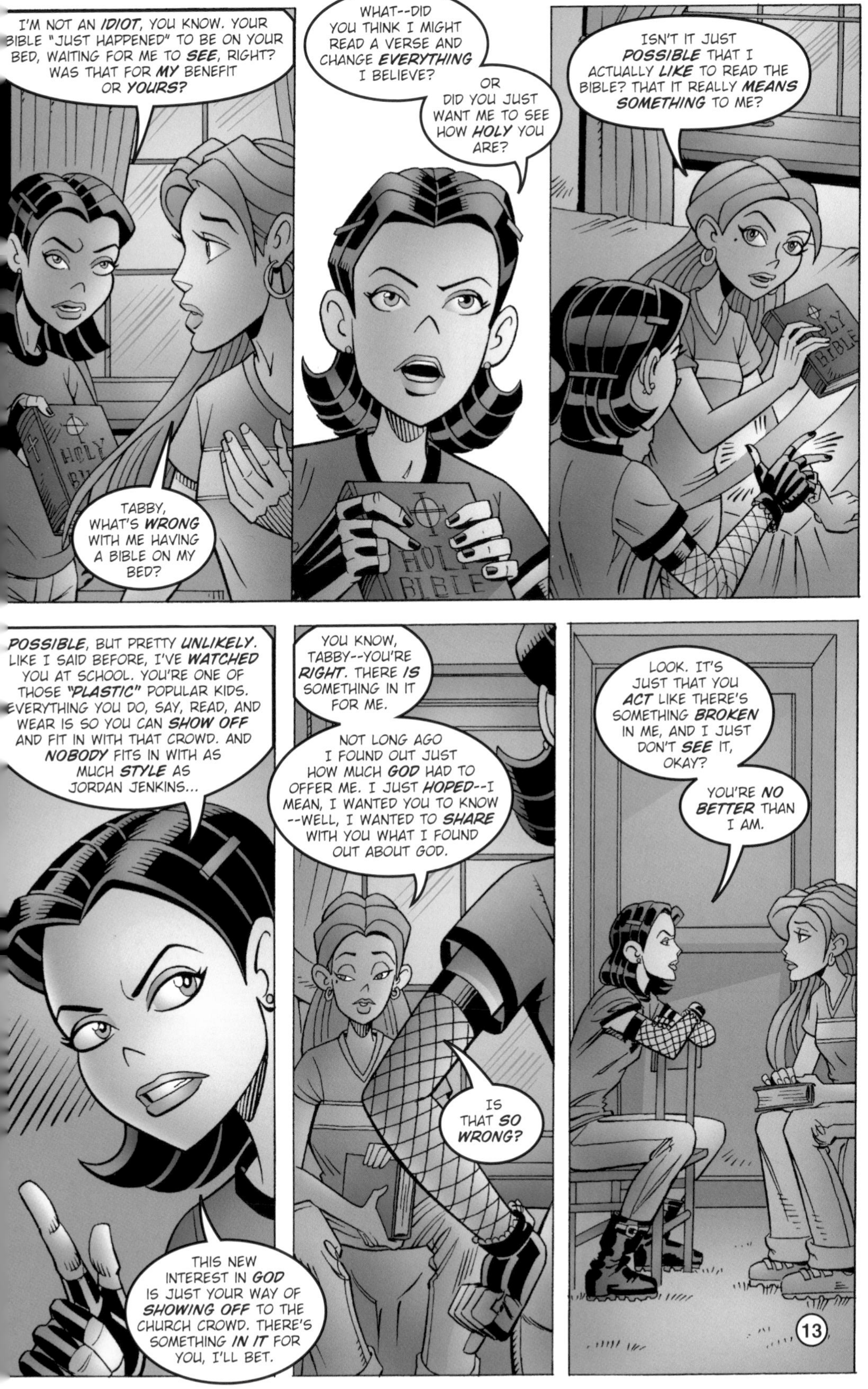
I'M NOT AN IDIOT, YOU KNOW. YOUR BIBLE "JUST HAPPENED" TO BE ON YOUR BED, WAITING FOR ME TO SEE, RIGHT? WAS THAT FOR MY BENEFIT OR YOURS?
TABBY, WHAT'S WRONG WITH ME HAVING A BIBLE ON MY BED?
WHAT--DID YOU THINK I MIGHT READ A VERSE AND CHANGE EVERYTHING I BELIEVE?
OR DID YOU JUST WANT ME TO SEE HOW HOLY YOU ARE?
ISN'T IT JUST POSSIBLE THAT I ACTUALLY LIKE TO READ THE BIBLE? THAT IT REALLY MEANS SOMETHING TO ME?
POSSIBLE, BUT PRETTY UNLIKELY. LIKE I SAID BEFORE, I'VE WATCHED YOU AT SCHOOL. YOU'RE ONE OF THOSE "PLASTIC" POPULAR KIDS. EVERYTHING YOU DO, SAY, READ, AND WEAR IS SO YOU CAN SHOW OFF AND FIT IN WITH THAT CROWD. AND NOBODY FITS IN WITH AS MUCH STYLE AS JORDAN JENKINS...
THIS NEW INTEREST IN GOD IS JUST YOUR WAY OF SHOWING OFF TO THE CHURCH CROWD. THERE'S SOMETHING IN IT FOR YOU, I'LL BET.
YOU KNOW, TABBY--YOU'RE RIGHT. THERE IS SOMETHING IN IT FOR ME.
NOT LONG AGO I FOUND OUT JUST HOW MUCH GOD HAD TO OFFER ME. I JUST HOPED--I MEAN, I WANTED YOU TO KNOW --WELL, I WANTED TO SHARE WITH YOU WHAT I FOUND OUT ABOUT GOD.
IS THAT SO WRONG?
LOOK. IT'S JUST THAT YOU ACT LIKE THERE'S SOMETHING BROKEN IN ME, AND I JUST DON'T SEE IT, OKAY?
YOU'RE NO BETTER THAN I AM.

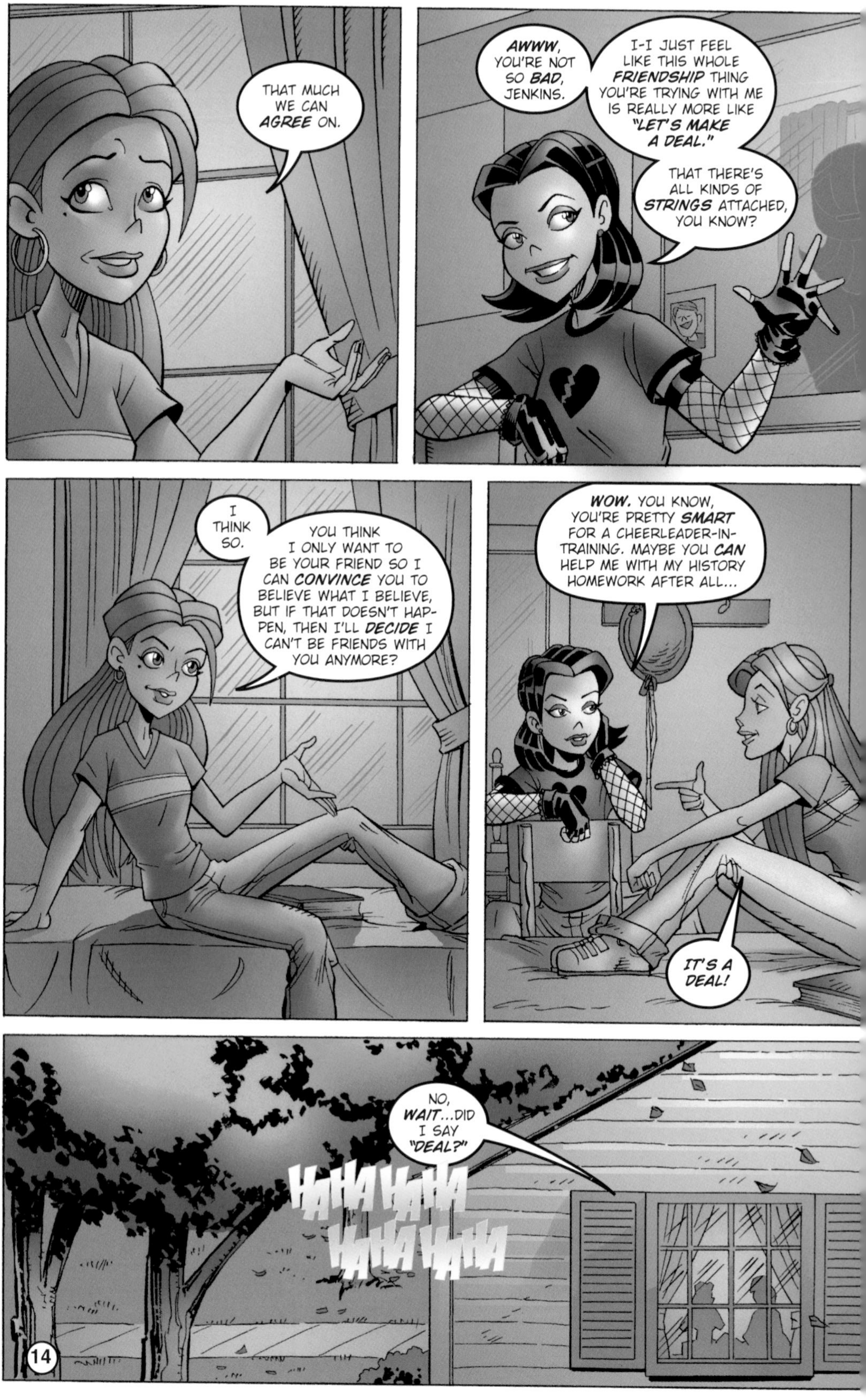
THAT MUCH WE CAN AGREE ON.
AWWW, YOU'RE NOT SO BAD, JENKINS.
I-I JUST FEEL LIKE THIS WHOLE FRIENDSHIP THING YOU'RE TRYING WITH ME IS REALLY MORE LIKE "LET'S MAKE A DEAL."
THAT THERE'S ALL KINDS OF STRINGS ATTACHED, YOU KNOW?
I THINK SO.
YOU THINK I ONLY WANT TO BE YOUR FRIEND SO I CAN CONVINCE YOU TO BELIEVE WHAT I BELIEVE, BUT IF THAT DOESN'T HAP-PEN, THEN I'LL DECIDE I CAN'T BE FRIENDS WITH YOU ANYMORE?
WOW. YOU KNOW, YOU'RE PRETTY SMART FOR A CHEERLEADER-IN-TRAINING. MAYBE YOU CAN HELP ME WITH MY HISTORY HOMEWORK AFTER ALL...
IT'S A DEAL!
NO, WAIT...DID I SAY "DEAL?"
HAHA HAHA HAHA HAHA

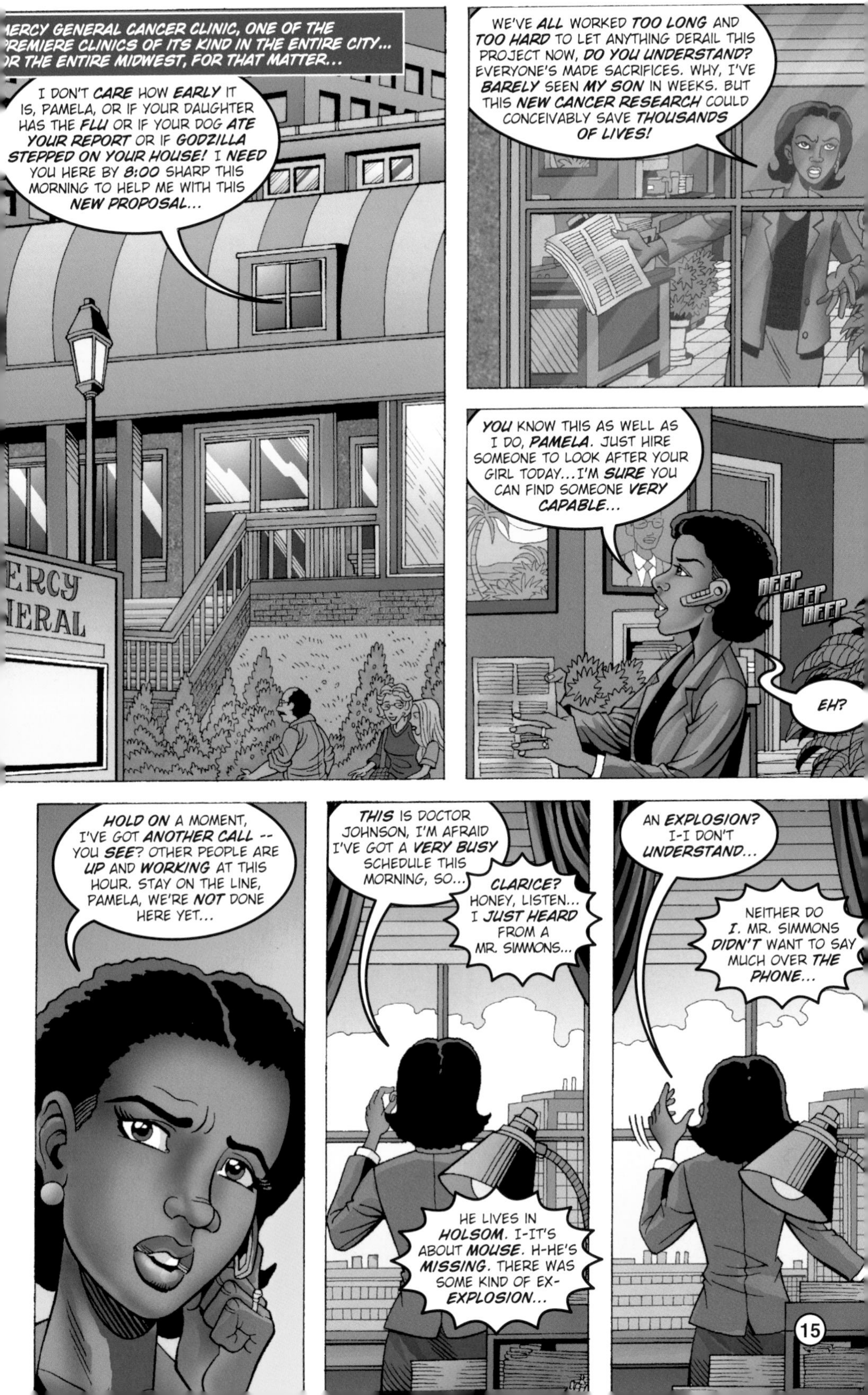
ERCY GENERAL CANCER CLINIC, ONE OF THE PREMIERE CLINICS OF ITS KIND IN THE ENTIRE CITY... R THE ENTIRE MIDWEST, FOR THAT MATTER...
I DON'T CARE HOW EARLY IT IS, PAMELA, OR IF YOUR DAUGHTER HAS THE FLU OR IF YOUR DOG ATE YOUR REPORT OR IF GODZILLA STEPPED ON YOUR HOUSE! I NEED YOU HERE BY 8:00 SHARP THIS MORNING TO HELP ME WITH THIS NEW PROPOSAL...
ERCY
IERAL
WE'VE ALL WORKED TOO LONG AND TOO HARD TO LET ANYTHING DERAIL THIS PROJECT NOW, DO YOU UNDERSTAND? EVERYONE'S MADE SACRIFICES. WHY, I'VE BARELY SEEN MY SON IN WEEKS. BUT THIS NEW CANCER RESEARCH COULD CONCEIVABLY SAVE THOUSANDS OF LIVES!
YOU KNOW THIS AS WELL AS I DO, PAMELA. JUST HIRE SOMEONE TO LOOK AFTER YOUR GIRL TODAY...I'M SURE YOU CAN FIND SOMEONE VERY CAPABLE...
BEEP BEEP BEEP
EH?
HOLD ON A MOMENT, I'VE GOT ANOTHER CALL -- YOU SEE? OTHER PEOPLE ARE UP AND WORKING AT THIS HOUR. STAY ON THE LINE, PAMELA, WE'RE NOT DONE HERE YET...
THIS IS DOCTOR JOHNSON, I'M AFRAID I'VE GOT A VERY BUSY SCHEDULE THIS MORNING, SO...
CLARICE? HONEY, LISTEN... I JUST HEARD FROM A MR. SIMMONS...
HE LIVES IN HOLSOM. I-IT'S ABOUT MOUSE. H-HE'S MISSING. THERE WAS SOME KIND OF EX- EXPLOSION...
AN EXPLOSION? I-I DON'T UNDERSTAND...
NEITHER DO I. MR. SIMMONS DIDN'T WANT TO SAY MUCH OVER THE PHONE...

WH-WHAT ABOUT THE *NANNY* WE HIRED? I-I'M *CONFUSED,* DAN...

NO ONE *KNOWS WHERE* SHE IS. THE LOCAL AUTHORITIES THINK MOUSE JUST *RAN AWAY* FROM HOME, BUT *MR. SIMMONS* DOESN'T BELIEVE THAT, AND *NEITHER DO I.*

JUST *HANG ON,* CLARICE... I JUST LEFT MY OFFICE... I'LL *PICK YOU UP* IN A FEW MINUTES. WE'LL GET TO THE *BOTTOM* OF THIS, *OKAY?*

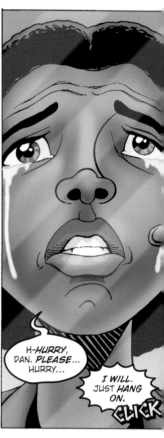

H-*HURRY,* DAN. *PLEASE...* HURRY...

I WILL. JUST *HANG* ON.

CLICK

DOCTOR JOHNSON? ARE YOU *STILL THERE?* LISTEN...I-I'LL GET SOMEONE TO *WATCH MY DAUGHTER,* OKAY?

I *MAY* BE A FEW MINUTES *LATE,* BUT I'LL BE THERE AS *SOON* AS I CAN. ...DOCTOR JOHNSON?

(16)

UMMMM... PAM... ERR... SOMETHING'S HAPPENED. UH... *STAY* WITH YOUR KID. *TAKE CARE* OF HER. DO WHAT YOU *NEED* TO DO.

BUT YOU SAID... ARE YOU *SURE?*

THAT'S THE *ONLY THING* I'M SURE ABOUT RIGHT NOW.

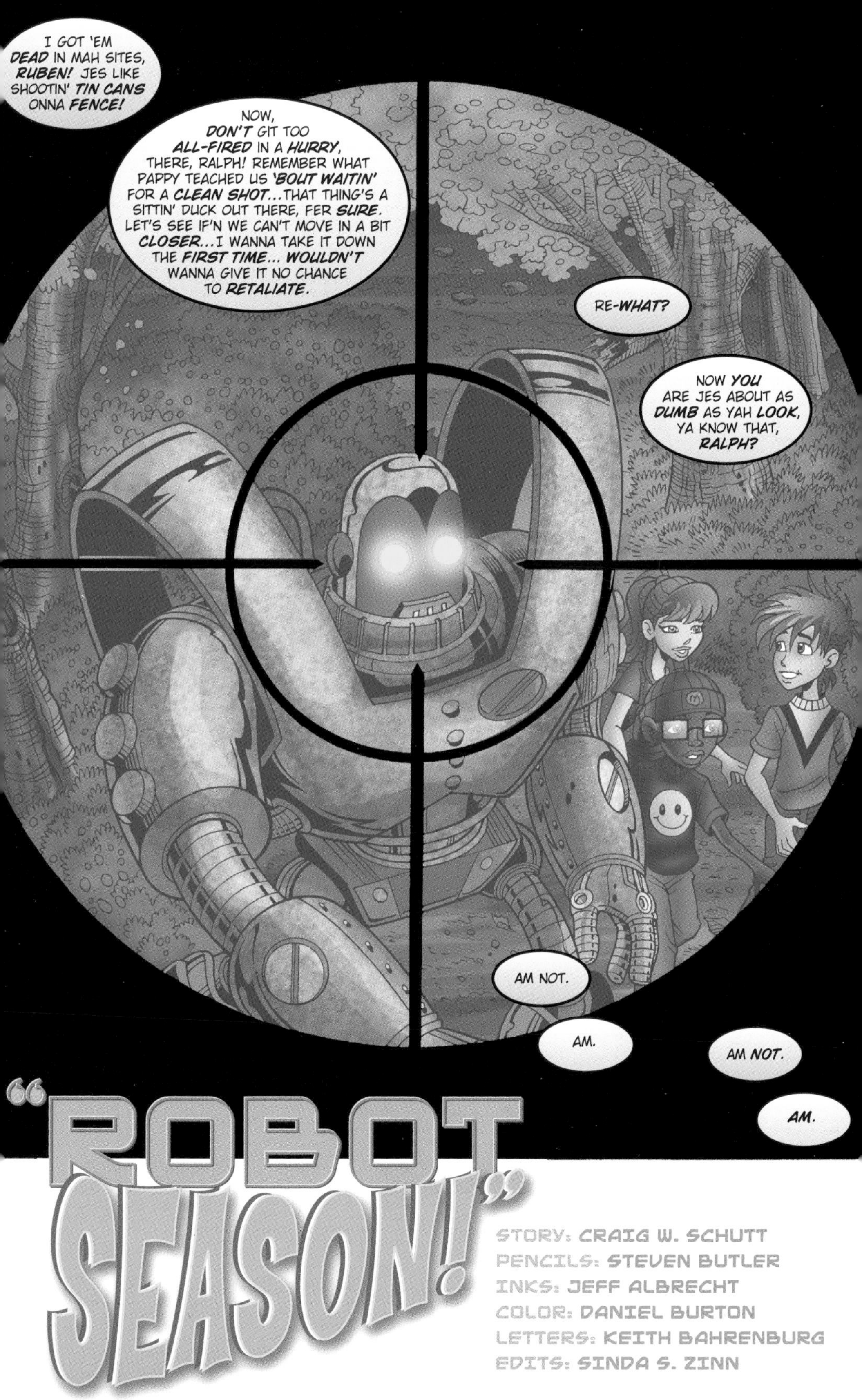
I GOT 'EM DEAD IN MAH SITES, RUBEN! JES LIKE SHOOTIN' TIN CANS ONNA FENCE!
NOW, DON'T GIT TOO ALL-FIRED IN A HURRY, THERE, RALPH! REMEMBER WHAT PAPPY TEACHED US 'BOUT WAITIN' FOR A CLEAN SHOT...THAT THING'S A SITTIN' DUCK OUT THERE, FER SURE. LET'S SEE IF'N WE CAN'T MOVE IN A BIT CLOSER...I WANNA TAKE IT DOWN THE FIRST TIME... WOULDN'T WANNA GIVE IT NO CHANCE TO RETALIATE.
RE-WHAT?
NOW YOU ARE JES ABOUT AS DUMB AS YAH LOOK, YA KNOW THAT, RALPH?
AM NOT.
AM.
AM NOT.
AM.

"ROBOT SEASON!"

STORY: CRAIG W. SCHUTT
PENCILS: STEVEN BUTLER
INKS: JEFF ALBRECHT
COLOR: DANIEL BURTON
LETTERS: KEITH BAHRENBURG
EDITS: SINDA S. ZINN

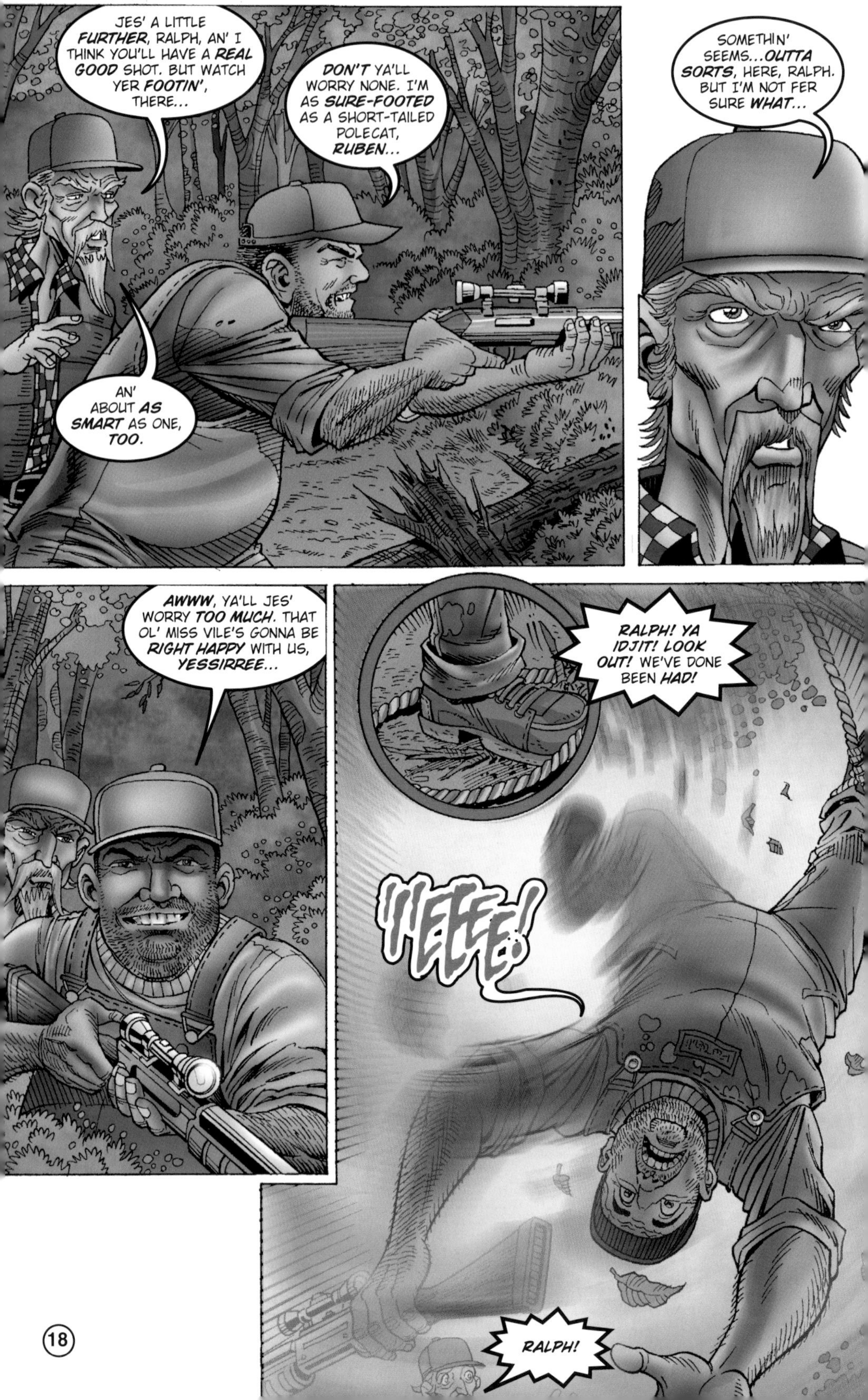
JES' A LITTLE FURTHER, RALPH, AN' I THINK YOU'LL HAVE A REAL GOOD SHOT. BUT WATCH YER FOOTIN', THERE...
DON'T YA'LL WORRY NONE. I'M AS SURE-FOOTED AS A SHORT-TAILED POLECAT, RUBEN...
AN' ABOUT AS SMART AS ONE, TOO.
SOMETHIN' SEEMS...OUTTA SORTS, HERE, RALPH. BUT I'M NOT FER SURE WHAT...
AWWW, YA'LL JES' WORRY TOO MUCH. THAT OL' MISS VILE'S GONNA BE RIGHT HAPPY WITH US, YESSIRREE...
RALPH! YA IDJIT! LOOK OUT! WE'VE DONE BEEN HAD!
IIEEE!
RALPH!

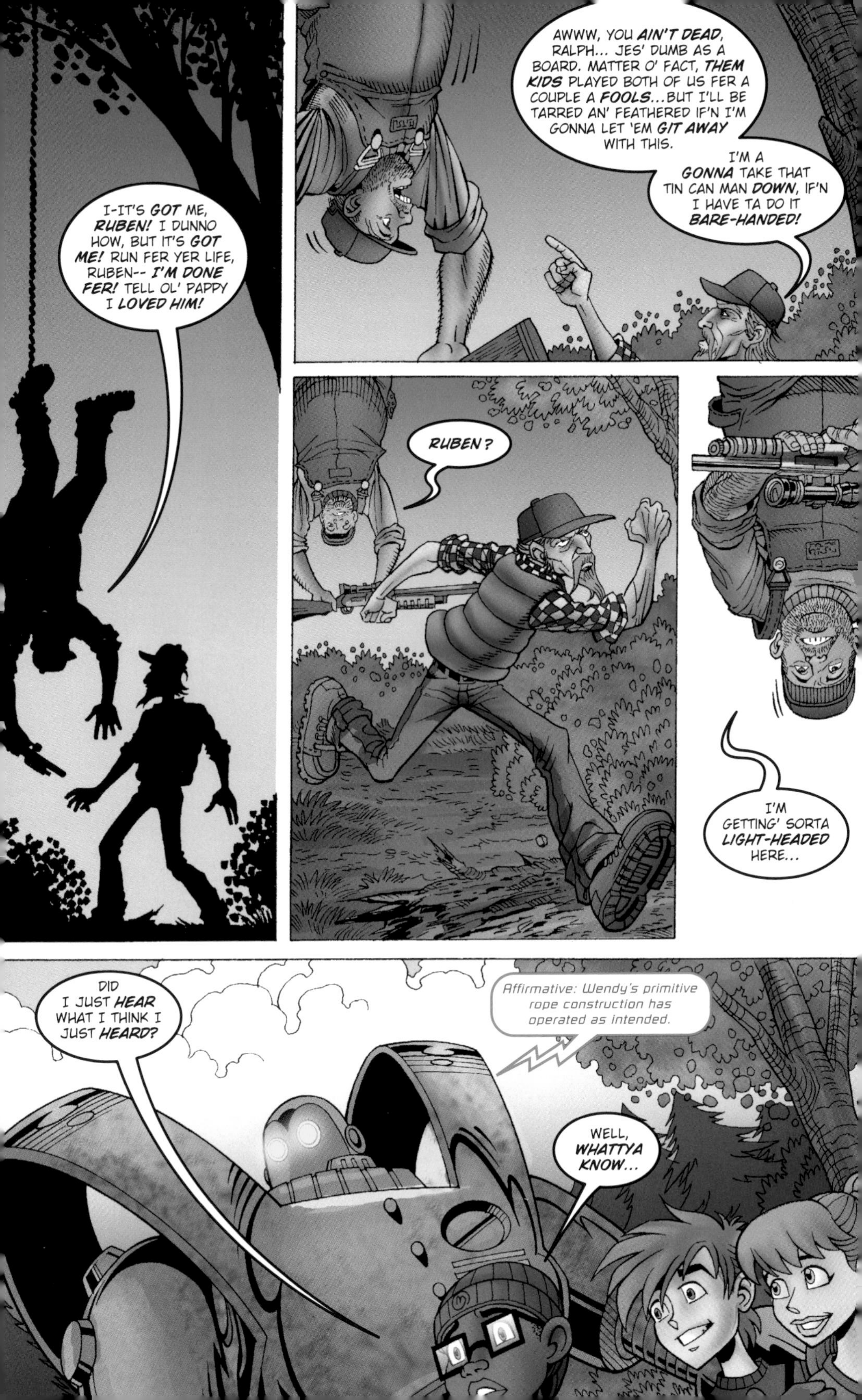
I-IT'S GOT ME, RUBEN! I DUNNO HOW, BUT IT'S GOT ME! RUN FER YER LIFE, RUBEN-- I'M DONE FER! TELL OL' PAPPY I LOVED HIM!
AWWW, YOU AIN'T DEAD, RALPH... JES' DUMB AS A BOARD. MATTER O' FACT, THEM KIDS PLAYED BOTH OF US FER A COUPLE A FOOLS...BUT I'LL BE TARRED AN' FEATHERED IF'N I'M GONNA LET 'EM GIT AWAY WITH THIS.
I'M A GONNA TAKE THAT TIN CAN MAN DOWN, IF'N I HAVE TA DO IT BARE-HANDED!
RUBEN?
I'M GETTING' SORTA LIGHT-HEADED HERE...
DID I JUST HEAR WHAT I THINK I JUST HEARD?
Affirmative: Wendy's primitive rope construction has operated as intended.
WELL, WHATTYA KNOW...

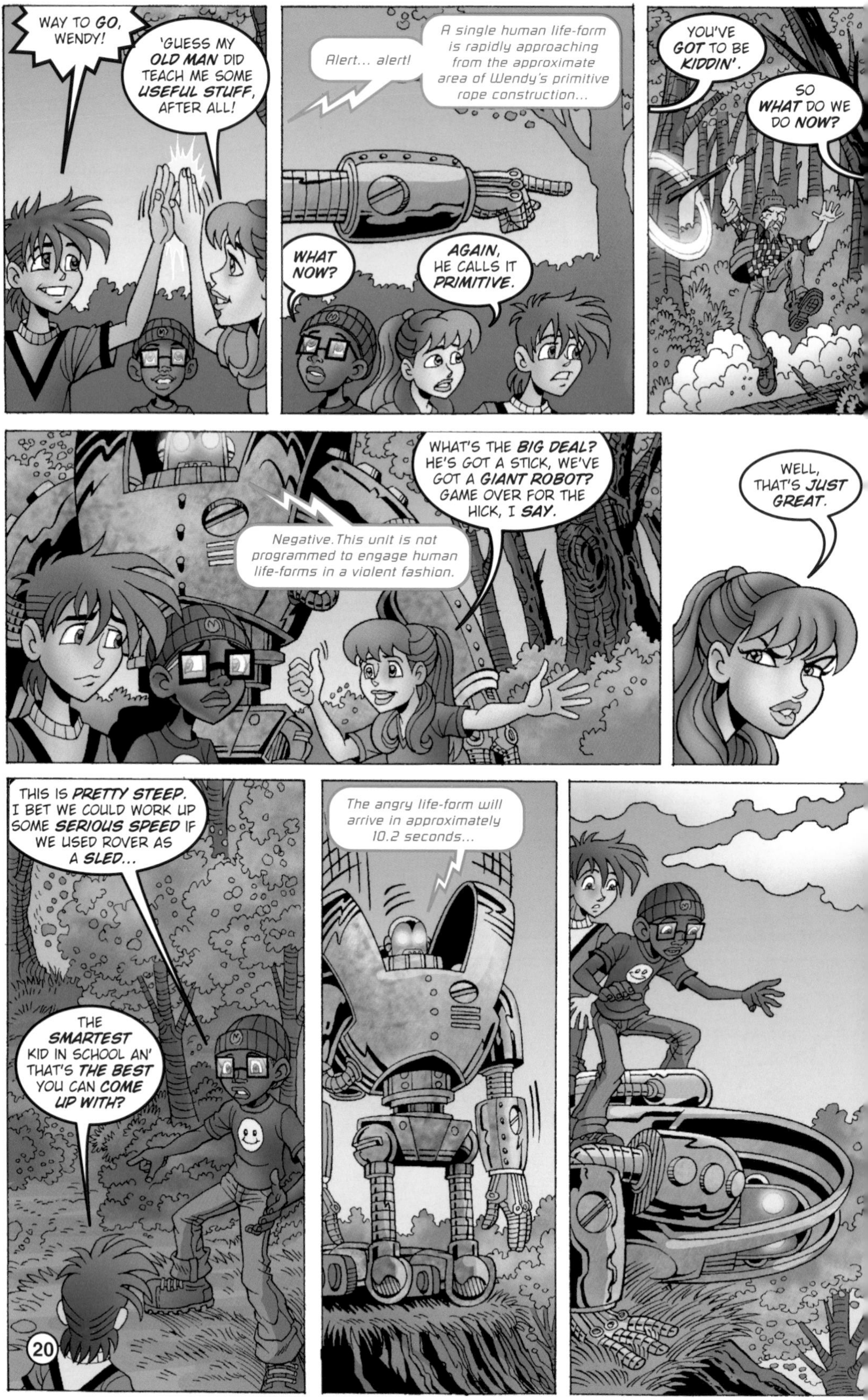
WAY TO GO, WENDY!
'GUESS MY OLD MAN DID TEACH ME SOME USEFUL STUFF, AFTER ALL!
Alert... alert!
A single human life-form is rapidly approaching from the approximate area of Wendy's primitive rope construction...
WHAT NOW?
AGAIN, HE CALLS IT PRIMITIVE.
YOU'VE GOT TO BE KIDDIN'.
SO WHAT DO WE DO NOW?
WHAT'S THE BIG DEAL? HE'S GOT A STICK, WE'VE GOT A GIANT ROBOT? GAME OVER FOR THE HICK, I SAY.
Negative. This unit is not programmed to engage human life-forms in a violent fashion.
WELL, THAT'S JUST GREAT.
THIS IS PRETTY STEEP. I BET WE COULD WORK UP SOME SERIOUS SPEED IF WE USED ROVER AS A SLED...
THE SMARTEST KID IN SCHOOL AN' THAT'S THE BEST YOU CAN COME UP WITH?
The angry life-form will arrive in approximately 10.2 seconds...

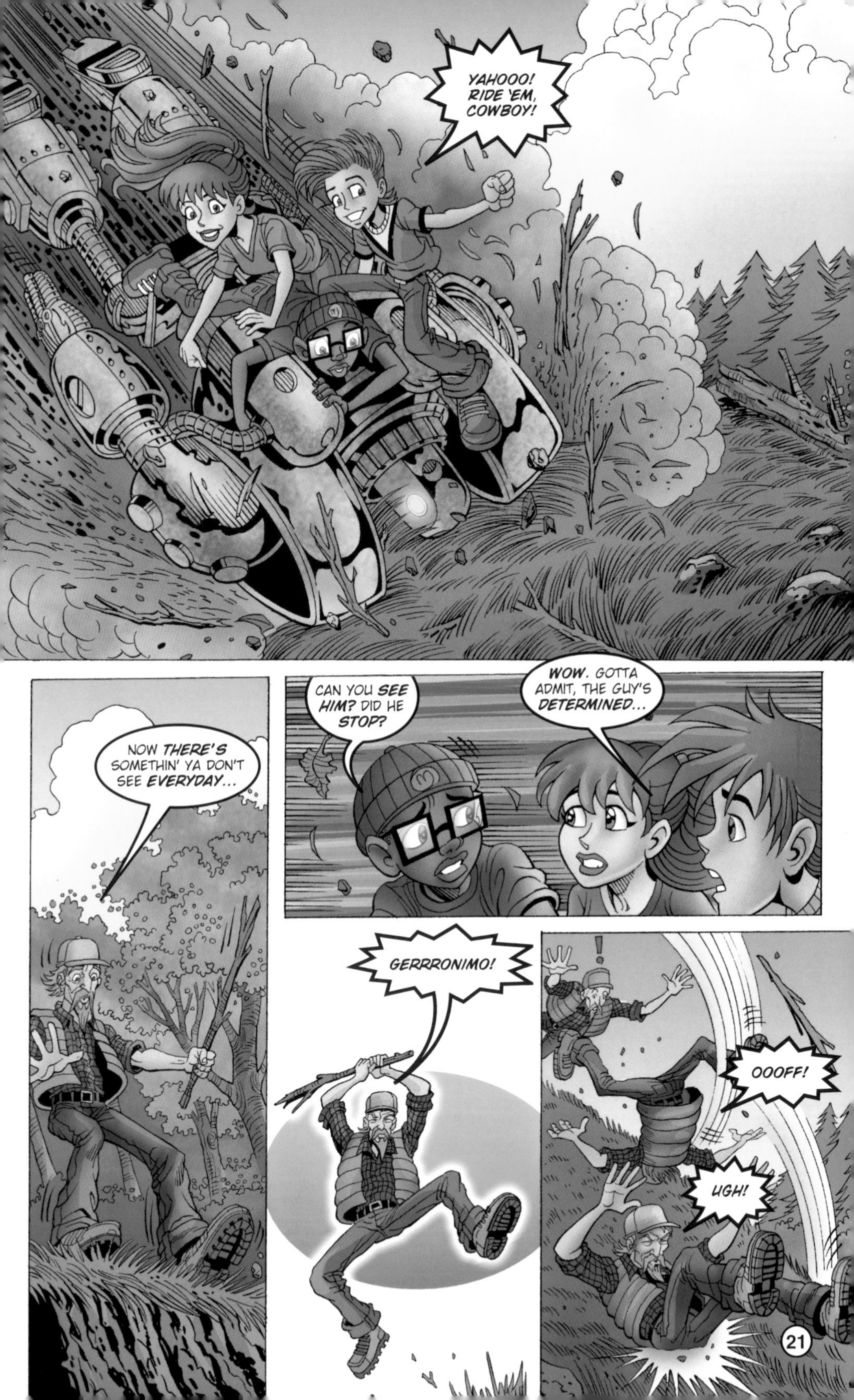
YAHOOO! RIDE 'EM, COWBOY!
NOW THERE'S SOMETHIN' YA DON'T SEE EVERYDAY...
CAN YOU SEE HIM? DID HE STOP?
WOW. GOTTA ADMIT, THE GUY'S DETERMINED...
GERRRONIMO!
!
OOOFF!
UGH!

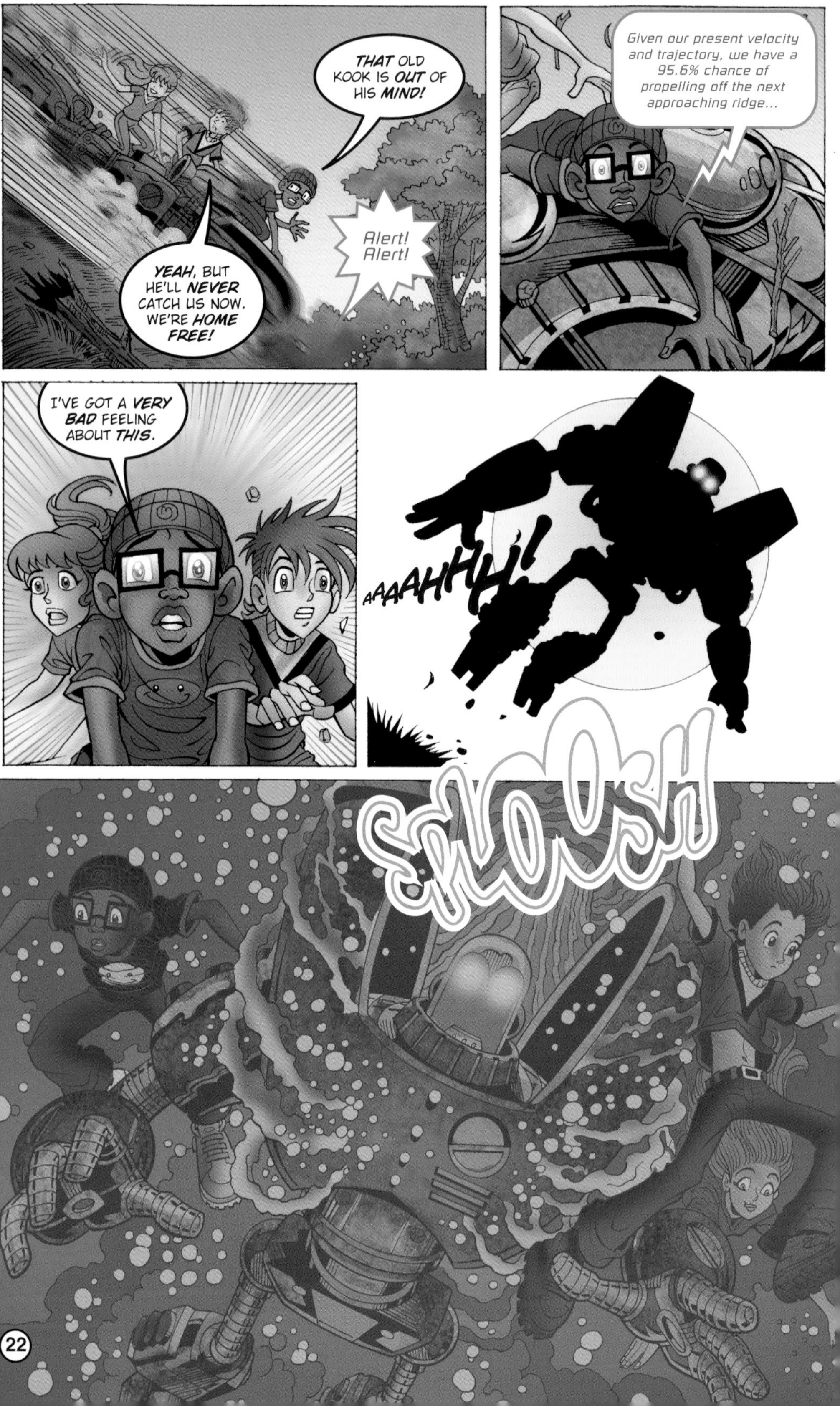

THAT OLD KOOK IS OUT OF HIS MIND!
YEAH, BUT HE'LL NEVER CATCH US NOW. WE'RE HOME FREE!
Alert! Alert!
Given our present velocity and trajectory, we have a 95.6% chance of propelling off the next approaching ridge...
I'VE GOT A VERY BAD FEELING ABOUT THIS.
AAAAHHH!
SPLOOSH

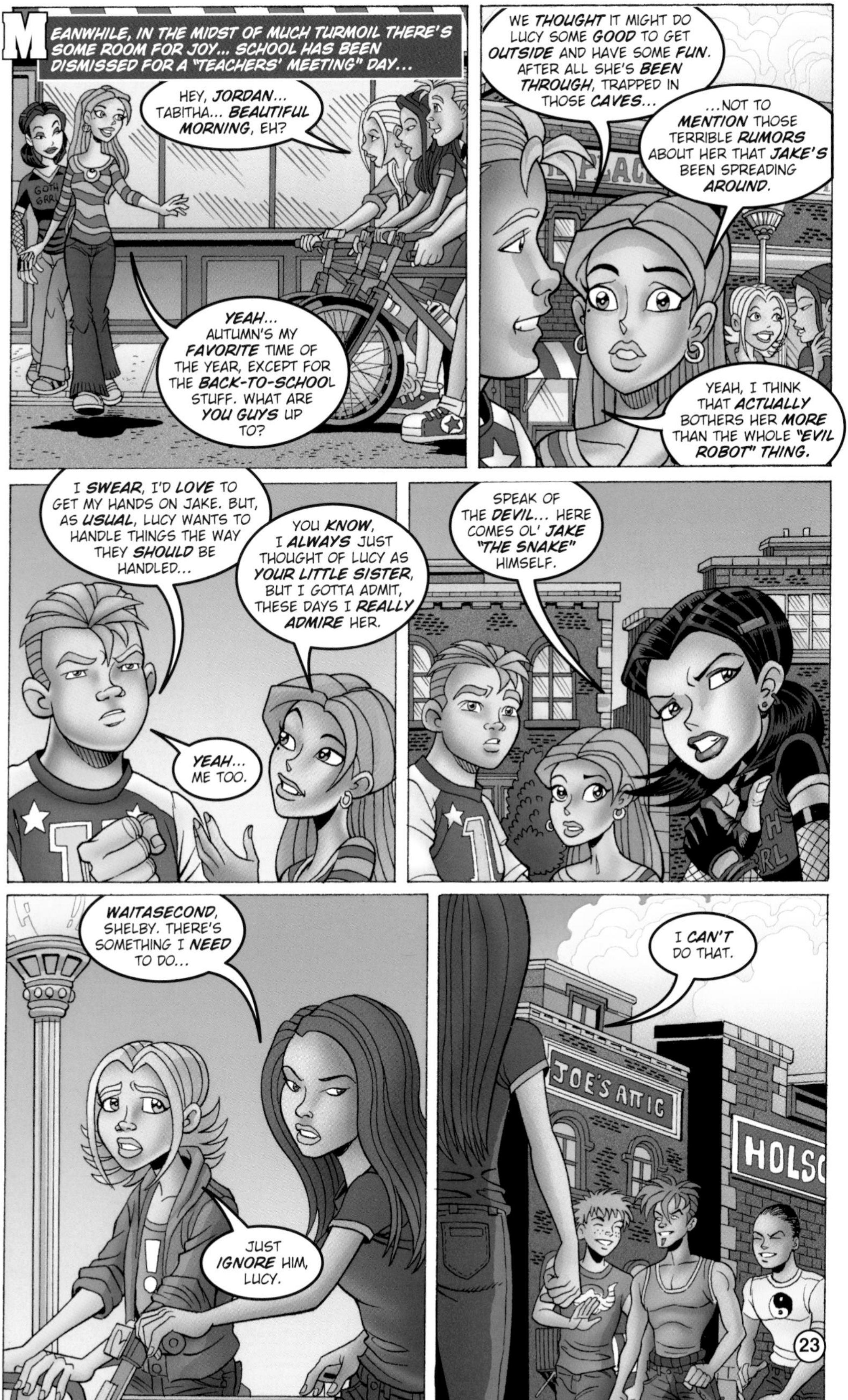
MEANWHILE, IN THE MIDST OF MUCH TURMOIL THERE'S SOME ROOM FOR JOY... SCHOOL HAS BEEN DISMISSED FOR A "TEACHERS' MEETING" DAY...
HEY, JORDAN... TABITHA... BEAUTIFUL MORNING, EH?
YEAH... AUTUMN'S MY FAVORITE TIME OF THE YEAR, EXCEPT FOR THE BACK-TO-SCHOOL STUFF. WHAT ARE YOU GUYS UP TO?
GOTH GRRL
WE THOUGHT IT MIGHT DO LUCY SOME GOOD TO GET OUTSIDE AND HAVE SOME FUN. AFTER ALL SHE'S BEEN THROUGH, TRAPPED IN THOSE CAVES...
...NOT TO MENTION THOSE TERRIBLE RUMORS ABOUT HER THAT JAKE'S BEEN SPREADING AROUND.
YEAH, I THINK THAT ACTUALLY BOTHERS HER MORE THAN THE WHOLE "EVIL ROBOT" THING.
I SWEAR, I'D LOVE TO GET MY HANDS ON JAKE. BUT, AS USUAL, LUCY WANTS TO HANDLE THINGS THE WAY THEY SHOULD BE HANDLED...
YOU KNOW, I ALWAYS JUST THOUGHT OF LUCY AS YOUR LITTLE SISTER, BUT I GOTTA ADMIT, THESE DAYS I REALLY ADMIRE HER.
YEAH... ME TOO.
SPEAK OF THE DEVIL... HERE COMES OL' JAKE "THE SNAKE" HIMSELF.
WAITASECOND, SHELBY. THERE'S SOMETHING I NEED TO DO...
JUST IGNORE HIM, LUCY.
I CAN'T DO THAT.
JOE'S ATTIC
HOLSO

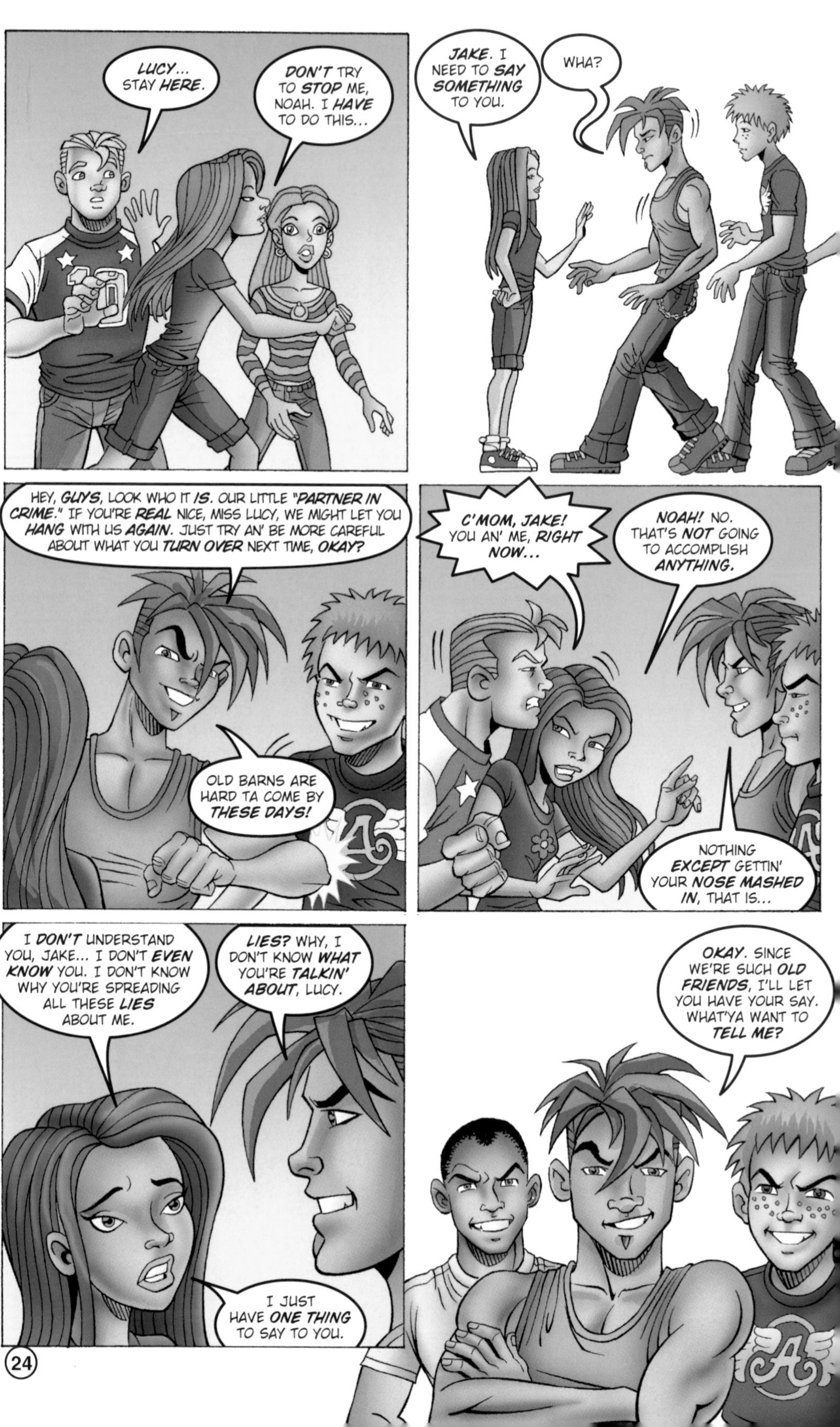

LUCY... STAY HERE.
DON'T TRY TO STOP ME, NOAH. I HAVE TO DO THIS...
JAKE. I NEED TO SAY SOMETHING TO YOU.
WHA?
HEY, GUYS, LOOK WHO IT IS. OUR LITTLE "PARTNER IN CRIME." IF YOU'RE REAL NICE, MISS LUCY, WE MIGHT LET YOU HANG WITH US AGAIN. JUST TRY AN' BE MORE CAREFUL ABOUT WHAT YOU TURN OVER NEXT TIME, OKAY?
OLD BARNS ARE HARD TA COME BY THESE DAYS!
C'MOM, JAKE! YOU AN' ME, RIGHT NOW...
NOAH! NO. THAT'S NOT GOING TO ACCOMPLISH ANYTHING.
NOTHING EXCEPT GETTIN' YOUR NOSE MASHED IN, THAT IS...
I DON'T UNDERSTAND YOU, JAKE... I DON'T EVEN KNOW YOU. I DON'T KNOW WHY YOU'RE SPREADING ALL THESE LIES ABOUT ME.
LIES? WHY, I DON'T KNOW WHAT YOU'RE TALKIN' ABOUT, LUCY.
I JUST HAVE ONE THING TO SAY TO YOU.
OKAY. SINCE WE'RE SUCH OLD FRIENDS, I'LL LET YOU HAVE YOUR SAY. WHAT'YA WANT TO TELL ME?

I FORGIVE YOU.

I DON'T **KNOW** YOU. I DON'T KNOW WHY YOU **FEEL** LIKE YOU **HAVE** TO BE THE WAY YOU **ARE**.

I WISH YOU HAD A **BETTER LIFE**. I WISH YOU HAD BETTER THINGS TO **DO**.

BUT I CAN'T **CHANGE** YOU, AND I CAN'T **MAKE** YOU TAKE BACK WHAT YOU'VE **SAID** AND **DONE**.

BUT I CAN **FORGIVE** YOU. AND I DO.

WOW.

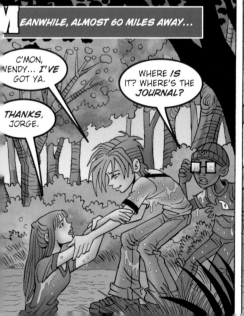

MEANWHILE, ALMOST 60 MILES AWAY...

C'MON, WENDY... **I'VE** GOT YA.

THANKS, JORGE.

WHERE **IS** IT? WHERE'S THE **JOURNAL?**

The Maker's journal is unharmed.

"**UNHARMED?**" BRING IT HERE... **QUICK!**

25

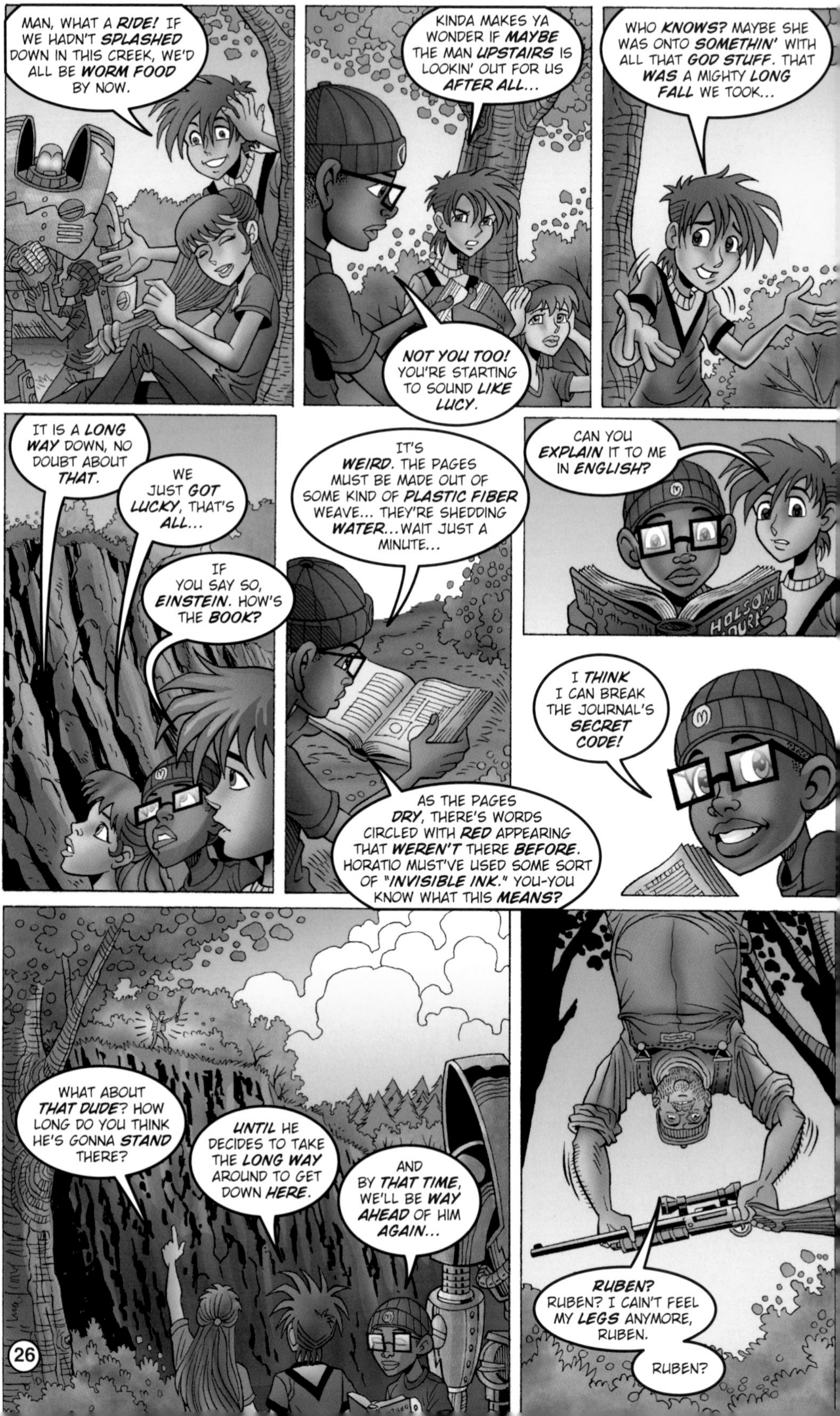
MAN, WHAT A RIDE! IF WE HADN'T SPLASHED DOWN IN THIS CREEK, WE'D ALL BE WORM FOOD BY NOW.
KINDA MAKES YA WONDER IF MAYBE THE MAN UPSTAIRS IS LOOKIN' OUT FOR US AFTER ALL...
NOT YOU TOO! YOU'RE STARTING TO SOUND LIKE LUCY.
WHO KNOWS? MAYBE SHE WAS ONTO SOMETHIN' WITH ALL THAT GOD STUFF. THAT WAS A MIGHTY LONG FALL WE TOOK...
IT IS A LONG WAY DOWN, NO DOUBT ABOUT THAT.
WE JUST GOT LUCKY, THAT'S ALL...
IF YOU SAY SO, EINSTEIN. HOW'S THE BOOK?
IT'S WEIRD. THE PAGES MUST BE MADE OUT OF SOME KIND OF PLASTIC FIBER WEAVE... THEY'RE SHEDDING WATER... WAIT JUST A MINUTE...
AS THE PAGES DRY, THERE'S WORDS CIRCLED WITH RED APPEARING THAT WEREN'T THERE BEFORE. HORATIO MUST'VE USED SOME SORT OF "INVISIBLE INK." YOU-YOU KNOW WHAT THIS MEANS?
CAN YOU EXPLAIN IT TO ME IN ENGLISH?
I THINK I CAN BREAK THE JOURNAL'S SECRET CODE!
WHAT ABOUT THAT DUDE? HOW LONG DO YOU THINK HE'S GONNA STAND THERE?
UNTIL HE DECIDES TO TAKE THE LONG WAY AROUND TO GET DOWN HERE.
AND BY THAT TIME, WE'LL BE WAY AHEAD OF HIM AGAIN...
RUBEN? RUBEN? I CAIN'T FEEL MY LEGS ANYMORE, RUBEN.
RUBEN?

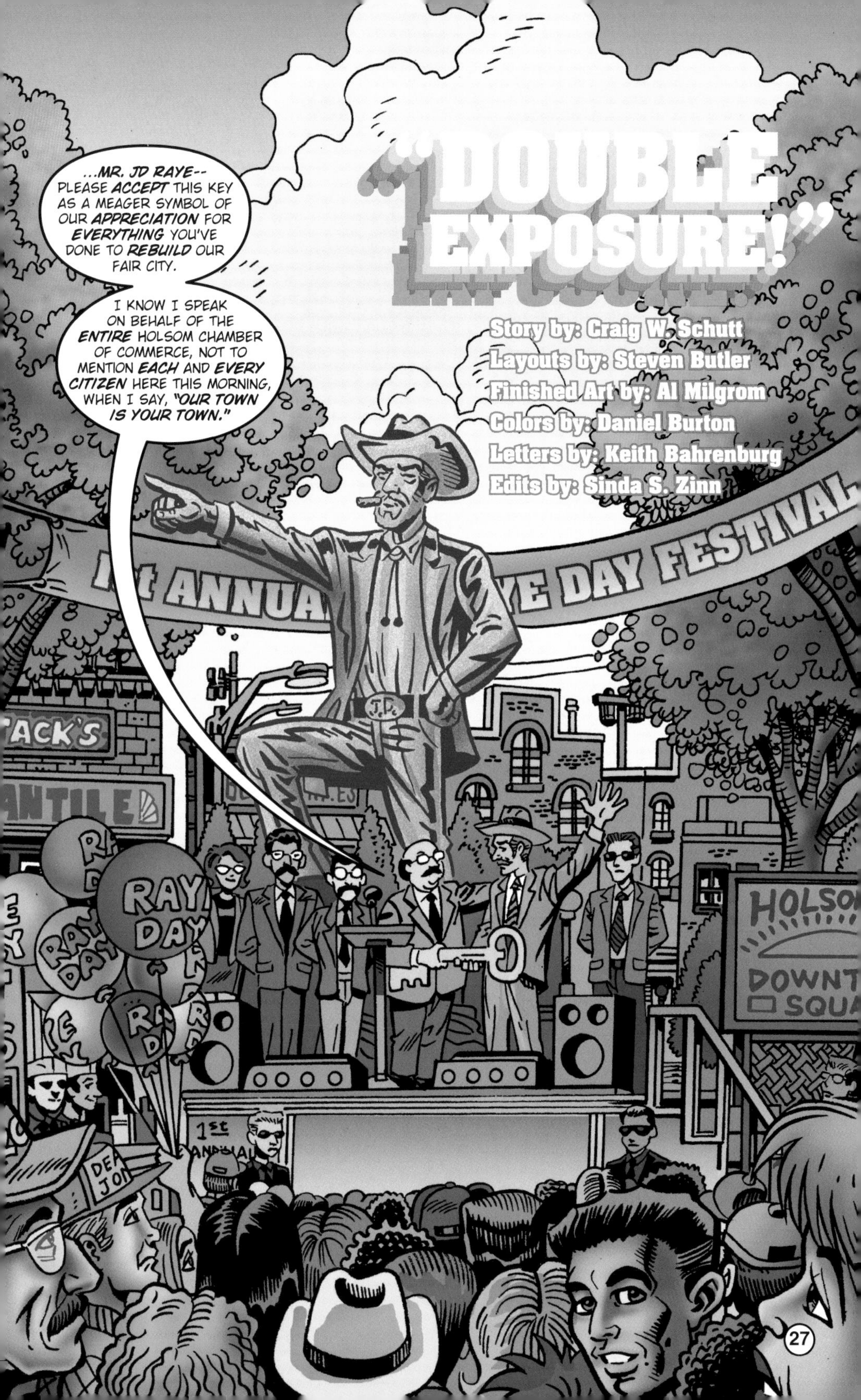
"DOUBLE EXPOSURE!"
Story by: Craig W. Schutt
Layouts by: Steven Butler
Finished Art by: Al Milgrom
Colors by: Daniel Burton
Letters by: Keith Bahrenburg
Edits by: Sinda S. Zinn
...MR. JD RAYE-- PLEASE ACCEPT THIS KEY AS A MEAGER SYMBOL OF OUR APPRECIATION FOR EVERYTHING YOU'VE DONE TO REBUILD OUR FAIR CITY.
I KNOW I SPEAK ON BEHALF OF THE ENTIRE HOLSOM CHAMBER OF COMMERCE, NOT TO MENTION EACH AND EVERY CITIZEN HERE THIS MORNING, WHEN I SAY, "OUR TOWN IS YOUR TOWN."
DAY FESTIVAL
RAYE DAY
1st ANNUAL

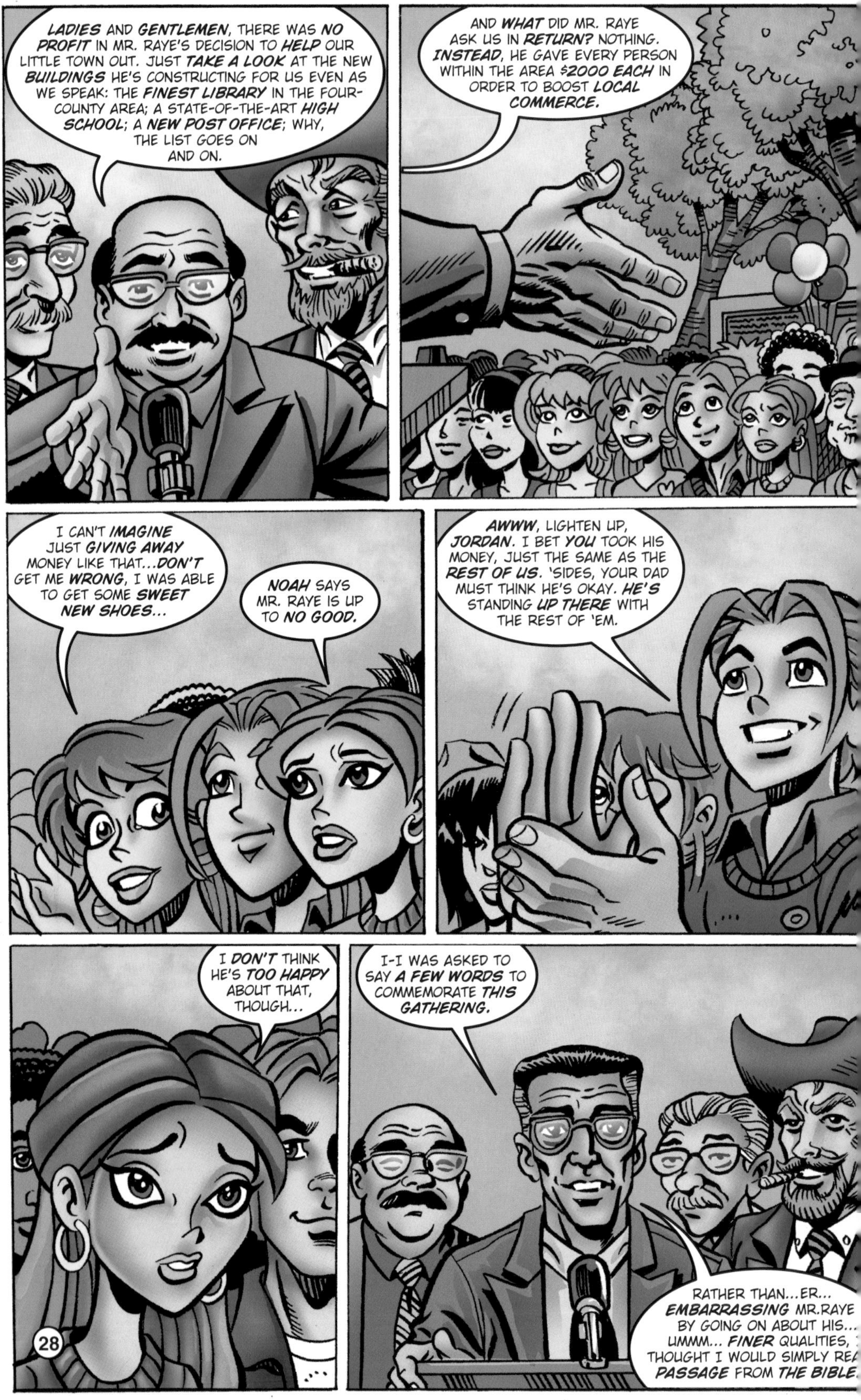
LADIES AND GENTLEMEN, THERE WAS NO PROFIT IN MR. RAYE'S DECISION TO HELP OUR LITTLE TOWN OUT. JUST TAKE A LOOK AT THE NEW BUILDINGS HE'S CONSTRUCTING FOR US EVEN AS WE SPEAK: THE FINEST LIBRARY IN THE FOUR-COUNTY AREA; A STATE-OF-THE-ART HIGH SCHOOL; A NEW POST OFFICE; WHY, THE LIST GOES ON AND ON.
AND WHAT DID MR. RAYE ASK US IN RETURN? NOTHING. INSTEAD, HE GAVE EVERY PERSON WITHIN THE AREA $2000 EACH IN ORDER TO BOOST LOCAL COMMERCE.
I CAN'T IMAGINE JUST GIVING AWAY MONEY LIKE THAT...DON'T GET ME WRONG, I WAS ABLE TO GET SOME SWEET NEW SHOES...
NOAH SAYS MR. RAYE IS UP TO NO GOOD.
AWWW, LIGHTEN UP, JORDAN. I BET YOU TOOK HIS MONEY, JUST THE SAME AS THE REST OF US. 'SIDES, YOUR DAD MUST THINK HE'S OKAY. HE'S STANDING UP THERE WITH THE REST OF 'EM.
I DON'T THINK HE'S TOO HAPPY ABOUT THAT, THOUGH...
I-I WAS ASKED TO SAY A FEW WORDS TO COMMEMORATE THIS GATHERING.
RATHER THAN...ER... EMBARRASSING MR.RAYE BY GOING ON ABOUT HIS... UMMM... FINER QUALITIES, I THOUGHT I WOULD SIMPLY REA PASSAGE FROM THE BIBLE

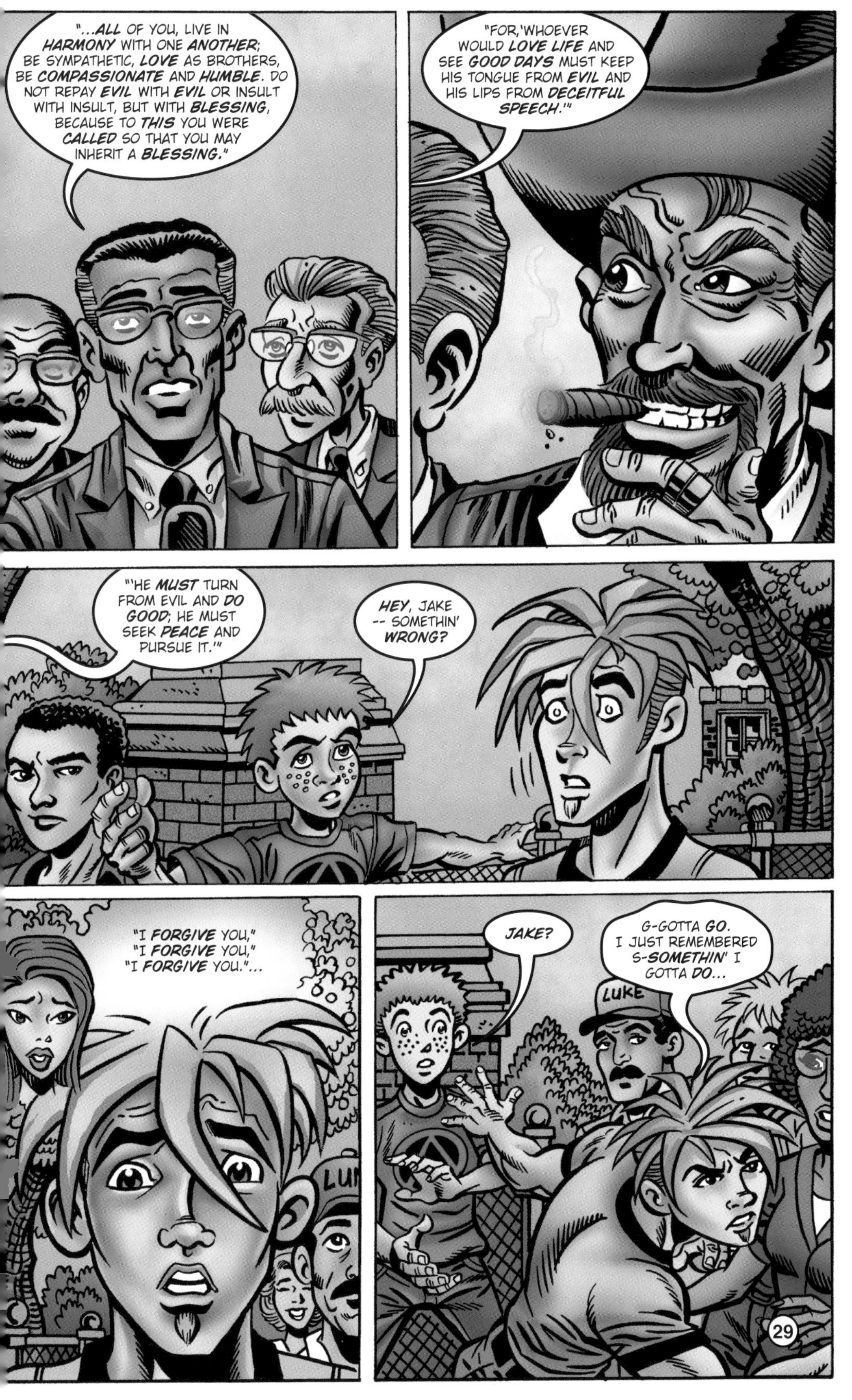
"...ALL OF YOU, LIVE IN HARMONY WITH ONE ANOTHER; BE SYMPATHETIC, LOVE AS BROTHERS, BE COMPASSIONATE AND HUMBLE. DO NOT REPAY EVIL WITH EVIL OR INSULT WITH INSULT, BUT WITH BLESSING, BECAUSE TO THIS YOU WERE CALLED SO THAT YOU MAY INHERIT A BLESSING."
"FOR,'WHOEVER WOULD LOVE LIFE AND SEE GOOD DAYS MUST KEEP HIS TONGUE FROM EVIL AND HIS LIPS FROM DECEITFUL SPEECH.'"
"'HE MUST TURN FROM EVIL AND DO GOOD; HE MUST SEEK PEACE AND PURSUE IT.'"
HEY, JAKE -- SOMETHIN' WRONG?
"I FORGIVE YOU," "I FORGIVE YOU," "I FORGIVE YOU."...
JAKE?
G-GOTTA GO. I JUST REMEMBERED S-SOMETHIN' I GOTTA DO...
LUKE

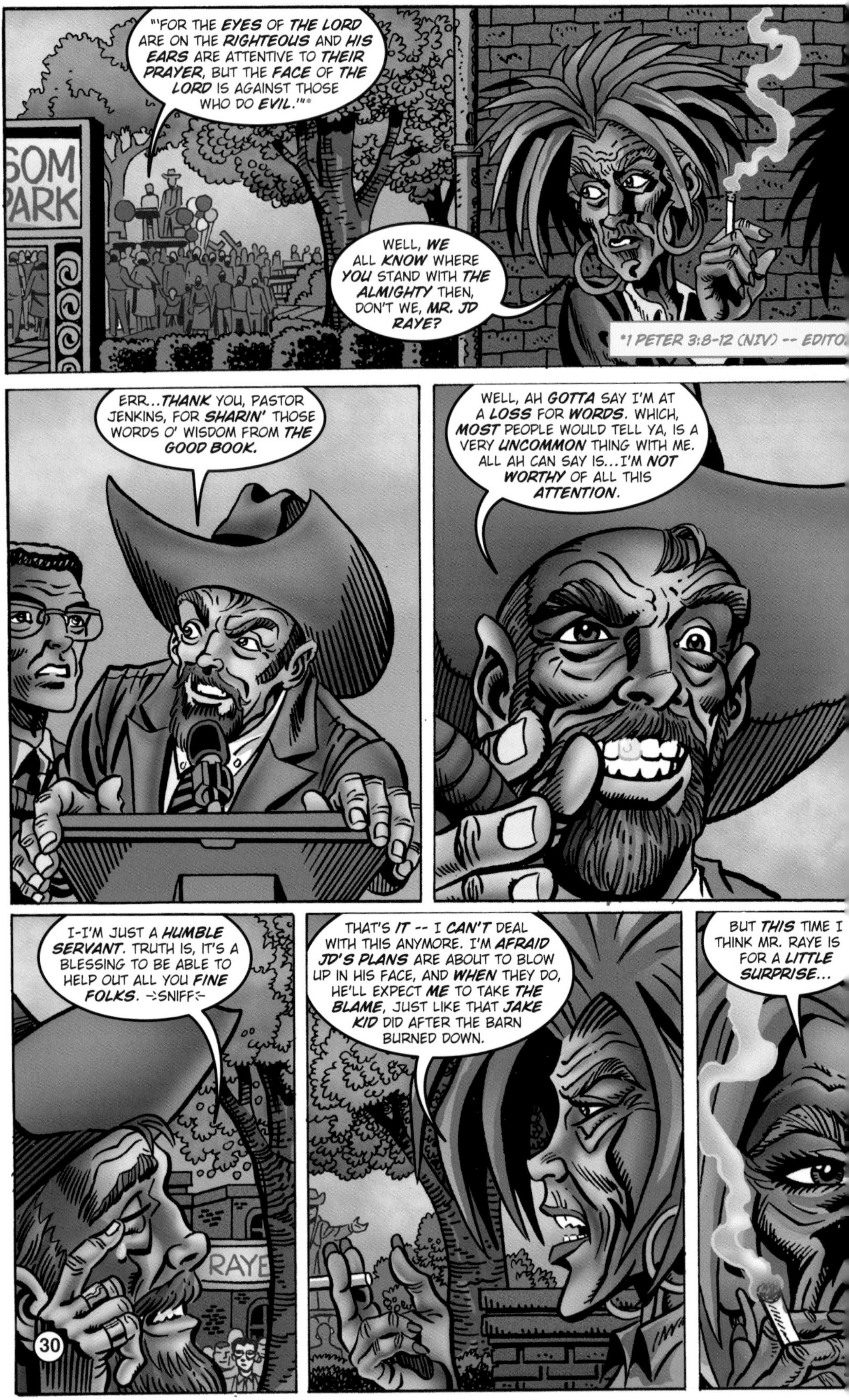
"'FOR THE EYES OF THE LORD ARE ON THE RIGHTEOUS AND HIS EARS ARE ATTENTIVE TO THEIR PRAYER, BUT THE FACE OF THE LORD IS AGAINST THOSE WHO DO EVIL.'"*
WELL, WE ALL KNOW WHERE YOU STAND WITH THE ALMIGHTY THEN, DON'T WE, MR. JD RAYE?
*1 PETER 3:8-12 (NIV) -- EDITO
ERR...THANK YOU, PASTOR JENKINS, FOR SHARIN' THOSE WORDS O' WISDOM FROM THE GOOD BOOK.
WELL, AH GOTTA SAY I'M AT A LOSS FOR WORDS. WHICH, MOST PEOPLE WOULD TELL YA, IS A VERY UNCOMMON THING WITH ME. ALL AH CAN SAY IS...I'M NOT WORTHY OF ALL THIS ATTENTION.
I-I'M JUST A HUMBLE SERVANT. TRUTH IS, IT'S A BLESSING TO BE ABLE TO HELP OUT ALL YOU FINE FOLKS. -SNIFF-
RAYE
THAT'S IT -- I CAN'T DEAL WITH THIS ANYMORE. I'M AFRAID JD'S PLANS ARE ABOUT TO BLOW UP IN HIS FACE, AND WHEN THEY DO, HE'LL EXPECT ME TO TAKE THE BLAME, JUST LIKE THAT JAKE KID DID AFTER THE BARN BURNED DOWN.
BUT THIS TIME I THINK MR. RAYE IS FOR A LITTLE SURPRISE...

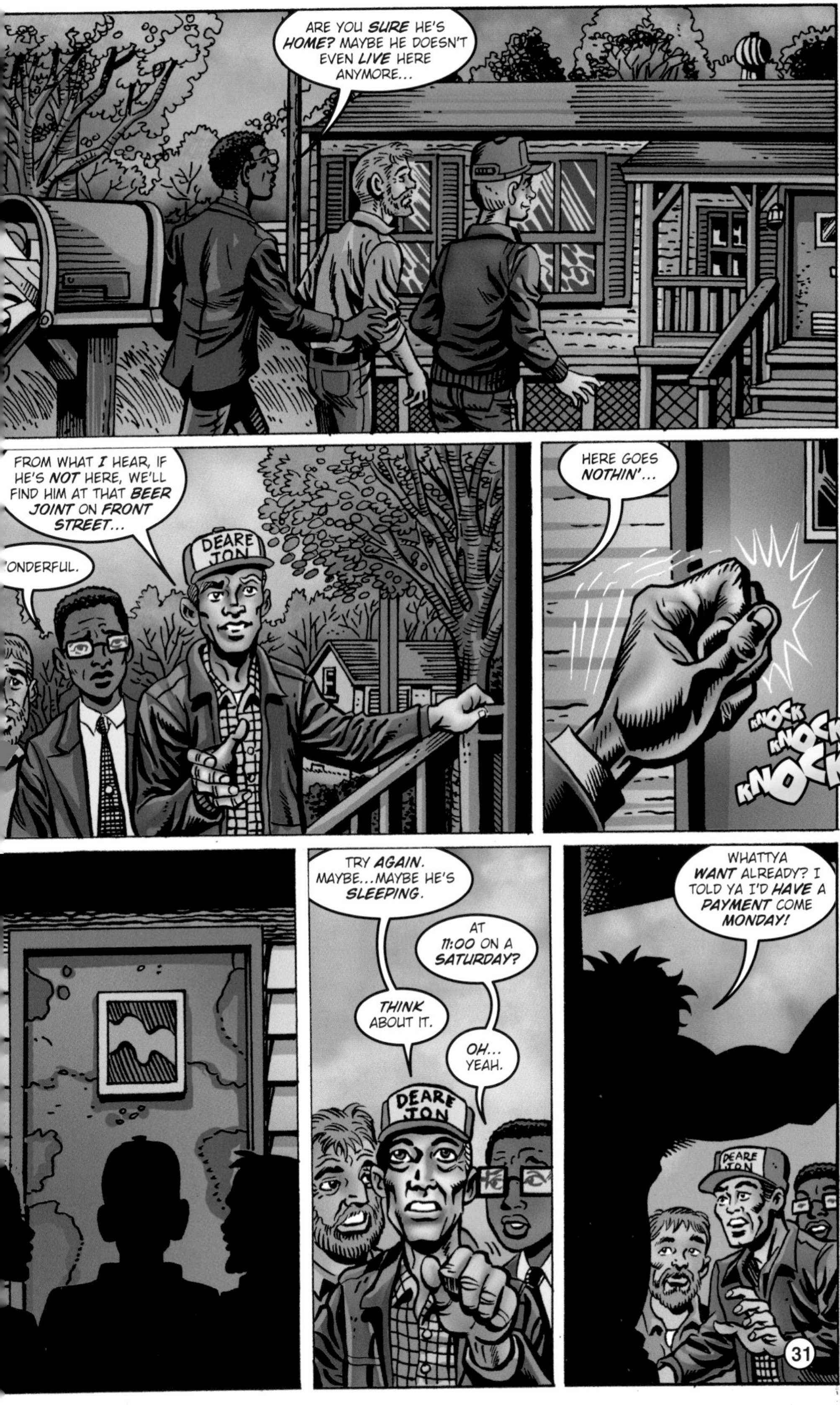

ARE YOU SURE HE'S HOME? MAYBE HE DOESN'T EVEN LIVE HERE ANYMORE...
FROM WHAT I HEAR, IF HE'S NOT HERE, WE'LL FIND HIM AT THAT BEER JOINT ON FRONT STREET...
DEARE JON
ONDERFUL.
HERE GOES NOTHIN'...
KNOCK KNOCK KNOCK
TRY AGAIN. MAYBE... MAYBE HE'S SLEEPING.
AT 11:00 ON A SATURDAY?
THINK ABOUT IT.
OH... YEAH.
DEARE JON
WHATTYA WANT ALREADY? I TOLD YA I'D HAVE A PAYMENT COME MONDAY!
DEARE JON

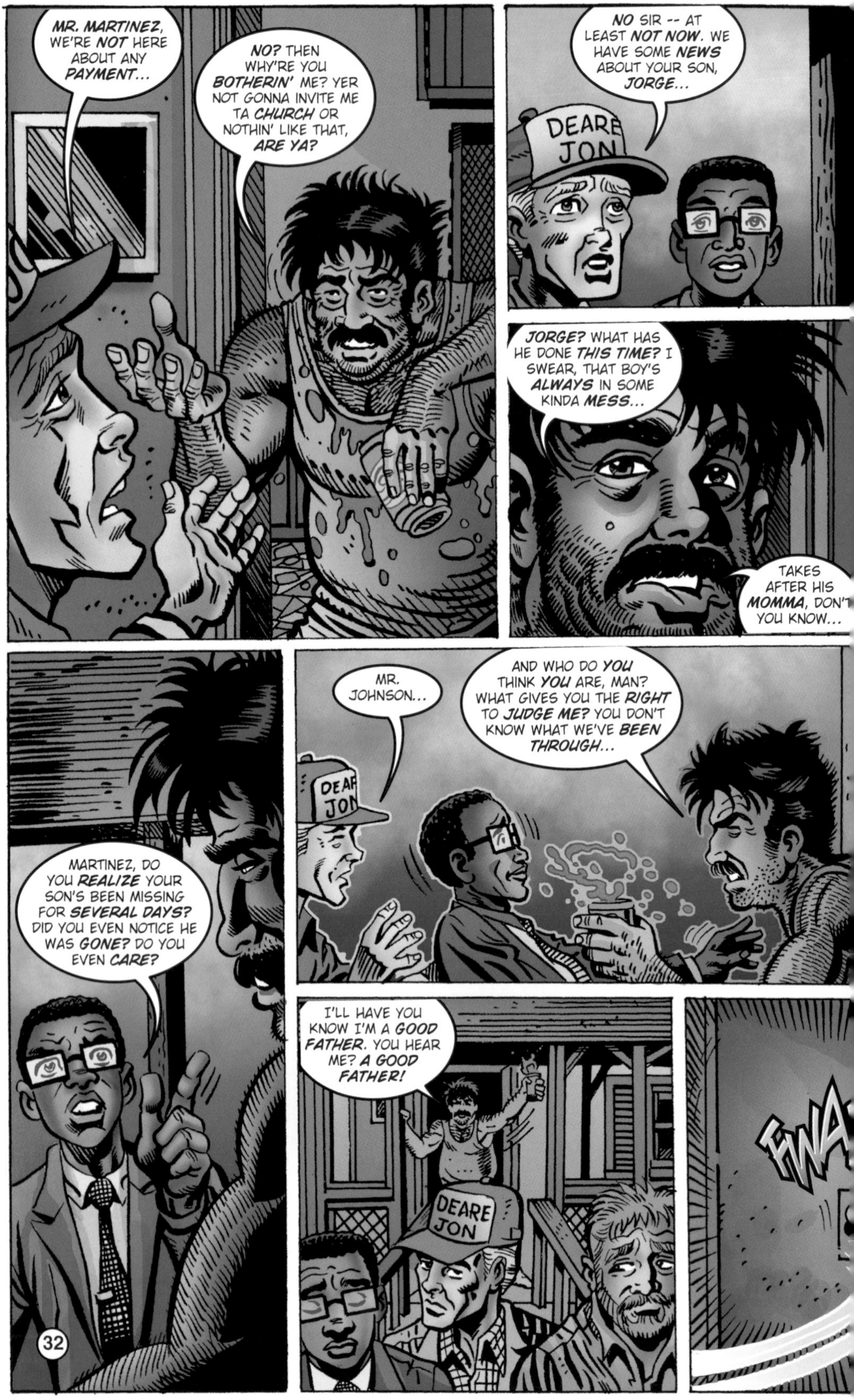
MR. MARTINEZ, WE'RE NOT HERE ABOUT ANY PAYMENT...
NO? THEN WHY'RE YOU BOTHERIN' ME? YER NOT GONNA INVITE ME TA CHURCH OR NOTHIN' LIKE THAT, ARE YA?
NO SIR -- AT LEAST NOT NOW. WE HAVE SOME NEWS ABOUT YOUR SON, JORGE...
DEARE JON
JORGE? WHAT HAS HE DONE THIS TIME? I SWEAR, THAT BOY'S ALWAYS IN SOME KINDA MESS...
TAKES AFTER HIS MOMMA, DON'T YOU KNOW...
MARTINEZ, DO YOU REALIZE YOUR SON'S BEEN MISSING FOR SEVERAL DAYS? DID YOU EVEN NOTICE HE WAS GONE? DO YOU EVEN CARE?
MR. JOHNSON...
AND WHO DO YOU THINK YOU ARE, MAN? WHAT GIVES YOU THE RIGHT TO JUDGE ME? YOU DON'T KNOW WHAT WE'VE BEEN THROUGH...
I'LL HAVE YOU KNOW I'M A GOOD FATHER. YOU HEAR ME? A GOOD FATHER!
DEARE JON
FWA

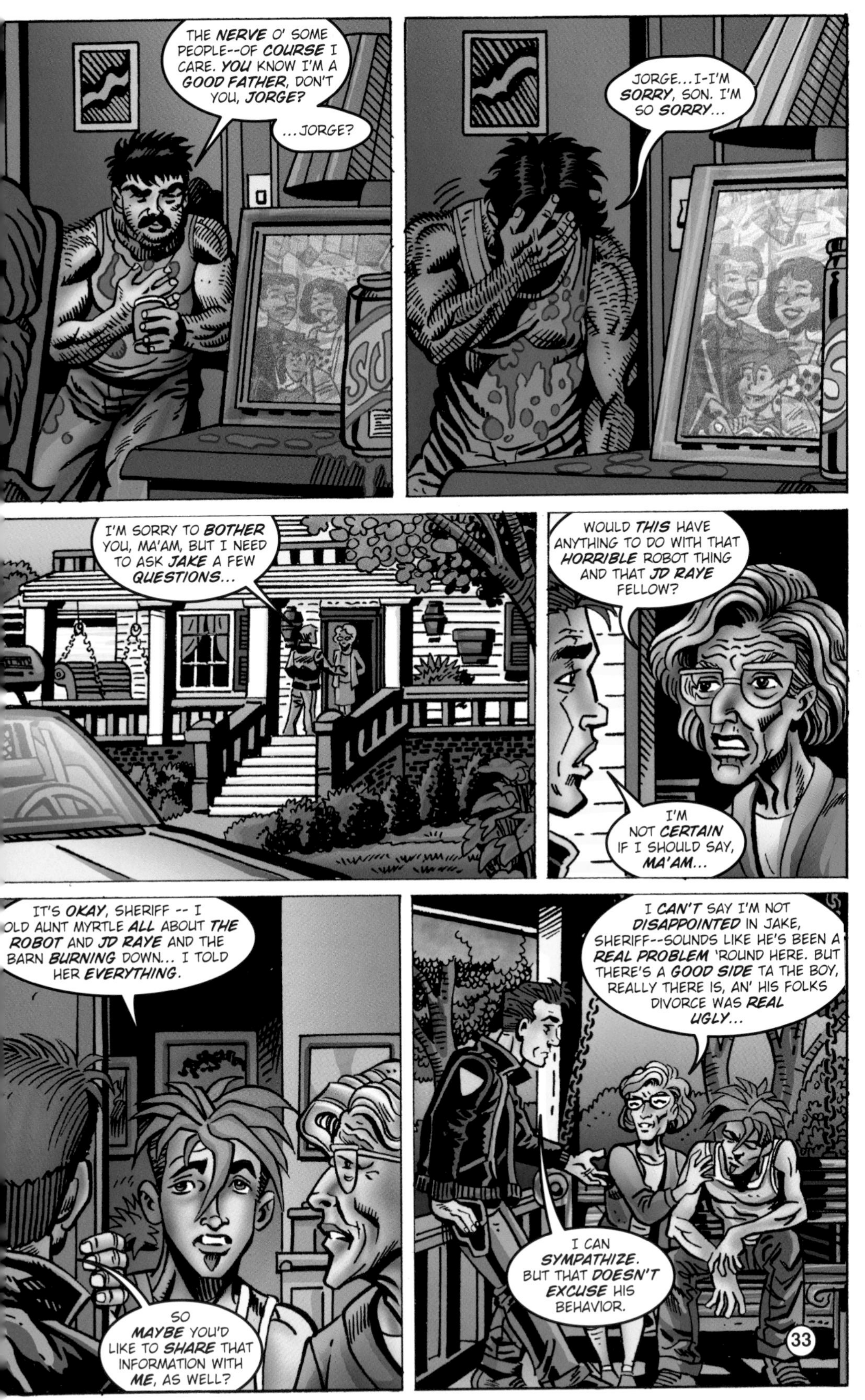
THE NERVE O' SOME PEOPLE--OF COURSE I CARE. YOU KNOW I'M A GOOD FATHER, DON'T YOU, JORGE?
...JORGE?
JORGE...I-I'M SORRY, SON. I'M SO SORRY...
I'M SORRY TO BOTHER YOU, MA'AM, BUT I NEED TO ASK JAKE A FEW QUESTIONS...
WOULD THIS HAVE ANYTHING TO DO WITH THAT HORRIBLE ROBOT THING AND THAT JD RAYE FELLOW?
I'M NOT CERTAIN IF I SHOULD SAY, MA'AM...
IT'S OKAY, SHERIFF -- I OLD AUNT MYRTLE ALL ABOUT THE ROBOT AND JD RAYE AND THE BARN BURNING DOWN... I TOLD HER EVERYTHING.
SO MAYBE YOU'D LIKE TO SHARE THAT INFORMATION WITH ME, AS WELL?
I CAN'T SAY I'M NOT DISAPPOINTED IN JAKE, SHERIFF--SOUNDS LIKE HE'S BEEN A REAL PROBLEM 'ROUND HERE. BUT THERE'S A GOOD SIDE TA THE BOY, REALLY THERE IS, AN' HIS FOLKS DIVORCE WAS REAL UGLY...
I CAN SYMPATHIZE. BUT THAT DOESN'T EXCUSE HIS BEHAVIOR.

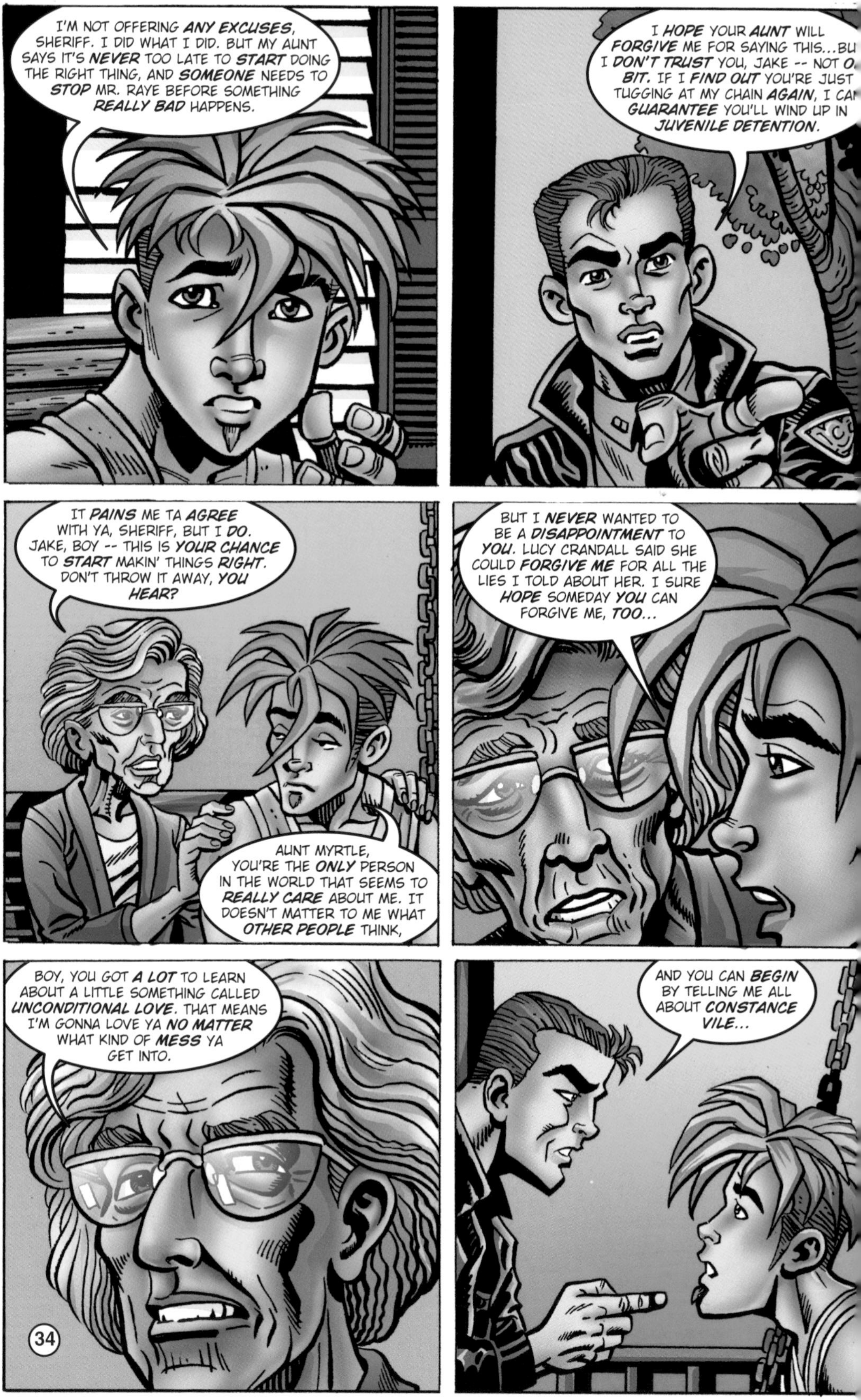
I'M NOT OFFERING ANY EXCUSES, SHERIFF. I DID WHAT I DID. BUT MY AUNT SAYS IT'S NEVER TOO LATE TO START DOING THE RIGHT THING, AND SOMEONE NEEDS TO STOP MR. RAYE BEFORE SOMETHING REALLY BAD HAPPENS.
I HOPE YOUR AUNT WILL FORGIVE ME FOR SAYING THIS...BU I DON'T TRUST YOU, JAKE -- NOT O BIT. IF I FIND OUT YOU'RE JUST TUGGING AT MY CHAIN AGAIN, I CA GUARANTEE YOU'LL WIND UP IN JUVENILE DETENTION.
IT PAINS ME TA AGREE WITH YA, SHERIFF, BUT I DO. JAKE, BOY -- THIS IS YOUR CHANCE TO START MAKIN' THINGS RIGHT. DON'T THROW IT AWAY, YOU HEAR?
AUNT MYRTLE, YOU'RE THE ONLY PERSON IN THE WORLD THAT SEEMS TO REALLY CARE ABOUT ME. IT DOESN'T MATTER TO ME WHAT OTHER PEOPLE THINK,
BUT I NEVER WANTED TO BE A DISAPPOINTMENT TO YOU. LUCY CRANDALL SAID SHE COULD FORGIVE ME FOR ALL THE LIES I TOLD ABOUT HER. I SURE HOPE SOMEDAY YOU CAN FORGIVE ME, TOO...
BOY, YOU GOT A LOT TO LEARN ABOUT A LITTLE SOMETHING CALLED UNCONDITIONAL LOVE. THAT MEANS I'M GONNA LOVE YA NO MATTER WHAT KIND OF MESS YA GET INTO.
AND YOU CAN BEGIN BY TELLING ME ALL ABOUT CONSTANCE VILE...

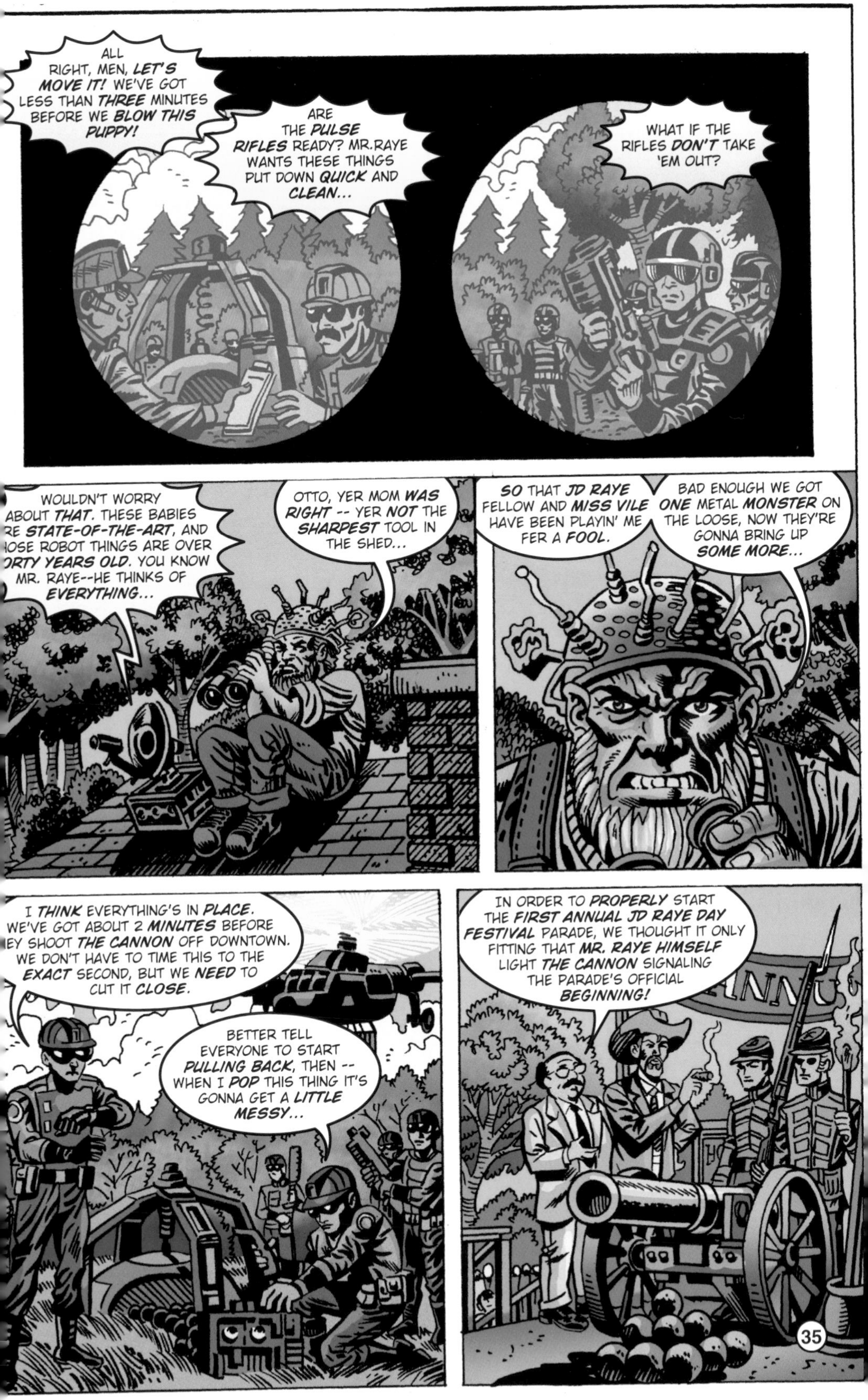

ALL RIGHT, MEN, LET'S MOVE IT! WE'VE GOT LESS THAN THREE MINUTES BEFORE WE BLOW THIS PUPPY!
ARE THE PULSE RIFLES READY? MR.RAYE WANTS THESE THINGS PUT DOWN QUICK AND CLEAN...
WHAT IF THE RIFLES DON'T TAKE 'EM OUT?
WOULDN'T WORRY ABOUT THAT. THESE BABIES RE STATE-OF-THE-ART, AND IOSE ROBOT THINGS ARE OVER ORTY YEARS OLD. YOU KNOW MR. RAYE--HE THINKS OF EVERYTHING...
OTTO, YER MOM WAS RIGHT -- YER NOT THE SHARPEST TOOL IN THE SHED...
SO THAT JD RAYE FELLOW AND MISS VILE HAVE BEEN PLAYIN' ME FER A FOOL.
BAD ENOUGH WE GOT ONE METAL MONSTER ON THE LOOSE, NOW THEY'RE GONNA BRING UP SOME MORE...
I THINK EVERYTHING'S IN PLACE. WE'VE GOT ABOUT 2 MINUTES BEFORE EY SHOOT THE CANNON OFF DOWNTOWN. WE DON'T HAVE TO TIME THIS TO THE EXACT SECOND, BUT WE NEED TO CUT IT CLOSE.
BETTER TELL EVERYONE TO START PULLING BACK, THEN -- WHEN I POP THIS THING IT'S GONNA GET A LITTLE MESSY...
IN ORDER TO PROPERLY START THE FIRST ANNUAL JD RAYE DAY FESTIVAL PARADE, WE THOUGHT IT ONLY FITTING THAT MR. RAYE HIMSELF LIGHT THE CANNON SIGNALING THE PARADE'S OFFICIAL BEGINNING!

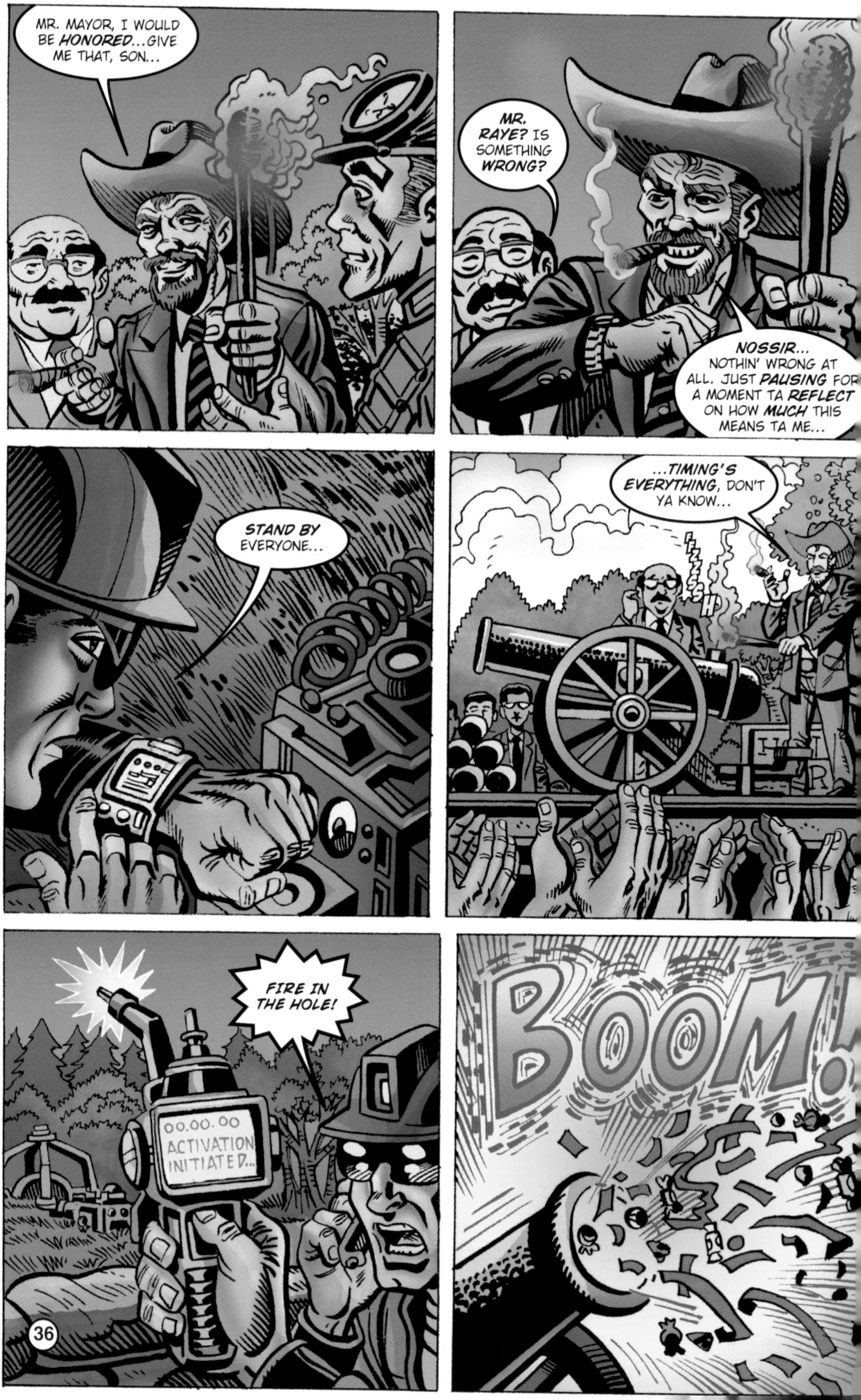
MR. MAYOR, I WOULD BE HONORED...GIVE ME THAT, SON...
MR. RAYE? IS SOMETHING WRONG?
NOSSIR... NOTHIN' WRONG AT ALL. JUST PAUSING FOR A MOMENT TA REFLECT ON HOW MUCH THIS MEANS TA ME...
STAND BY EVERYONE...
...TIMING'S EVERYTHING, DON'T YA KNOW...
FZZZSSH
FIRE IN THE HOLE!
00.00.00
ACTIVATION INITIATED...
BOOM!

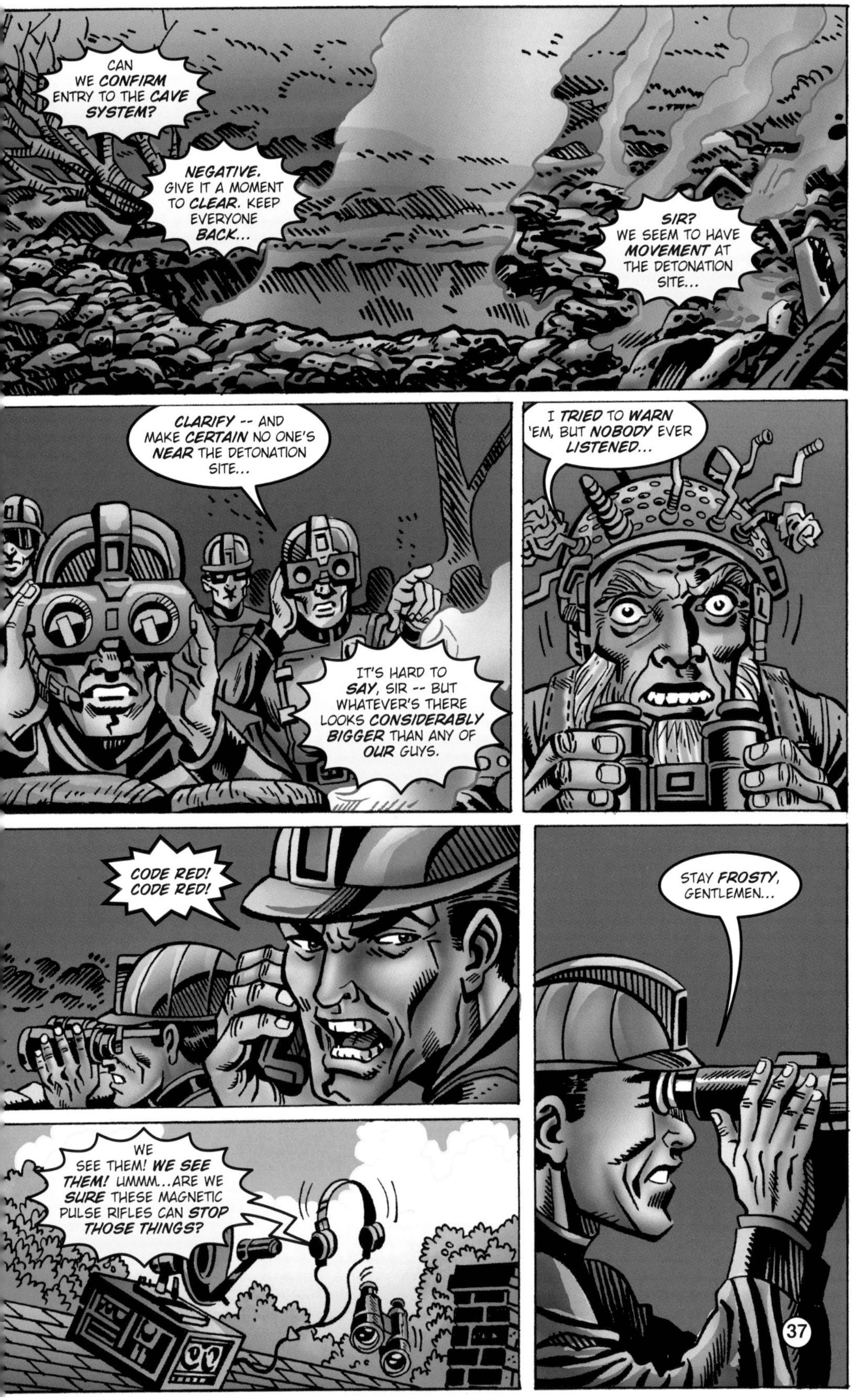
CAN WE CONFIRM ENTRY TO THE CAVE SYSTEM?
NEGATIVE. GIVE IT A MOMENT TO CLEAR. KEEP EVERYONE BACK...
SIR? WE SEEM TO HAVE MOVEMENT AT THE DETONATION SITE...
CLARIFY -- AND MAKE CERTAIN NO ONE'S NEAR THE DETONATION SITE...
IT'S HARD TO SAY, SIR -- BUT WHATEVER'S THERE LOOKS CONSIDERABLY BIGGER THAN ANY OF OUR GUYS.
I TRIED TO WARN 'EM, BUT NOBODY EVER LISTENED...
CODE RED! CODE RED!
WE SEE THEM! WE SEE THEM! UMMM...ARE WE SURE THESE MAGNETIC PULSE RIFLES CAN STOP THOSE THINGS?
STAY FROSTY, GENTLEMEN...

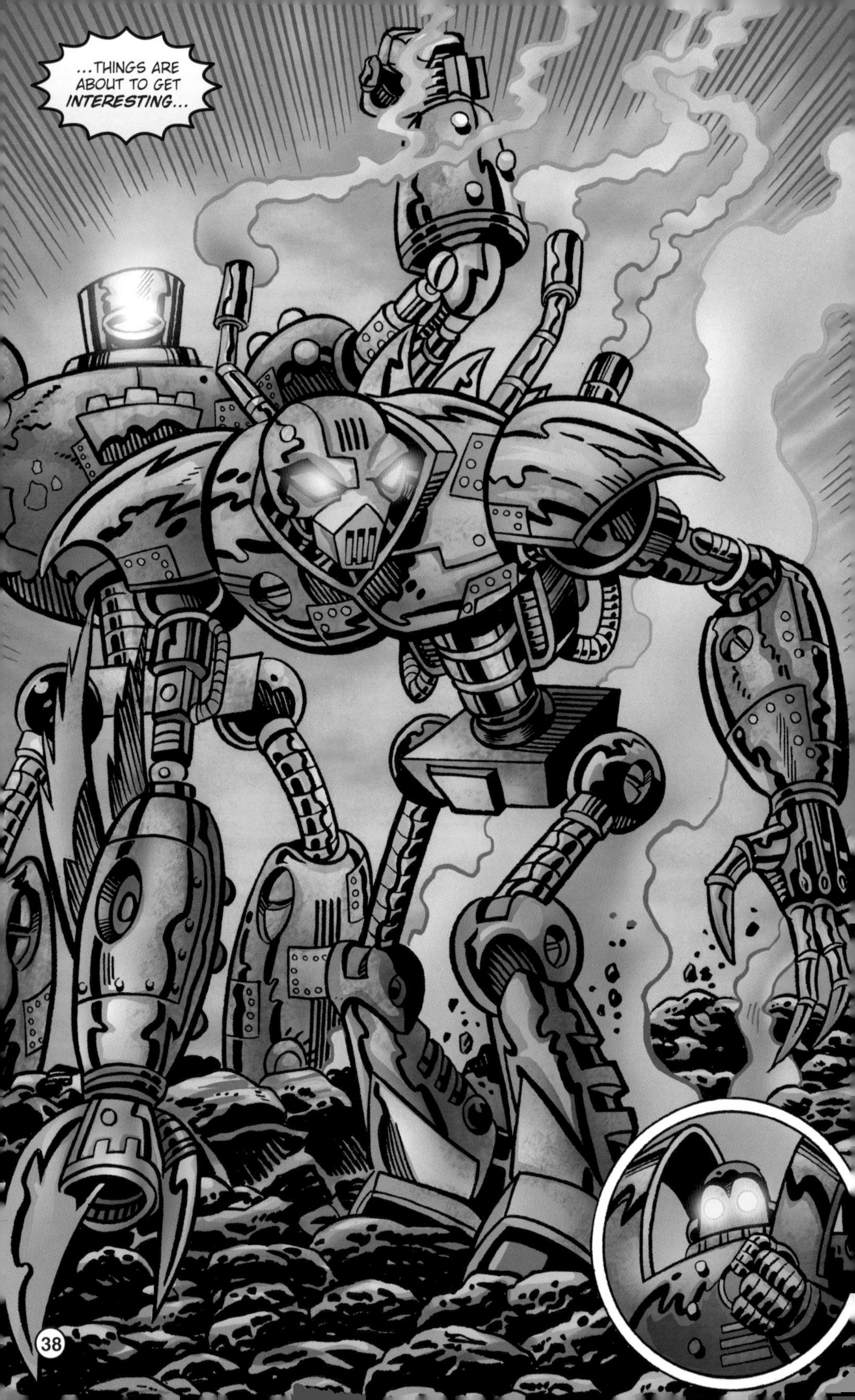
...THINGS ARE ABOUT TO GET *INTERESTING*...

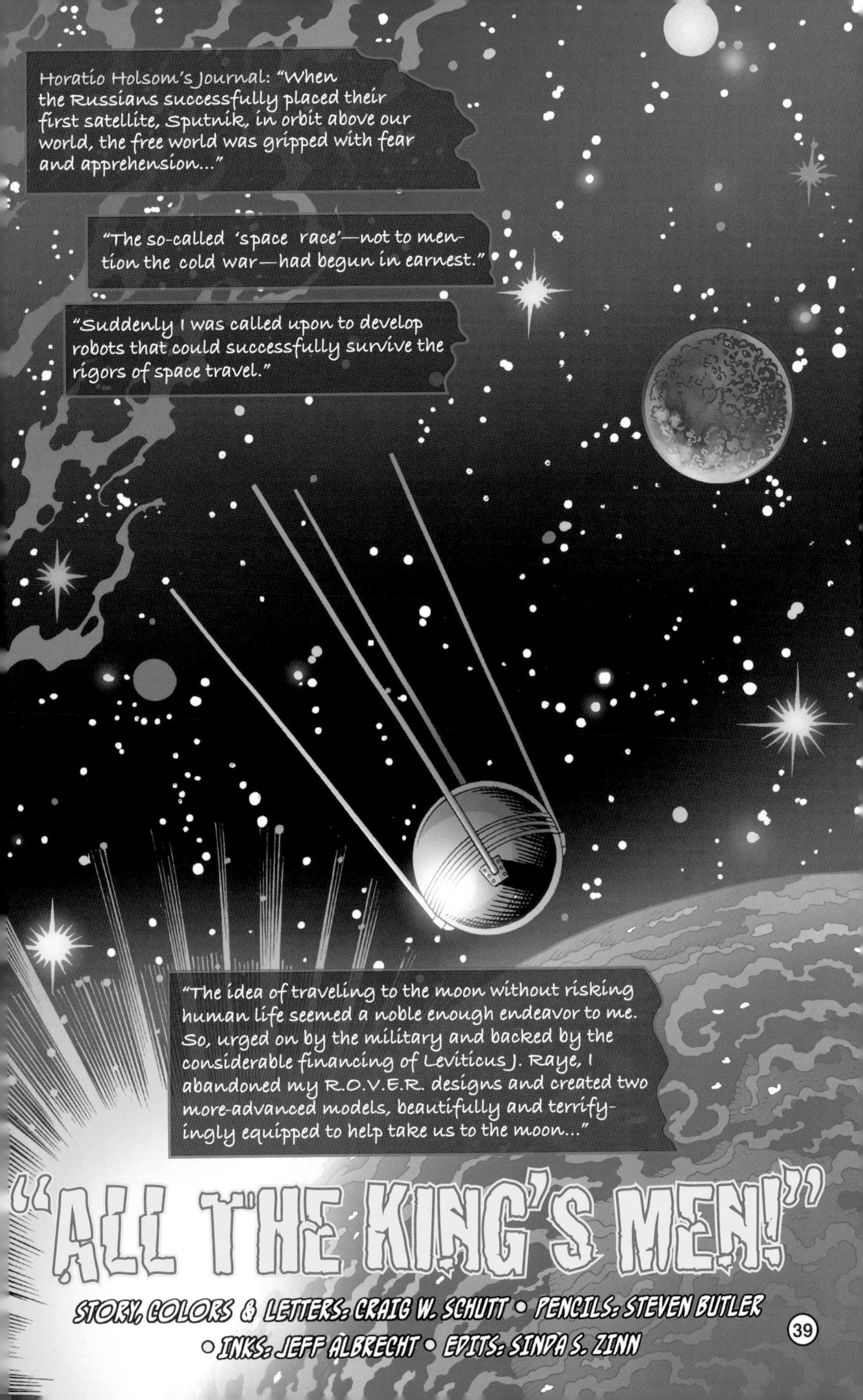
Horatio Holsom's Journal: "When the Russians successfully placed their first satellite, Sputnik, in orbit above our world, the free world was gripped with fear and apprehension..."
"The so-called 'space race'—not to mention the cold war—had begun in earnest."
"Suddenly I was called upon to develop robots that could successfully survive the rigors of space travel."
"The idea of traveling to the moon without risking human life seemed a noble enough endeavor to me. So, urged on by the military and backed by the considerable financing of Leviticus J. Raye, I abandoned my R.O.V.E.R. designs and created two more-advanced models, beautifully and terrifyingly equipped to help take us to the moon..."
"ALL THE KING'S MEN!"
STORY, COLORS & LETTERS: CRAIG W. SCHUTT • PENCILS: STEVEN BUTLER • INKS: JEFF ALBRECHT • EDITS: SINDA S. ZINN

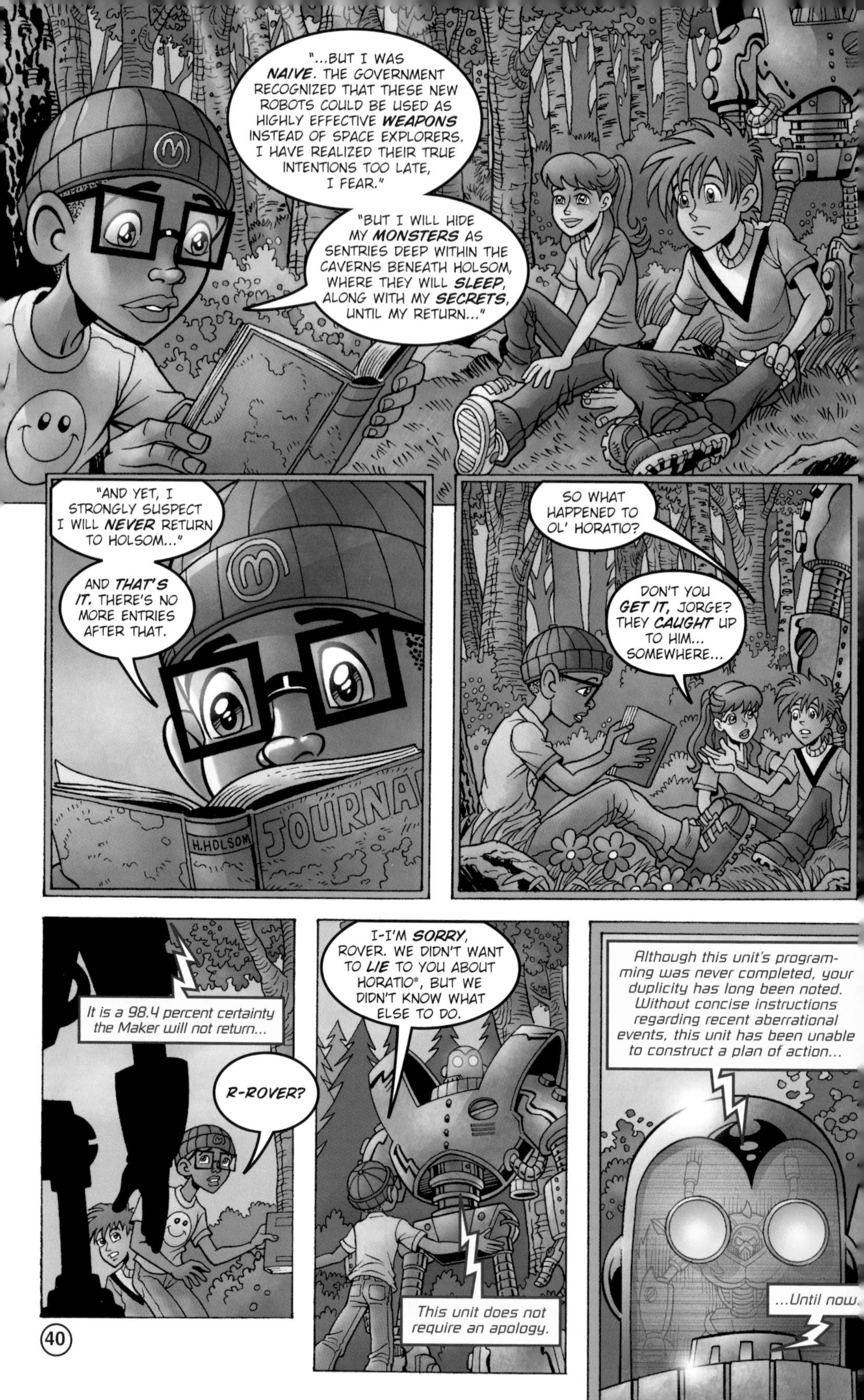

"...BUT I WAS NAIVE. THE GOVERNMENT RECOGNIZED THAT THESE NEW ROBOTS COULD BE USED AS HIGHLY EFFECTIVE WEAPONS INSTEAD OF SPACE EXPLORERS. I HAVE REALIZED THEIR TRUE INTENTIONS TOO LATE, I FEAR."
"BUT I WILL HIDE MY MONSTERS AS SENTRIES DEEP WITHIN THE CAVERNS BENEATH HOLSOM, WHERE THEY WILL SLEEP, ALONG WITH MY SECRETS, UNTIL MY RETURN..."
"AND YET, I STRONGLY SUSPECT I WILL NEVER RETURN TO HOLSOM..."
AND THAT'S IT. THERE'S NO MORE ENTRIES AFTER THAT.
JOURNAL
H. HOLSOM
SO WHAT HAPPENED TO OL' HORATIO?
DON'T YOU GET IT, JORGE? THEY CAUGHT UP TO HIM... SOMEWHERE...
It is a 98.4 percent certainty the Maker will not return...
R-ROVER?
I-I'M SORRY, ROVER. WE DIDN'T WANT TO LIE TO YOU ABOUT HORATIO*, BUT WE DIDN'T KNOW WHAT ELSE TO DO.
This unit does not require an apology.
Although this unit's programming was never completed, your duplicity has long been noted. Without concise instructions regarding recent aberrational events, this unit has been unable to construct a plan of action...
...Until now.

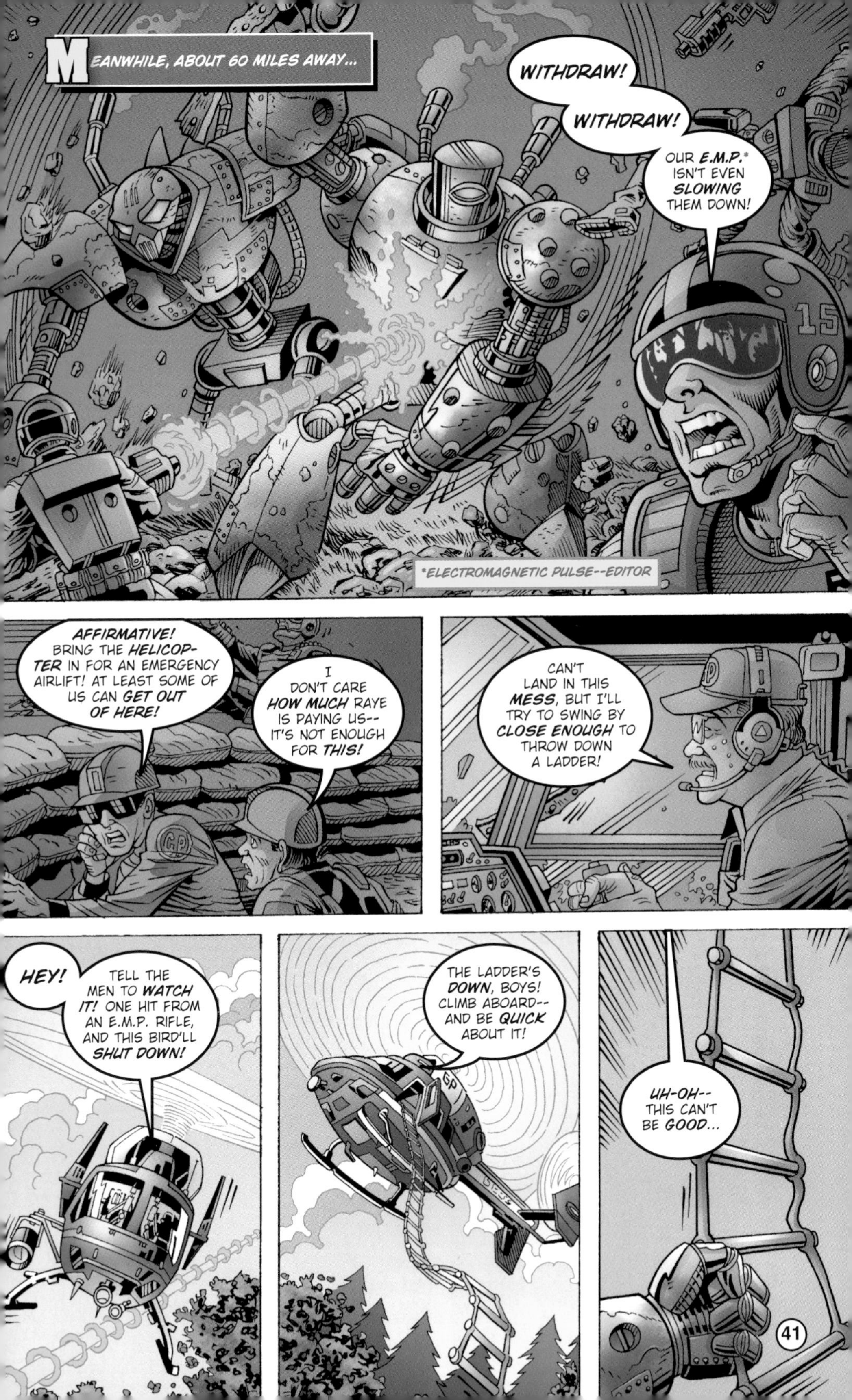

MEANWHILE, ABOUT 60 MILES AWAY...
WITHDRAW!
WITHDRAW!
OUR E.M.P.* ISN'T EVEN SLOWING THEM DOWN!
*ELECTROMAGNETIC PULSE--EDITOR
AFFIRMATIVE! BRING THE HELICOPTER IN FOR AN EMERGENCY AIRLIFT! AT LEAST SOME OF US CAN GET OUT OF HERE!
I DON'T CARE HOW MUCH RAYE IS PAYING US-- IT'S NOT ENOUGH FOR THIS!
CAN'T LAND IN THIS MESS, BUT I'LL TRY TO SWING BY CLOSE ENOUGH TO THROW DOWN A LADDER!
HEY!
TELL THE MEN TO WATCH IT! ONE HIT FROM AN E.M.P. RIFLE, AND THIS BIRD'LL SHUT DOWN!
THE LADDER'S DOWN, BOYS! CLIMB ABOARD-- AND BE QUICK ABOUT IT!
UH-OH-- THIS CAN'T BE GOOD...

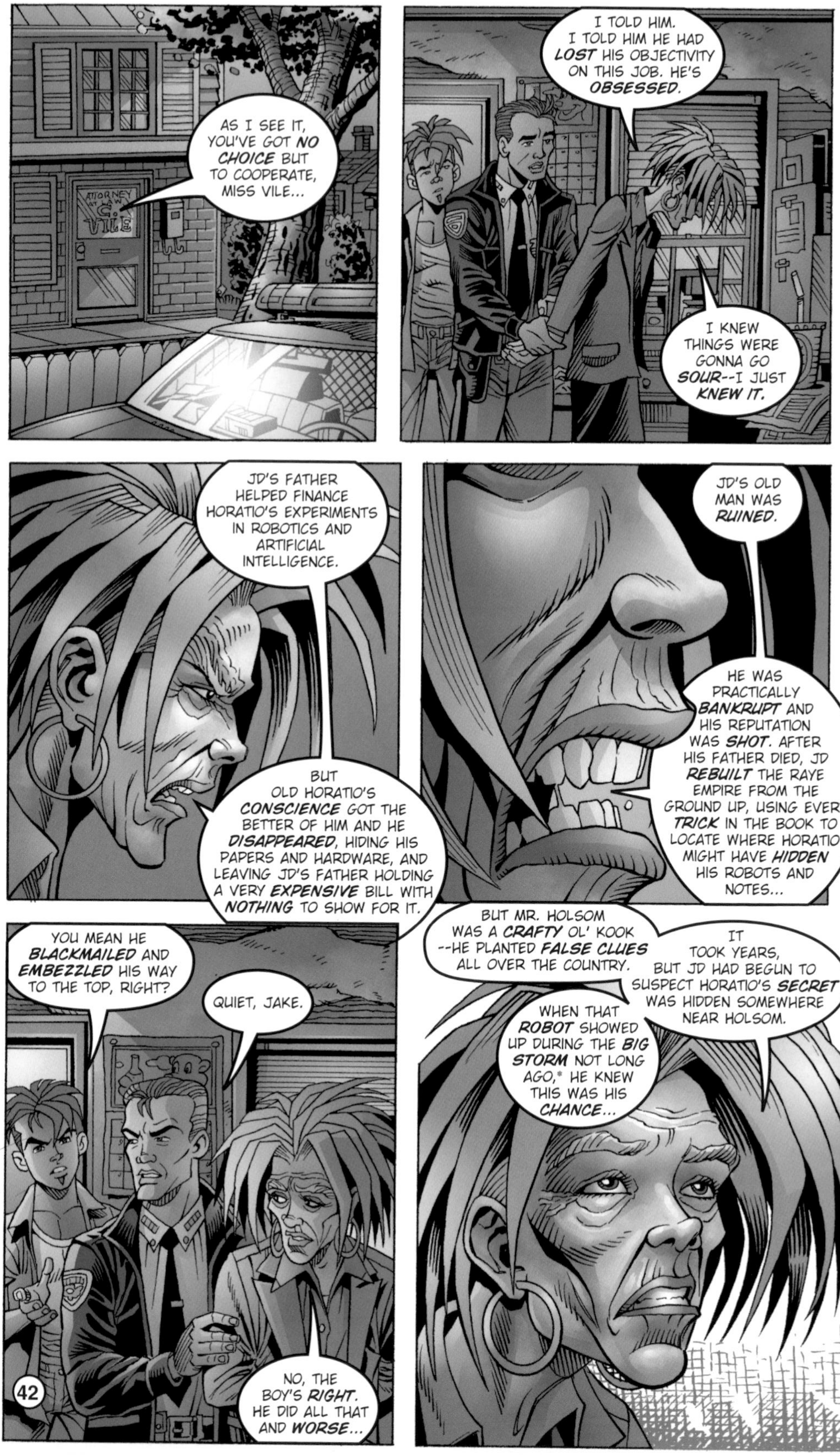
ATTORNEY AT LAW C. VILE
AS I SEE IT, YOU'VE GOT NO CHOICE BUT TO COOPERATE, MISS VILE...
I TOLD HIM. I TOLD HIM HE HAD LOST HIS OBJECTIVITY ON THIS JOB. HE'S OBSESSED.
I KNEW THINGS WERE GONNA GO SOUR--I JUST KNEW IT.
JD'S FATHER HELPED FINANCE HORATIO'S EXPERIMENTS IN ROBOTICS AND ARTIFICIAL INTELLIGENCE.
BUT OLD HORATIO'S CONSCIENCE GOT THE BETTER OF HIM AND HE DISAPPEARED, HIDING HIS PAPERS AND HARDWARE, AND LEAVING JD'S FATHER HOLDING A VERY EXPENSIVE BILL WITH NOTHING TO SHOW FOR IT.
JD'S OLD MAN WAS RUINED.
HE WAS PRACTICALLY BANKRUPT AND HIS REPUTATION WAS SHOT. AFTER HIS FATHER DIED, JD REBUILT THE RAYE EMPIRE FROM THE GROUND UP, USING EVERY TRICK IN THE BOOK TO LOCATE WHERE HORATIO MIGHT HAVE HIDDEN HIS ROBOTS AND NOTES...
YOU MEAN HE BLACKMAILED AND EMBEZZLED HIS WAY TO THE TOP, RIGHT?
QUIET, JAKE.
NO, THE BOY'S RIGHT. HE DID ALL THAT AND WORSE...
BUT MR. HOLSOM WAS A CRAFTY OL' KOOK --HE PLANTED FALSE CLUES ALL OVER THE COUNTRY.
IT TOOK YEARS, BUT JD HAD BEGUN TO SUSPECT HORATIO'S SECRET WAS HIDDEN SOMEWHERE NEAR HOLSOM.
WHEN THAT ROBOT SHOWED UP DURING THE BIG STORM NOT LONG AGO,* HE KNEW THIS WAS HIS CHANCE...

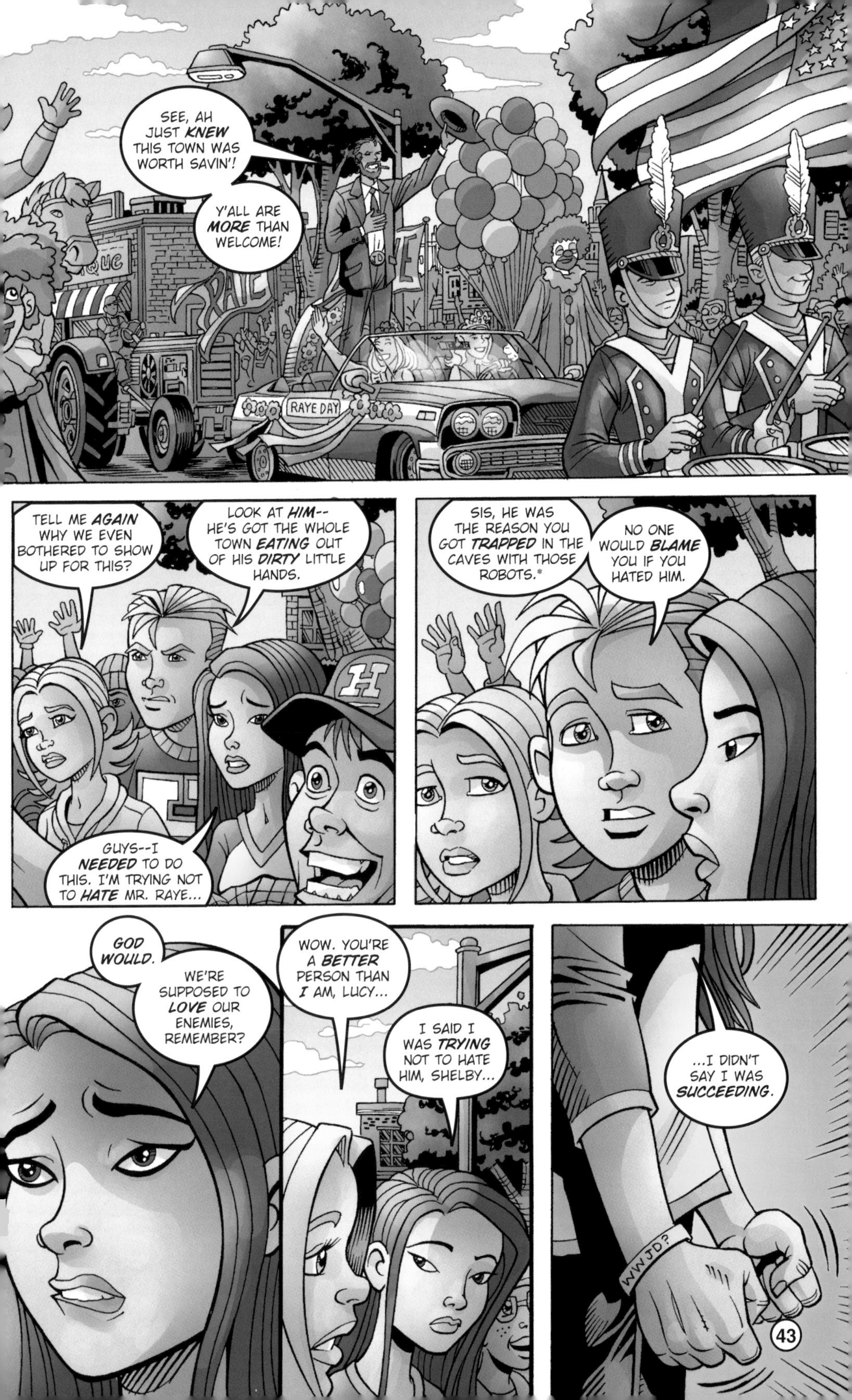

SEE, AH JUST KNEW THIS TOWN WAS WORTH SAVIN'!
Y'ALL ARE MORE THAN WELCOME!
RAYE DAY
TELL ME AGAIN WHY WE EVEN BOTHERED TO SHOW UP FOR THIS?
LOOK AT HIM-- HE'S GOT THE WHOLE TOWN EATING OUT OF HIS DIRTY LITTLE HANDS.
GUYS--I NEEDED TO DO THIS. I'M TRYING NOT TO HATE MR. RAYE...
SIS, HE WAS THE REASON YOU GOT TRAPPED IN THE CAVES WITH THOSE ROBOTS.*
NO ONE WOULD BLAME YOU IF YOU HATED HIM.
GOD WOULD.
WE'RE SUPPOSED TO LOVE OUR ENEMIES, REMEMBER?
WOW. YOU'RE A BETTER PERSON THAN I AM, LUCY...
I SAID I WAS TRYING NOT TO HATE HIM, SHELBY...
...I DIDN'T SAY I WAS SUCCEEDING.
WWJD?

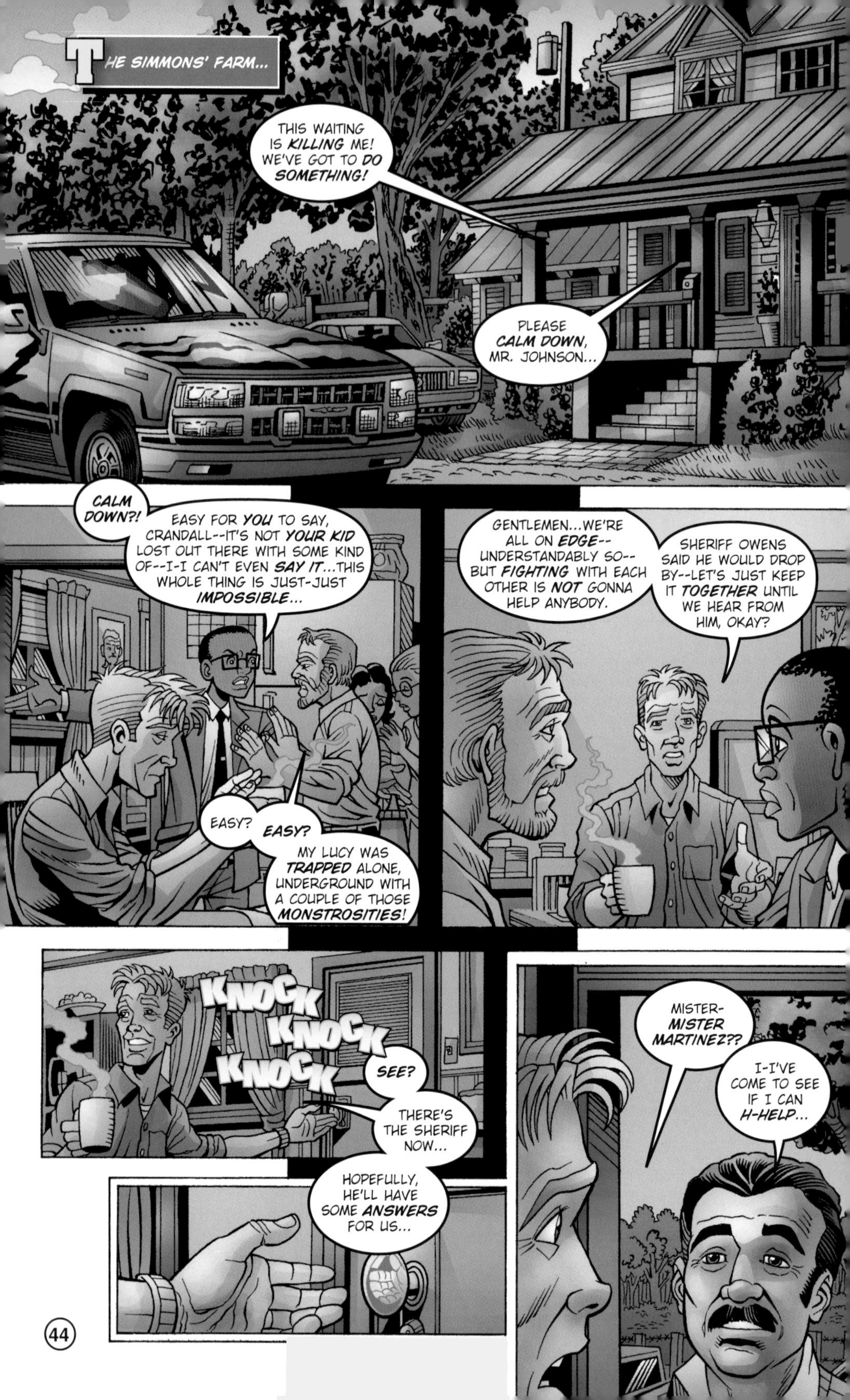
THE SIMMONS' FARM...
THIS WAITING IS KILLING ME! WE'VE GOT TO DO SOMETHING!
PLEASE CALM DOWN, MR. JOHNSON...
CALM DOWN?!
EASY FOR YOU TO SAY, CRANDALL--IT'S NOT YOUR KID LOST OUT THERE WITH SOME KIND OF--I-I CAN'T EVEN SAY IT...THIS WHOLE THING IS JUST-JUST IMPOSSIBLE...
EASY?
EASY?
MY LUCY WAS TRAPPED ALONE, UNDERGROUND WITH A COUPLE OF THOSE MONSTROSITIES!
GENTLEMEN...WE'RE ALL ON EDGE--UNDERSTANDABLY SO--BUT FIGHTING WITH EACH OTHER IS NOT GONNA HELP ANYBODY.
SHERIFF OWENS SAID HE WOULD DROP BY--LET'S JUST KEEP IT TOGETHER UNTIL WE HEAR FROM HIM, OKAY?
KNOCK
KNOCK
KNOCK
SEE?
THERE'S THE SHERIFF NOW...
HOPEFULLY, HE'LL HAVE SOME ANSWERS FOR US...
MISTER-MISTER MARTINEZ??
I-I'VE COME TO SEE IF I CAN H-HELP...

ROVER!

ROVER, WAIT UP!

WHAT'S WRONG WITH HIM?

I DUNNO! ALL HE SAID WAS THAT HE HAD TO GET BACK TO HOLSOM--FAST!

HOLSOM?! BUT ISN'T THAT WHERE YOU'VE BEEN RUNNING AWAY FROM ALL THIS TIME?

I KNOW! I KNOW!

THIS IS NUTS!

OUCH!

NOW WHAT?

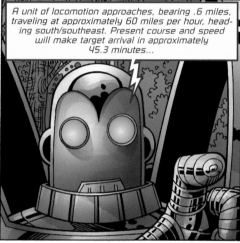

A unit of locomotion approaches, bearing .6 miles, traveling at approximately 60 miles per hour, heading south/southeast. Present course and speed will make target arrival in approximately 45.3 minutes...

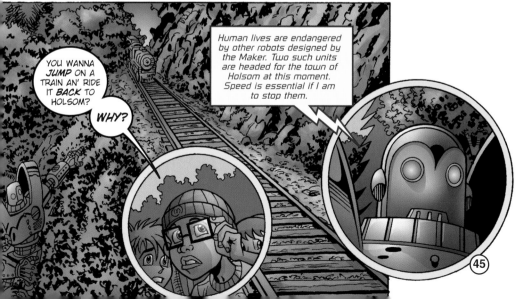

YOU WANNA JUMP ON A TRAIN AN' RIDE IT BACK TO HOLSOM?

WHY?

Human lives are endangered by other robots designed by the Maker. Two such units are headed for the town of Holsom at this moment. Speed is essential if I am to stop them.

45

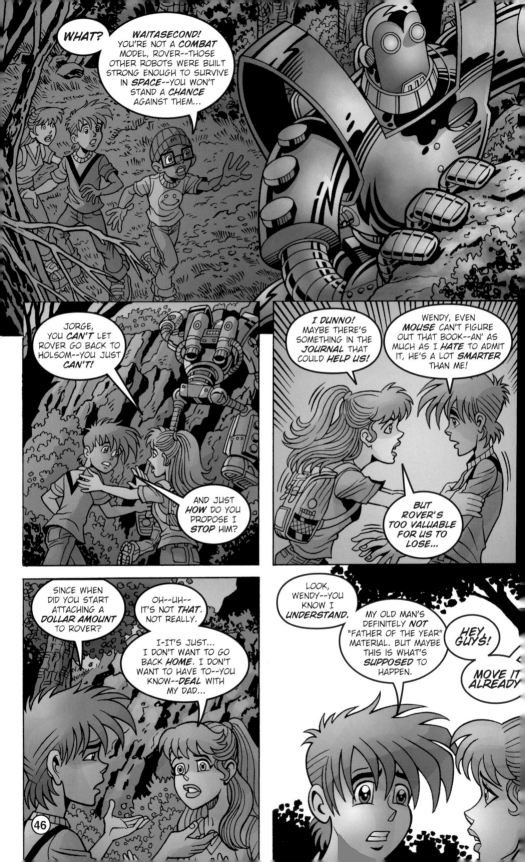

WHAT?

WAITASECOND! YOU'RE NOT A *COMBAT* MODEL, ROVER--THOSE OTHER ROBOTS WERE BUILT STRONG ENOUGH TO SURVIVE IN *SPACE*--YOU WON'T STAND A *CHANCE* AGAINST THEM...

JORGE, YOU *CAN'T* LET ROVER GO BACK TO HOLSOM--YOU JUST *CAN'T!*

AND JUST *HOW* DO YOU PROPOSE I *STOP* HIM?

I *DUNNO!* MAYBE THERE'S SOMETHING IN THE *JOURNAL* THAT COULD *HELP US!*

WENDY, EVEN *MOUSE* CAN'T FIGURE OUT THAT BOOK--AN' AS MUCH AS I *HATE* TO ADMIT IT, HE'S A LOT *SMARTER* THAN ME!

BUT ROVER'S TOO VALUABLE FOR US TO LOSE...

SINCE WHEN DID YOU START ATTACHING A *DOLLAR AMOUNT* TO ROVER?

OH--UH-- IT'S NOT *THAT.* NOT REALLY.

I-IT'S JUST... I DON'T WANT TO GO BACK *HOME.* I DON'T WANT TO HAVE TO--YOU KNOW--*DEAL* WITH MY DAD...

LOOK, WENDY--YOU KNOW I *UNDERSTAND.*

MY OLD MAN'S DEFINITELY *NOT* "FATHER OF THE YEAR" MATERIAL. BUT MAYBE THIS IS WHAT'S *SUPPOSED* TO HAPPEN.

HEY GUYS!

MOVE IT ALREADY

46

THE TRAIN'S ALMOST HERE!

HOW ARE WE SUPPOSED TO *GET ON* THAT THING?

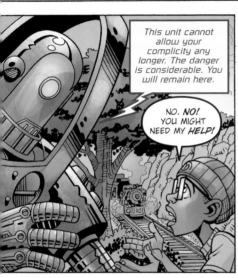

This unit cannot allow your complicity any longer. The danger is considerable. You will remain here.

NO. *NO!* YOU MIGHT NEED MY *HELP!*

BIG BRAIN'S RIGHT, ROVER-- WE'RE COMIN' ALONG WHETHER YOU *LIKE IT* OR *NOT.*

WE MAY GET *HURT* TRYING TO JUMP ONTO THE TRAIN WITHOUT YOUR HELP, BUT THAT'S WHAT WE'RE GONNA DO!

Consequently, this unit has no recourse. Please obtain a substantial grasp...

HERE WE GO AGAIN...

WHAT IN THE WORLD IS *THAT?!*

I'M SEEIN' IT, BUT THERE'S NO WAY I'M GONNA LOG THIS INTO A REPORT --THEY'D *THROW* US BOTH IN THE *LOONY BIN!*

47

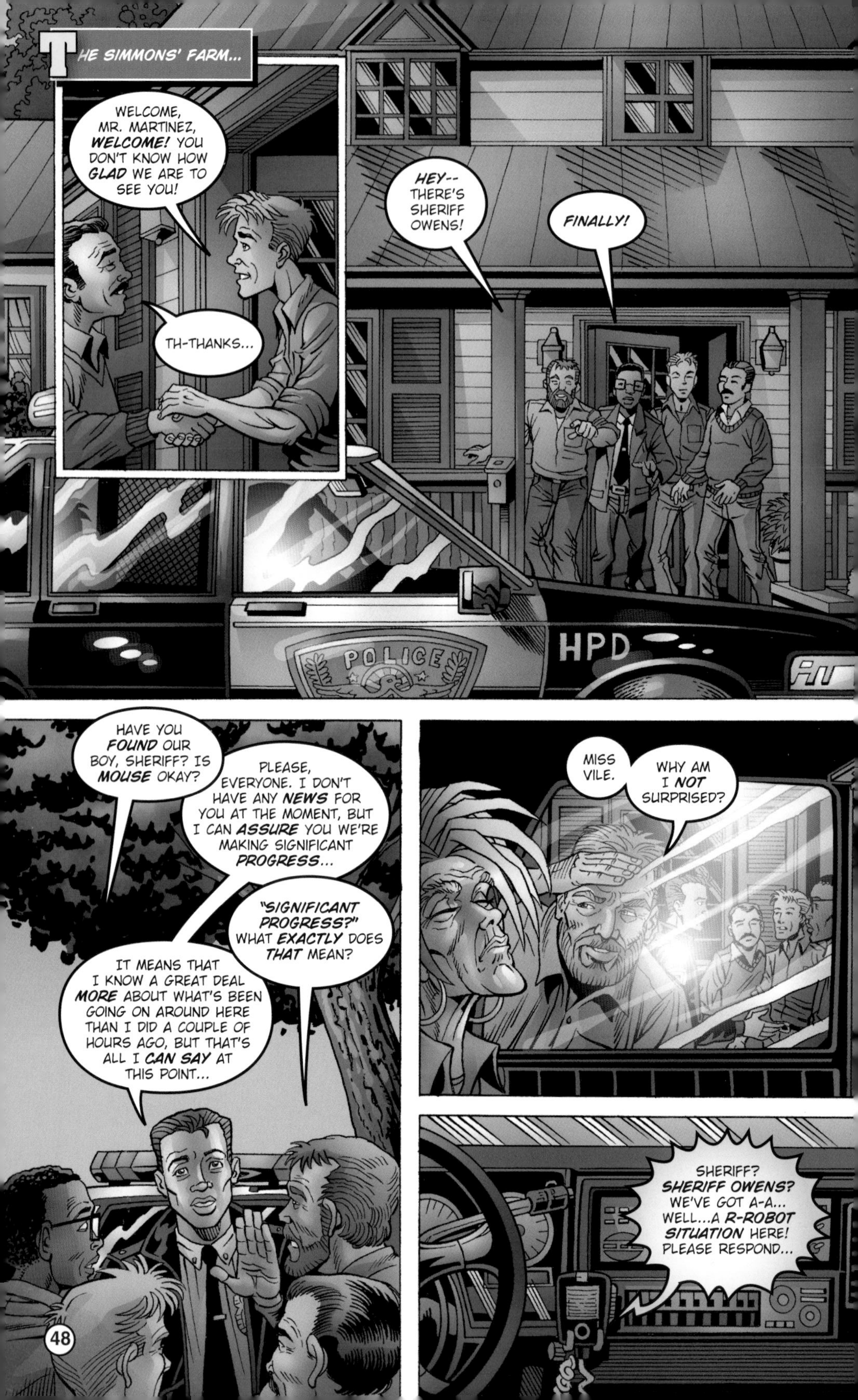
THE SIMMONS' FARM...
WELCOME, MR. MARTINEZ, WELCOME! YOU DON'T KNOW HOW GLAD WE ARE TO SEE YOU!
TH-THANKS...
HEY-- THERE'S SHERIFF OWENS!
FINALLY!
HPD
POLICE
HAVE YOU FOUND OUR BOY, SHERIFF? IS MOUSE OKAY?
PLEASE, EVERYONE. I DON'T HAVE ANY NEWS FOR YOU AT THE MOMENT, BUT I CAN ASSURE YOU WE'RE MAKING SIGNIFICANT PROGRESS...
"SIGNIFICANT PROGRESS?" WHAT EXACTLY DOES THAT MEAN?
IT MEANS THAT I KNOW A GREAT DEAL MORE ABOUT WHAT'S BEEN GOING ON AROUND HERE THAN I DID A COUPLE OF HOURS AGO, BUT THAT'S ALL I CAN SAY AT THIS POINT...
MISS VILE.
WHY AM I NOT SURPRISED?
SHERIFF? SHERIFF OWENS? WE'VE GOT A-A... WELL...A R-ROBOT SITUATION HERE! PLEASE RESPOND...

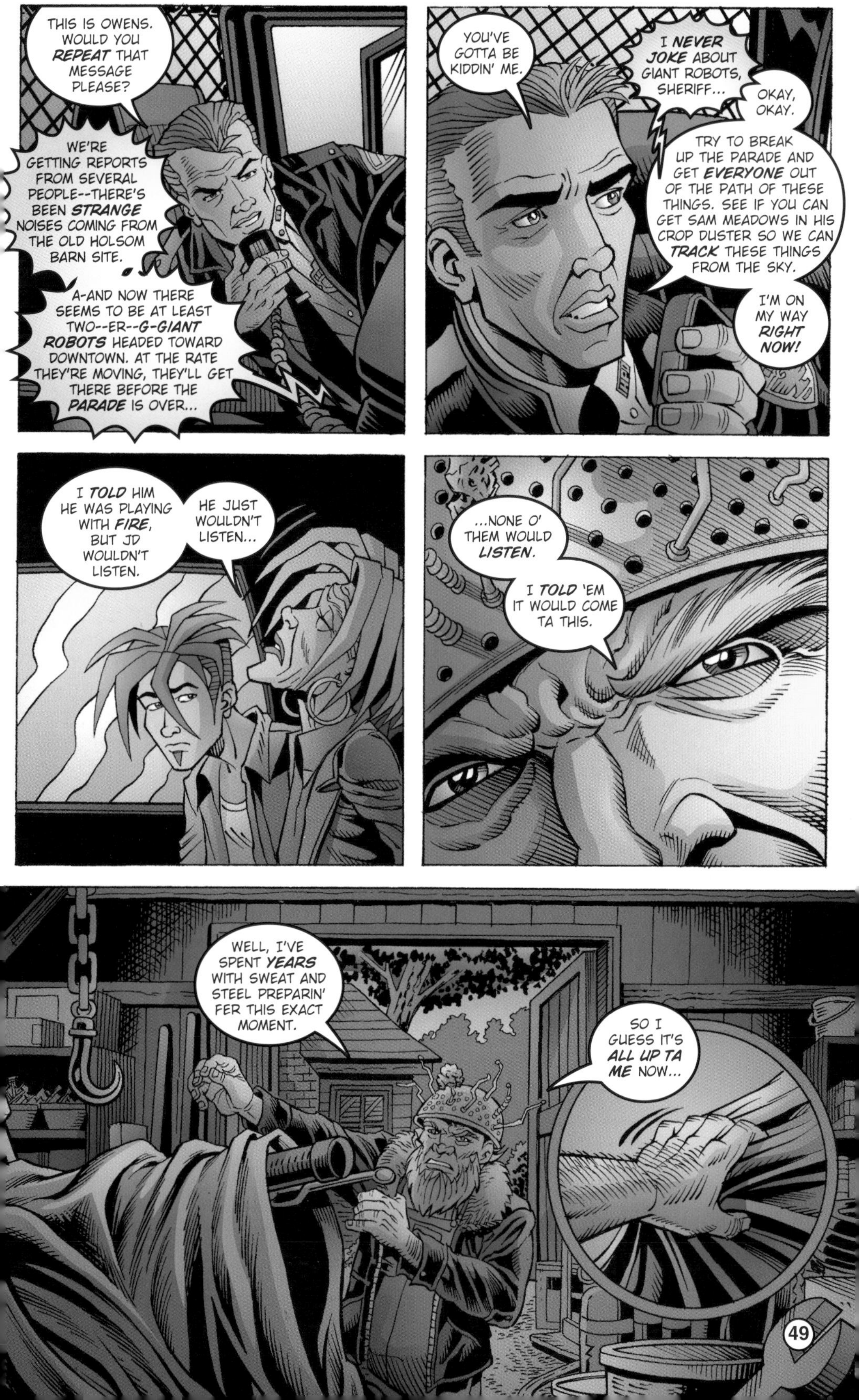
THIS IS OWENS. WOULD YOU REPEAT THAT MESSAGE PLEASE?
WE'RE GETTING REPORTS FROM SEVERAL PEOPLE--THERE'S BEEN STRANGE NOISES COMING FROM THE OLD HOLSOM BARN SITE.
A-AND NOW THERE SEEMS TO BE AT LEAST TWO--ER--G-GIANT ROBOTS HEADED TOWARD DOWNTOWN. AT THE RATE THEY'RE MOVING, THEY'LL GET THERE BEFORE THE PARADE IS OVER...
YOU'VE GOTTA BE KIDDIN' ME.
I NEVER JOKE ABOUT GIANT ROBOTS, SHERIFF...
OKAY, OKAY.
TRY TO BREAK UP THE PARADE AND GET EVERYONE OUT OF THE PATH OF THESE THINGS. SEE IF YOU CAN GET SAM MEADOWS IN HIS CROP DUSTER SO WE CAN TRACK THESE THINGS FROM THE SKY.
I'M ON MY WAY RIGHT NOW!
I TOLD HIM HE WAS PLAYING WITH FIRE, BUT JD WOULDN'T LISTEN.
HE JUST WOULDN'T LISTEN...
...NONE O' THEM WOULD LISTEN.
I TOLD 'EM IT WOULD COME TA THIS.
WELL, I'VE SPENT YEARS WITH SWEAT AND STEEL PREPARIN' FER THIS EXACT MOMENT.
SO I GUESS IT'S ALL UP TA ME NOW...

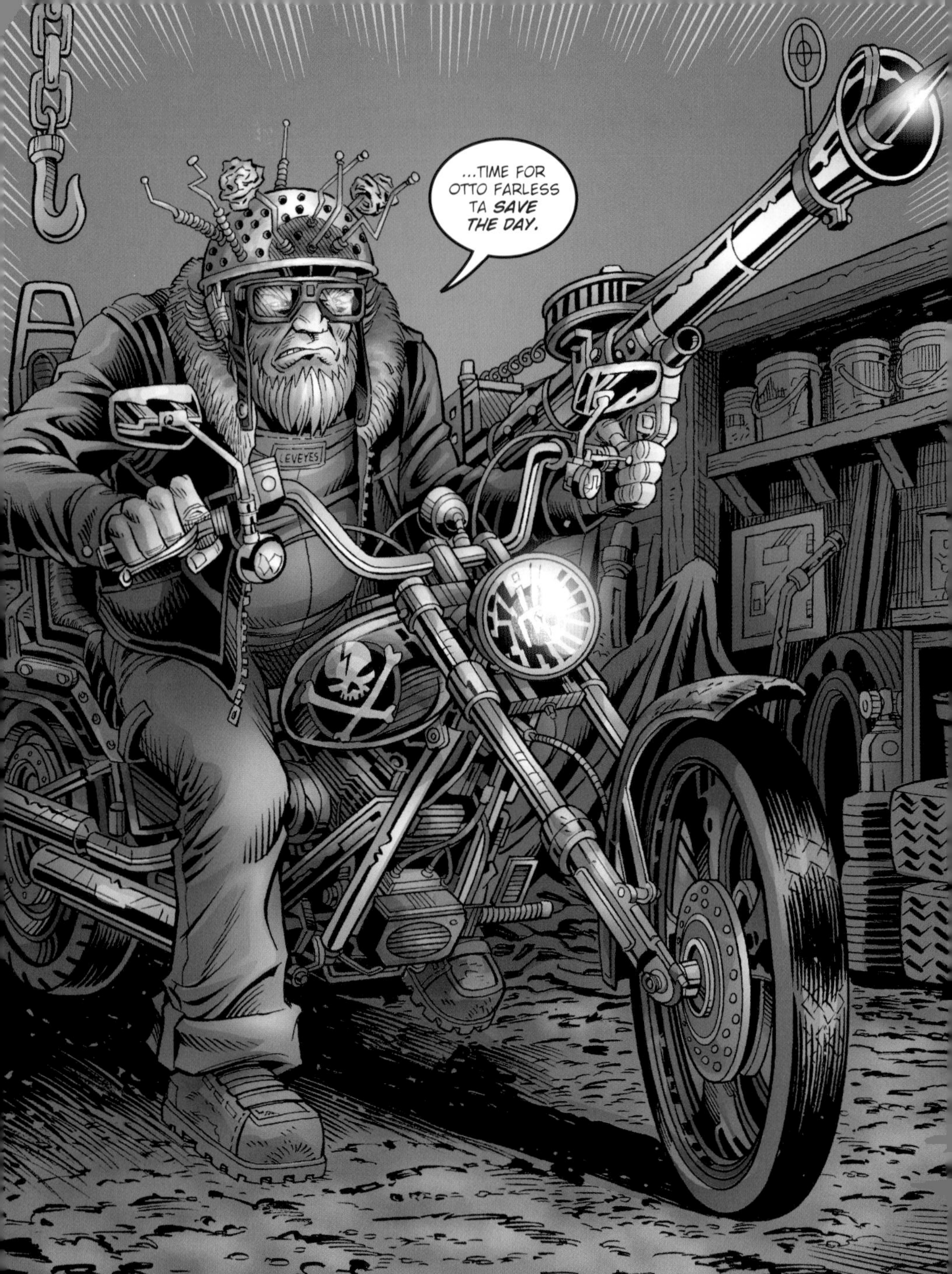
...TIME FOR OTTO FARLESS TA *SAVE THE DAY.*

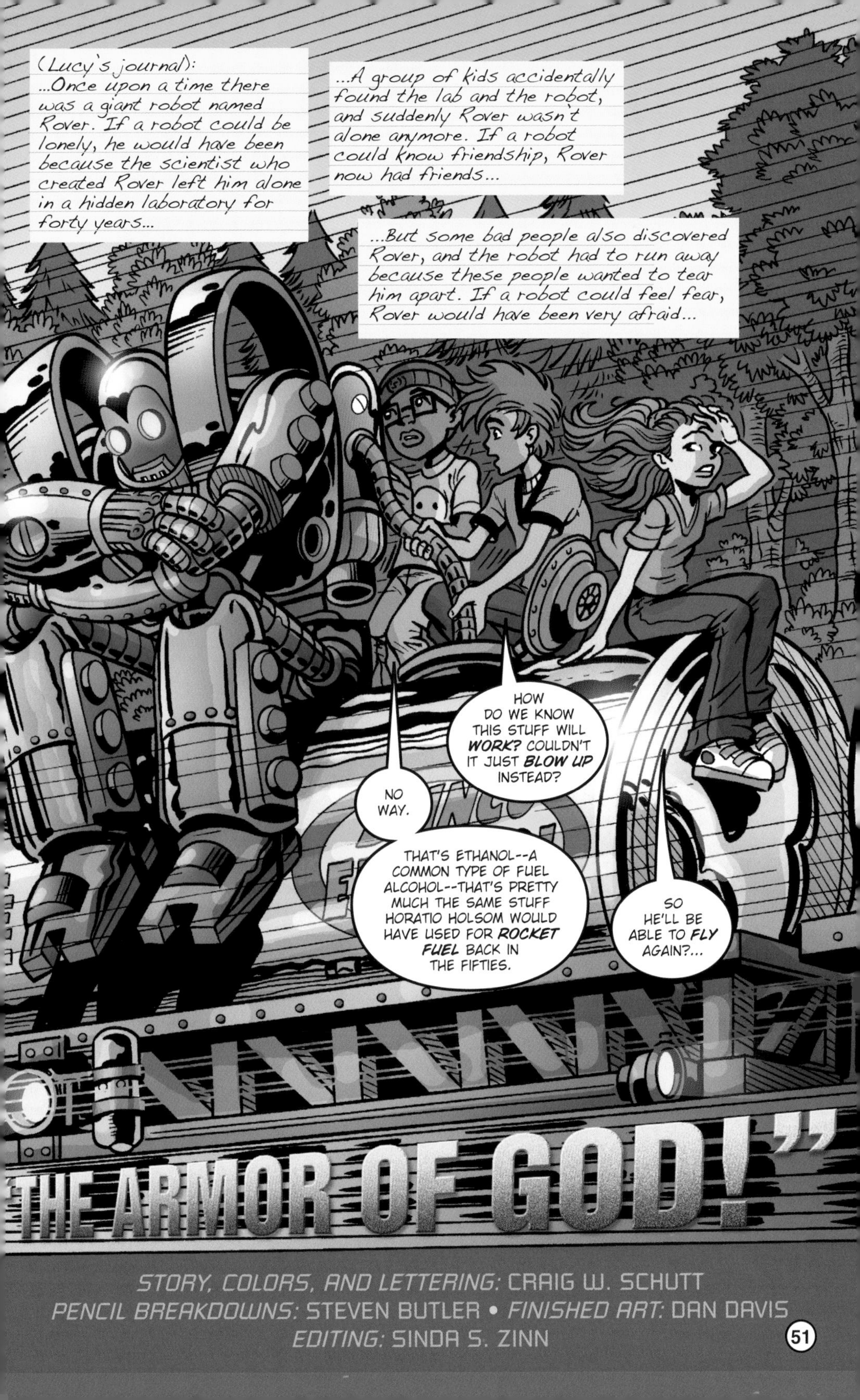
(Lucy's journal):
...Once upon a time there was a giant robot named Rover. If a robot could be lonely, he would have been because the scientist who created Rover left him alone in a hidden laboratory for forty years...
...A group of kids accidentally found the lab and the robot, and suddenly Rover wasn't alone anymore. If a robot could know friendship, Rover now had friends...
...But some bad people also discovered Rover, and the robot had to run away because these people wanted to tear him apart. If a robot could feel fear, Rover would have been very afraid...
HOW DO WE KNOW THIS STUFF WILL WORK? COULDN'T IT JUST BLOW UP INSTEAD?
NO WAY.
THAT'S ETHANOL--A COMMON TYPE OF FUEL ALCOHOL--THAT'S PRETTY MUCH THE SAME STUFF HORATIO HOLSOM WOULD HAVE USED FOR ROCKET FUEL BACK IN THE FIFTIES.
SO HE'LL BE ABLE TO FLY AGAIN?...
THE ARMOR OF GOD!”

STORY, COLORS, AND LETTERING: CRAIG W. SCHUTT
PENCIL BREAKDOWNS: STEVEN BUTLER • *FINISHED ART:* DAN DAVIS
EDITING: SINDA S. ZINN

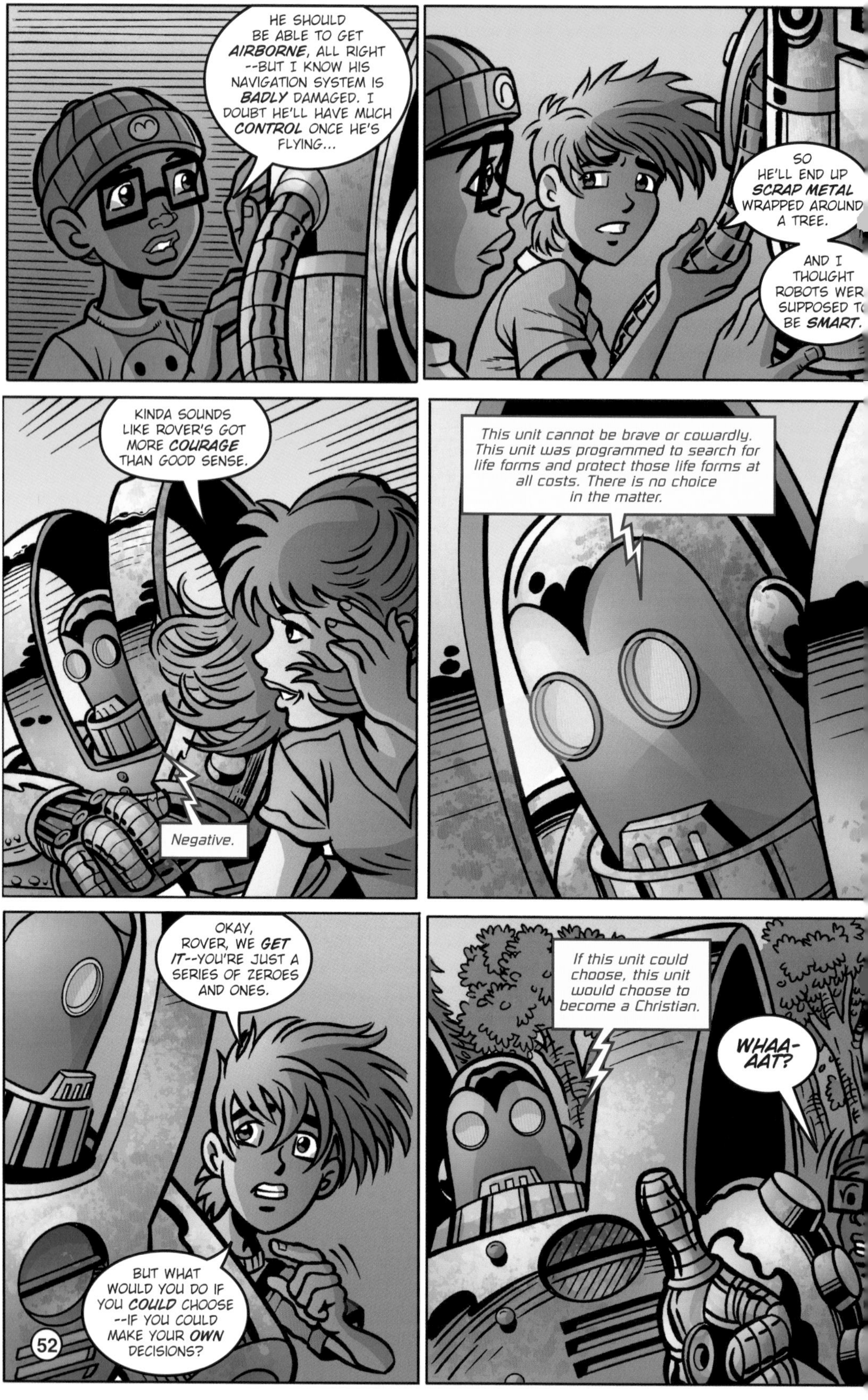
HE SHOULD BE ABLE TO GET AIRBORNE, ALL RIGHT --BUT I KNOW HIS NAVIGATION SYSTEM IS BADLY DAMAGED. I DOUBT HE'LL HAVE MUCH CONTROL ONCE HE'S FLYING...
SO HE'LL END UP SCRAP METAL WRAPPED AROUND A TREE.
AND I THOUGHT ROBOTS WER SUPPOSED T BE SMART.
KINDA SOUNDS LIKE ROVER'S GOT MORE COURAGE THAN GOOD SENSE.
Negative.
This unit cannot be brave or cowardly. This unit was programmed to search for life forms and protect those life forms at all costs. There is no choice in the matter.
OKAY, ROVER, WE GET IT--YOU'RE JUST A SERIES OF ZEROES AND ONES.
BUT WHAT WOULD YOU DO IF YOU COULD CHOOSE --IF YOU COULD MAKE YOUR OWN DECISIONS?
If this unit could choose, this unit would choose to become a Christian.
WHAA-AAT?

Like everything else that exists, human beings can physically be described and defined using equations and formulas. The universe has been designed mathematically, is this not so?

But if there is nothing more to existence than numbers, then why wrestle with morality?

WE'VE HAD THIS CONVERSATION *BEFORE*, ROVER® -- *"A DESIGN REQUIRES A DESIGNER."* I REMEMBER, BUT...

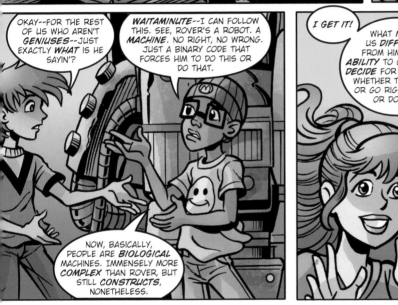

OKAY--FOR THE REST OF US WHO AREN'T *GENIUSES*--JUST EXACTLY *WHAT* IS HE SAYIN'?

WAITAMINUTE--I CAN FOLLOW THIS. SEE, ROVER'S A ROBOT. A *MACHINE*. NO RIGHT, NO WRONG. JUST A BINARY CODE THAT FORCES HIM TO DO THIS OR DO THAT.

NOW, BASICALLY, PEOPLE ARE *BIOLOGICAL* MACHINES. IMMENSELY MORE *COMPLEX* THAN ROVER, BUT STILL *CONSTRUCTS*, NONETHELESS.

I *GET IT!*

WHAT MAKES US *DIFFERENT* FROM HIM IS OUR *ABILITY* TO CHOOSE--TO *DECIDE* FOR OURSELVES WHETHER TO GO LEFT OR GO RIGHT, OR UP OR DOWN...

HUH-UH. ROVER'S NOT TALKIN' ABOUT *THAT KIND* OF DIRECTION. HE'S TALKIN' ABOUT CHOOSING BETWEEN BEIN' A *GOOD* GUY OR A *BAD* GUY...

MORE THAN THAT, EVEN-- THE FACT THAT WE *RECOGNIZE* THAT SOME THINGS ARE "RIGHT" AND OTHER THINGS ARE "WRONG" COMES FROM SOMEWHERE *BEYOND* JUST NUMBERS--SOMEWHERE OUTSIDE JUST THE *FACTS* AND *FIGURES*...

HE MEANS *GOD*.

ROVER'S TALKIN' ABOUT *GOD* AGAIN...

53

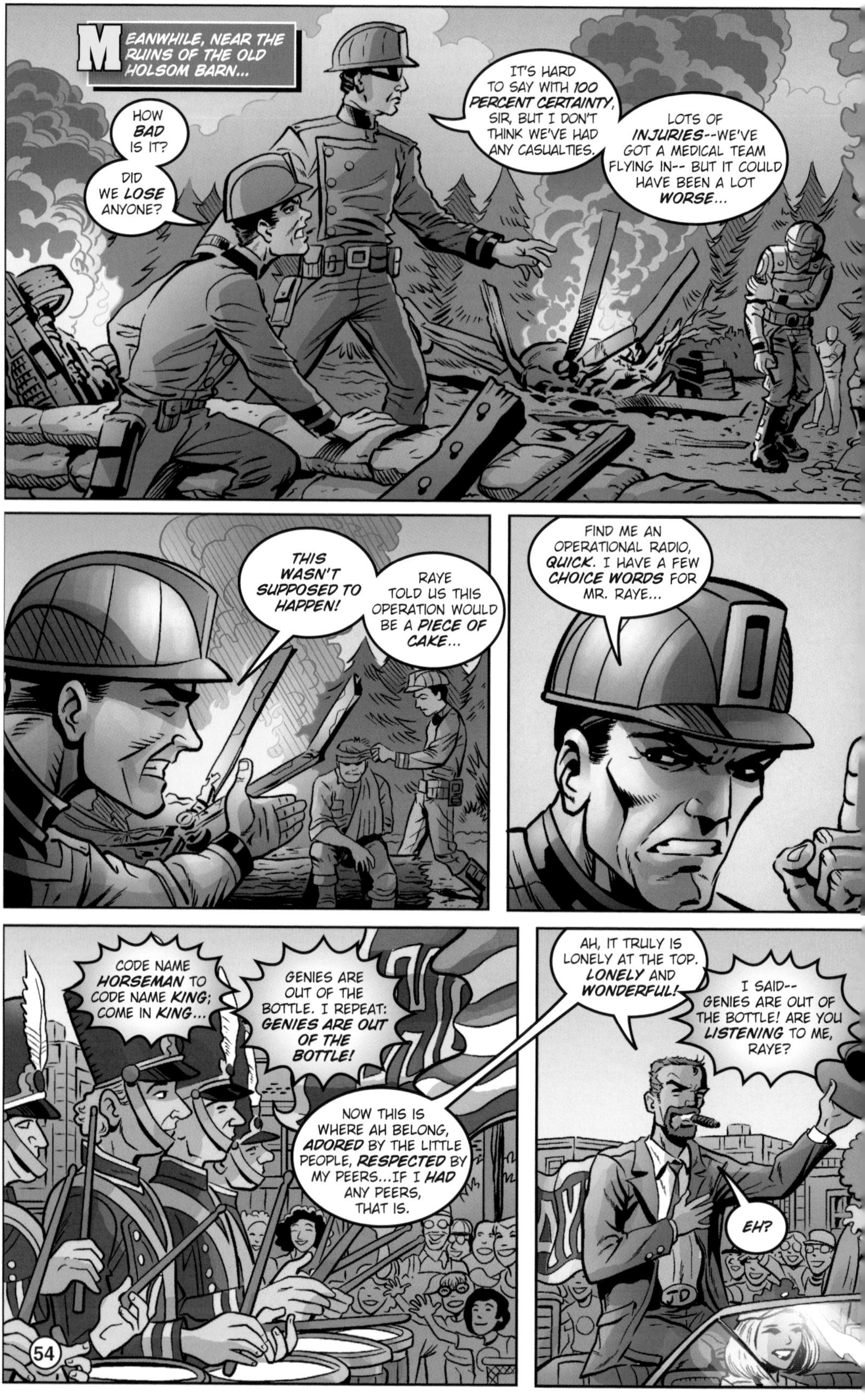
MEANWHILE, NEAR THE RUINS OF THE OLD HOLSOM BARN...
HOW BAD IS IT?
DID WE LOSE ANYONE?
IT'S HARD TO SAY WITH 100 PERCENT CERTAINTY, SIR, BUT I DON'T THINK WE'VE HAD ANY CASUALTIES.
LOTS OF INJURIES--WE'VE GOT A MEDICAL TEAM FLYING IN-- BUT IT COULD HAVE BEEN A LOT WORSE...
THIS WASN'T SUPPOSED TO HAPPEN!
RAYE TOLD US THIS OPERATION WOULD BE A PIECE OF CAKE...
FIND ME AN OPERATIONAL RADIO, QUICK. I HAVE A FEW CHOICE WORDS FOR MR. RAYE...
CODE NAME HORSEMAN TO CODE NAME KING; COME IN KING...
GENIES ARE OUT OF THE BOTTLE. I REPEAT: GENIES ARE OUT OF THE BOTTLE!
NOW THIS IS WHERE AH BELONG, ADORED BY THE LITTLE PEOPLE, RESPECTED BY MY PEERS...IF I HAD ANY PEERS, THAT IS.
AH, IT TRULY IS LONELY AT THE TOP. LONELY AND WONDERFUL!
I SAID-- GENIES ARE OUT OF THE BOTTLE! ARE YOU LISTENING TO ME, RAYE?
EH?

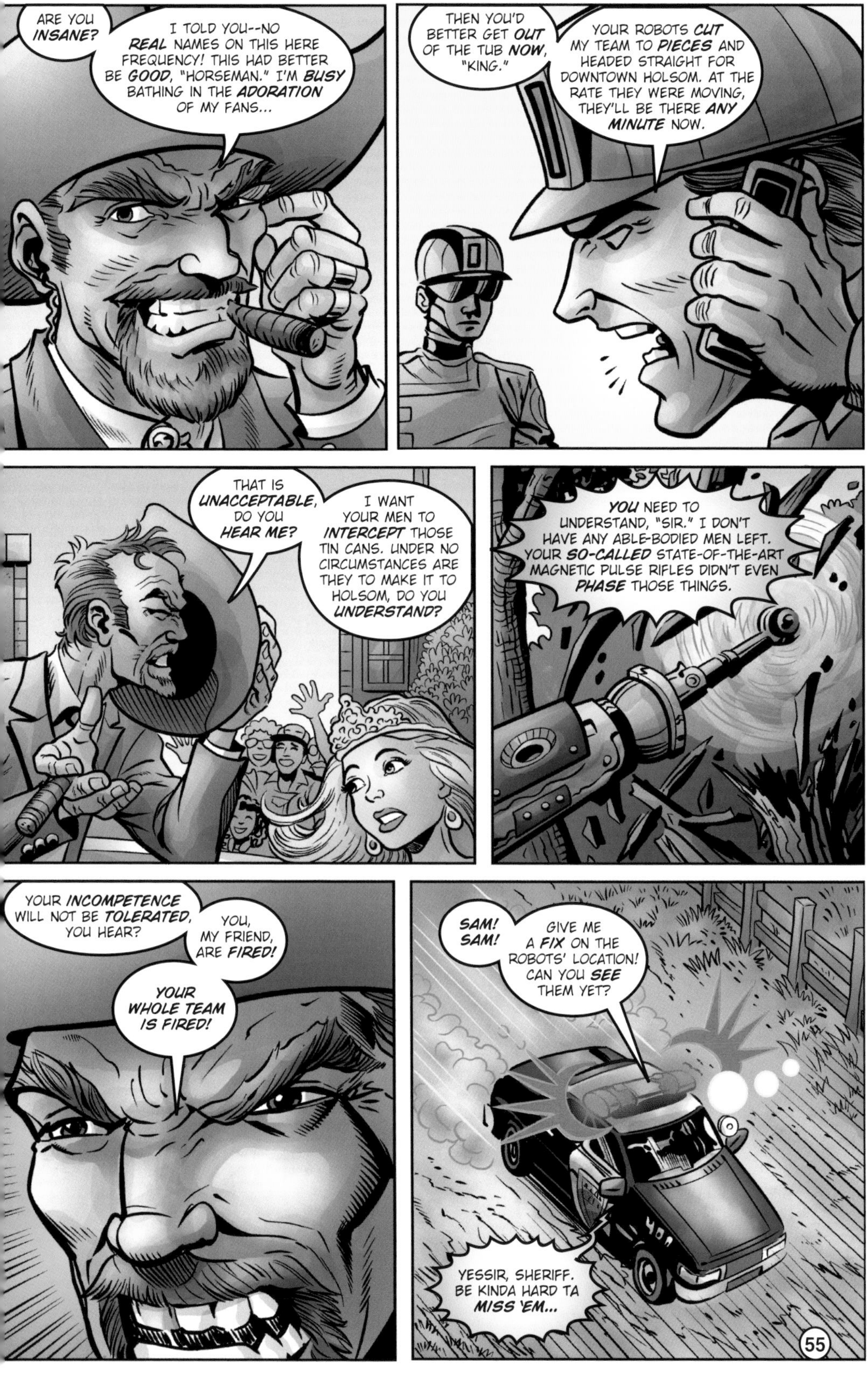
ARE YOU INSANE?
I TOLD YOU--NO REAL NAMES ON THIS HERE FREQUENCY! THIS HAD BETTER BE GOOD, "HORSEMAN." I'M BUSY BATHING IN THE ADORATION OF MY FANS...
THEN YOU'D BETTER GET OUT OF THE TUB NOW, "KING."
YOUR ROBOTS CUT MY TEAM TO PIECES AND HEADED STRAIGHT FOR DOWNTOWN HOLSOM. AT THE RATE THEY WERE MOVING, THEY'LL BE THERE ANY MINUTE NOW.
THAT IS UNACCEPTABLE, DO YOU HEAR ME?
I WANT YOUR MEN TO INTERCEPT THOSE TIN CANS. UNDER NO CIRCUMSTANCES ARE THEY TO MAKE IT TO HOLSOM, DO YOU UNDERSTAND?
YOU NEED TO UNDERSTAND, "SIR." I DON'T HAVE ANY ABLE-BODIED MEN LEFT. YOUR SO-CALLED STATE-OF-THE-ART MAGNETIC PULSE RIFLES DIDN'T EVEN PHASE THOSE THINGS.
YOUR INCOMPETENCE WILL NOT BE TOLERATED, YOU HEAR?
YOU, MY FRIEND, ARE FIRED!
YOUR WHOLE TEAM IS FIRED!
SAM! SAM!
GIVE ME A FIX ON THE ROBOTS' LOCATION! CAN YOU SEE THEM YET?
YESSIR, SHERIFF. BE KINDA HARD TA MISS 'EM...

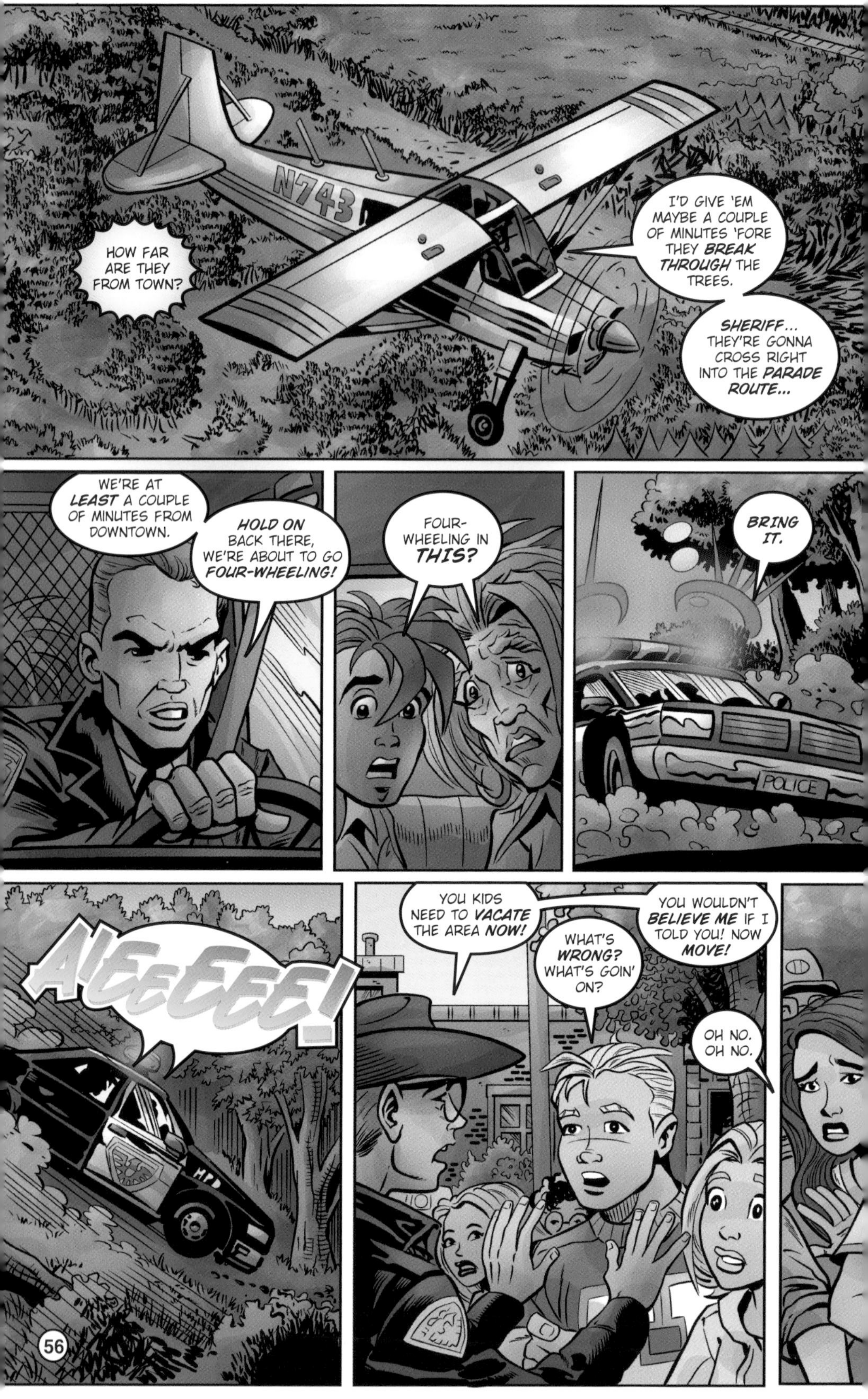
HOW FAR ARE THEY FROM TOWN?
I'D GIVE 'EM MAYBE A COUPLE OF MINUTES 'FORE THEY BREAK THROUGH THE TREES.
SHERIFF... THEY'RE GONNA CROSS RIGHT INTO THE PARADE ROUTE...
WE'RE AT LEAST A COUPLE OF MINUTES FROM DOWNTOWN.
HOLD ON BACK THERE, WE'RE ABOUT TO GO FOUR-WHEELING!
FOUR-WHEELING IN THIS?
BRING IT.
POLICE
AIEEEEE!
HPD
YOU KIDS NEED TO VACATE THE AREA NOW!
WHAT'S WRONG? WHAT'S GOIN' ON?
YOU WOULDN'T BELIEVE ME IF I TOLD YOU! NOW MOVE!
OH NO. OH NO.

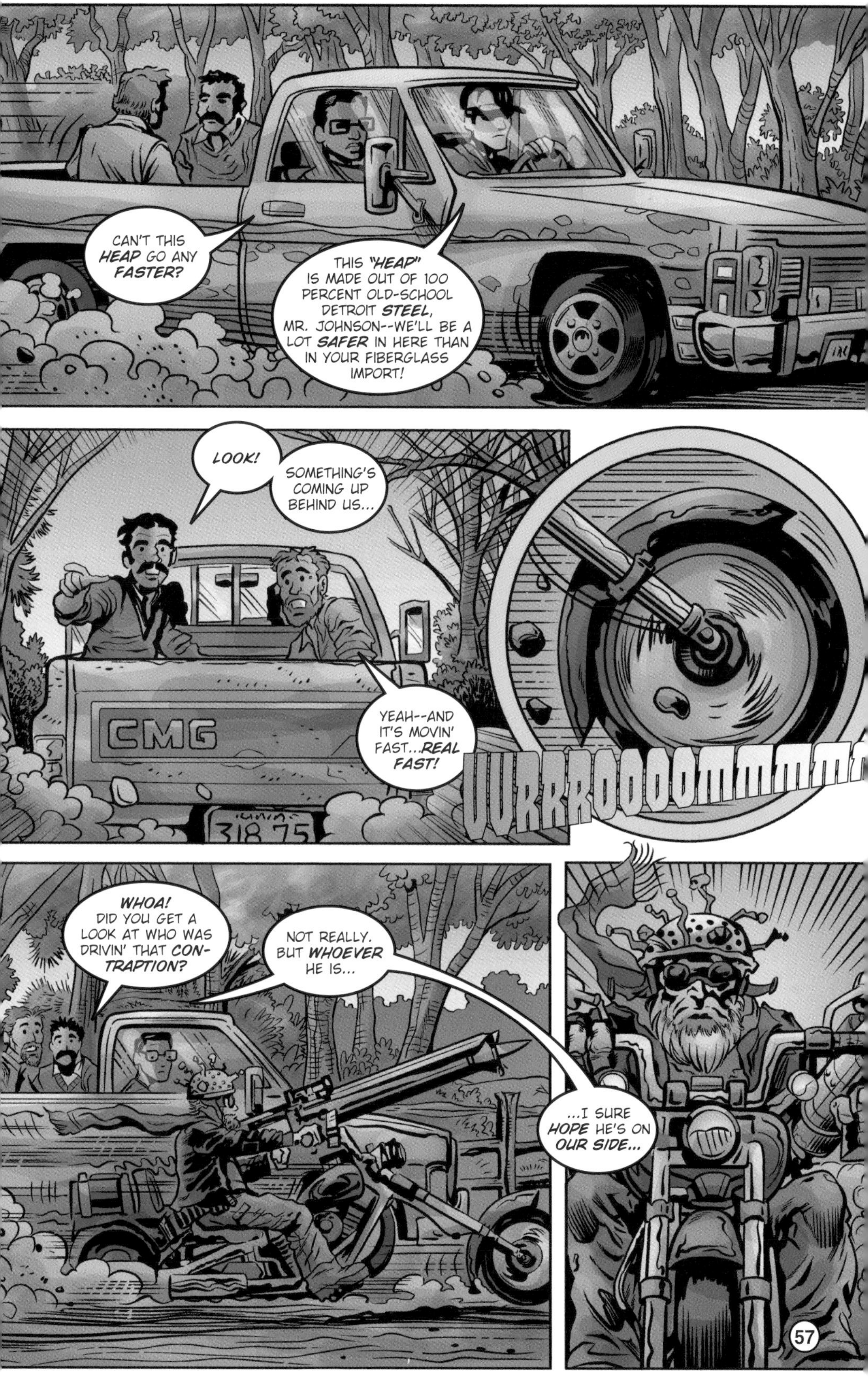
CAN'T THIS HEAP GO ANY FASTER?
THIS "HEAP" IS MADE OUT OF 100 PERCENT OLD-SCHOOL DETROIT STEEL, MR. JOHNSON--WE'LL BE A LOT SAFER IN HERE THAN IN YOUR FIBERGLASS IMPORT!
LOOK!
SOMETHING'S COMING UP BEHIND US...
CMG
YEAH--AND IT'S MOVIN' FAST...REAL FAST!
UURRROOOOMMMMM
WHOA! DID YOU GET A LOOK AT WHO WAS DRIVIN' THAT CON-TRAPTION?
NOT REALLY. BUT WHOEVER HE IS...
...I SURE HOPE HE'S ON OUR SIDE...

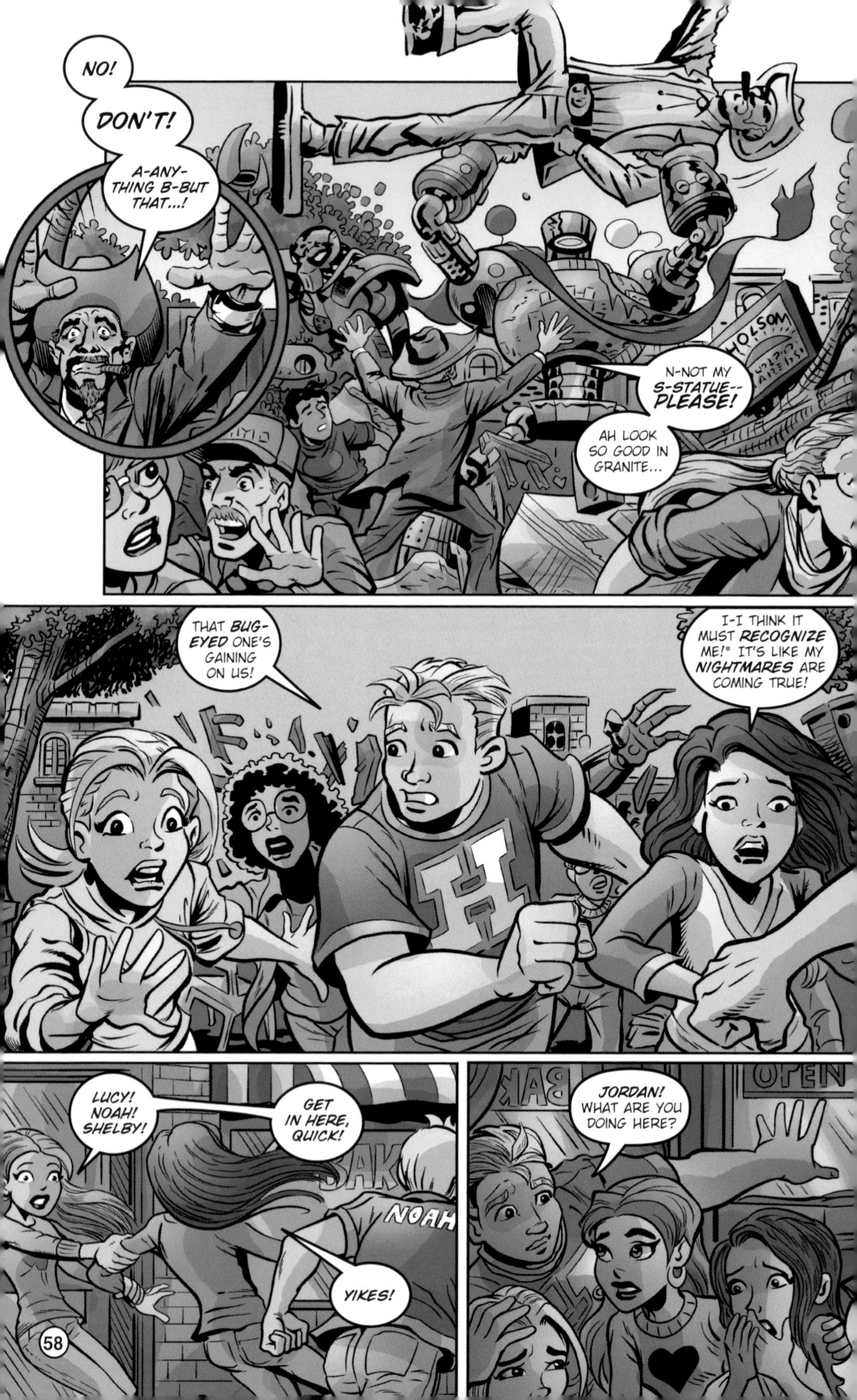
NO!
DON'T!
A-ANY-THING B-BUT THAT...!
HOLSOM
N-NOT MY S-STATUE-- PLEASE!
AH LOOK SO GOOD IN GRANITE...
THAT BUG-EYED ONE'S GAINING ON US!
I-I THINK IT MUST RECOGNIZE ME!* IT'S LIKE MY NIGHTMARES ARE COMING TRUE!
LUCY! NOAH! SHELBY!
GET IN HERE, QUICK!
NOAH
YIKES!
OPEN
JORDAN! WHAT ARE YOU DOING HERE?

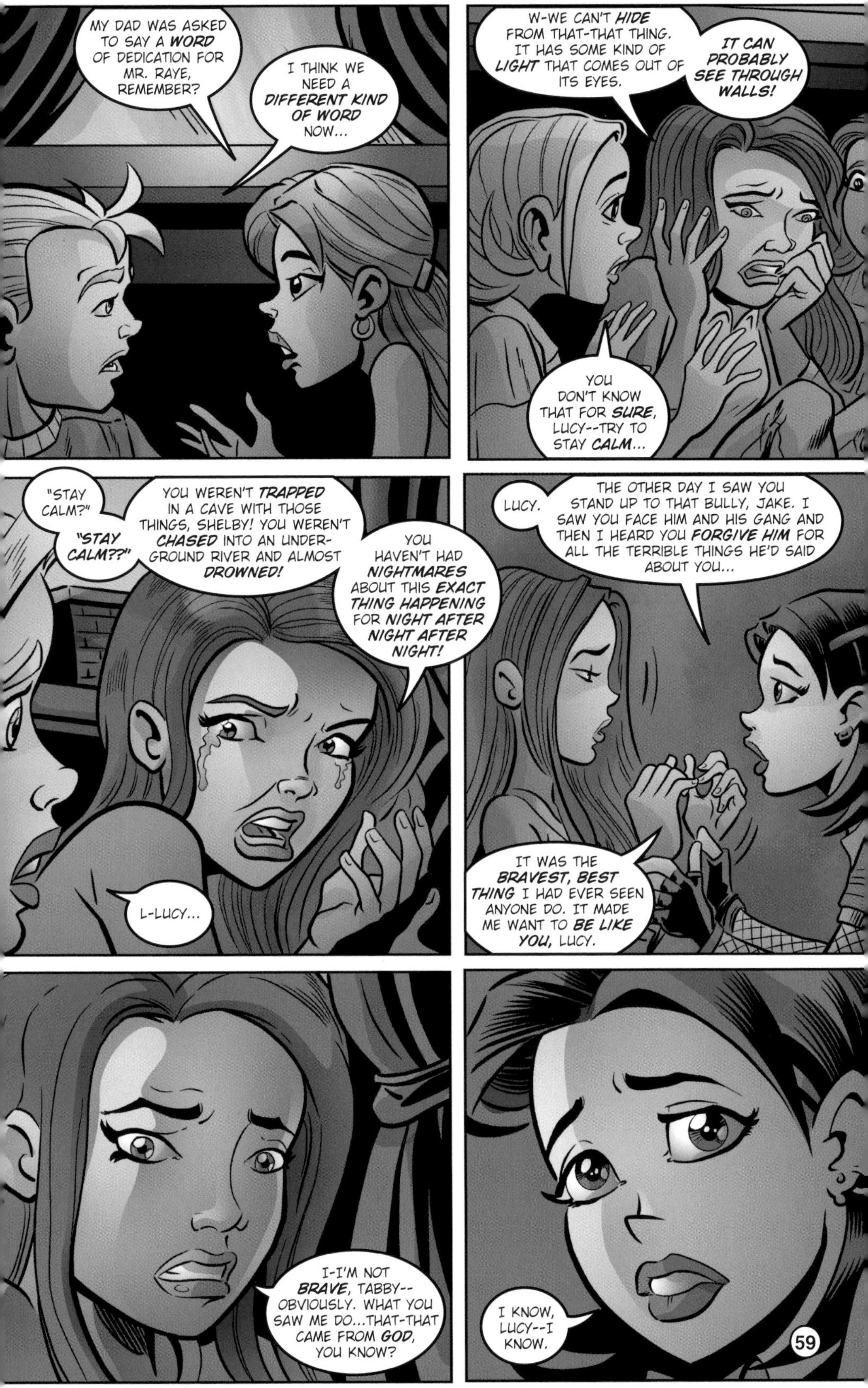

MY DAD WAS ASKED TO SAY A WORD OF DEDICATION FOR MR. RAYE, REMEMBER?
I THINK WE NEED A DIFFERENT KIND OF WORD NOW...
W-WE CAN'T HIDE FROM THAT-THAT THING. IT HAS SOME KIND OF LIGHT THAT COMES OUT OF ITS EYES.
IT CAN PROBABLY SEE THROUGH WALLS!
YOU DON'T KNOW THAT FOR SURE, LUCY--TRY TO STAY CALM...
"STAY CALM?"
"STAY CALM??"
YOU WEREN'T TRAPPED IN A CAVE WITH THOSE THINGS, SHELBY! YOU WEREN'T CHASED INTO AN UNDER-GROUND RIVER AND ALMOST DROWNED!
YOU HAVEN'T HAD NIGHTMARES ABOUT THIS EXACT THING HAPPENING FOR NIGHT AFTER NIGHT AFTER NIGHT!
L-LUCY...
LUCY.
THE OTHER DAY I SAW YOU STAND UP TO THAT BULLY, JAKE. I SAW YOU FACE HIM AND HIS GANG AND THEN I HEARD YOU FORGIVE HIM FOR ALL THE TERRIBLE THINGS HE'D SAID ABOUT YOU...
IT WAS THE BRAVEST, BEST THING I HAD EVER SEEN ANYONE DO. IT MADE ME WANT TO BE LIKE YOU, LUCY.
I-I'M NOT BRAVE, TABBY-- OBVIOUSLY. WHAT YOU SAW ME DO...THAT-THAT CAME FROM GOD, YOU KNOW?
I KNOW, LUCY--I KNOW.

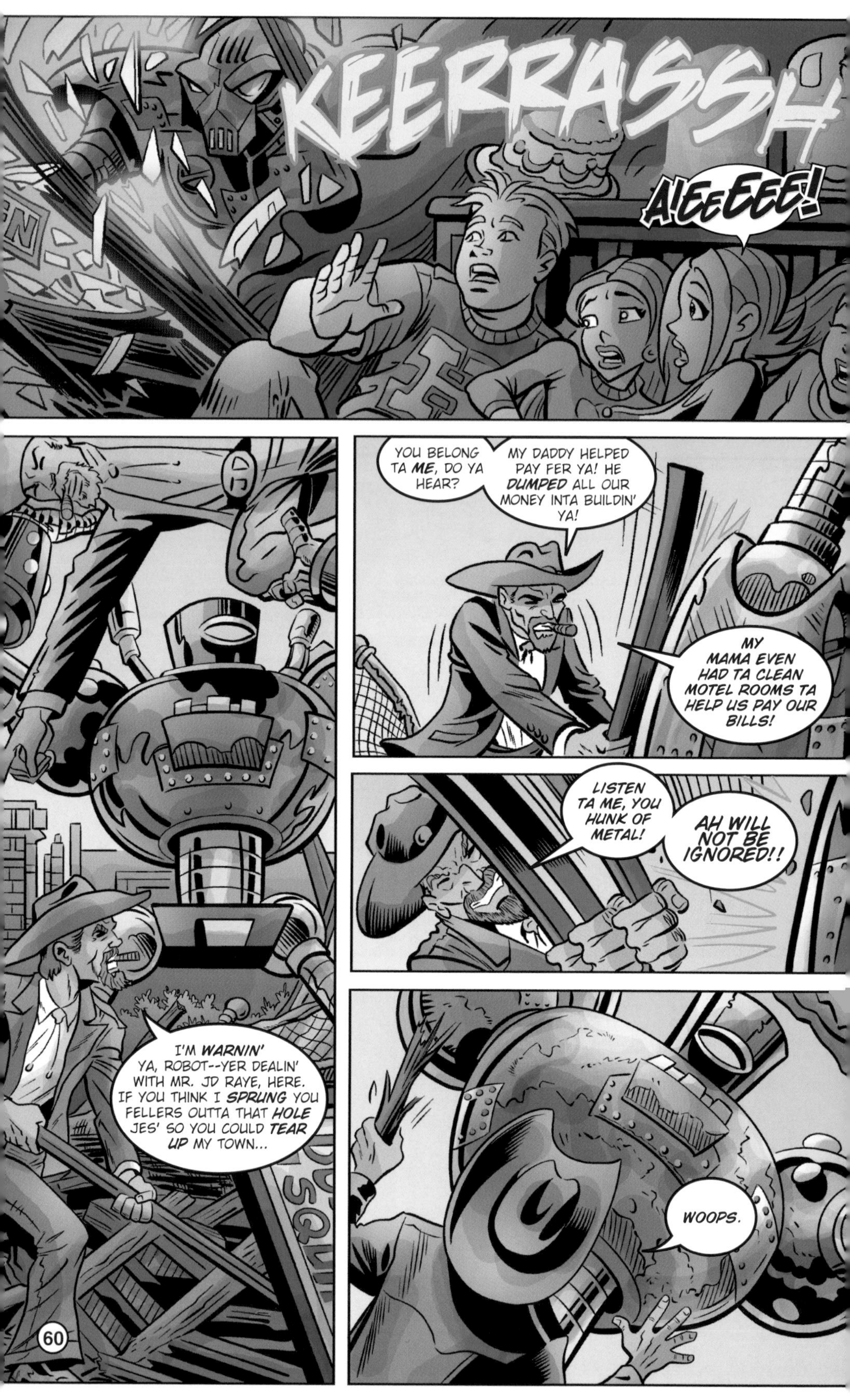
KEERRASSH
AIEEEEE!
I'M WARNIN' YA, ROBOT--YER DEALIN' WITH MR. JD RAYE, HERE. IF YOU THINK I SPRUNG YOU FELLERS OUTTA THAT HOLE JES' SO YOU COULD TEAR UP MY TOWN...
YOU BELONG TA ME, DO YA HEAR?
MY DADDY HELPED PAY FER YA! HE DUMPED ALL OUR MONEY INTA BUILDIN' YA!
MY MAMA EVEN HAD TA CLEAN MOTEL ROOMS TA HELP US PAY OUR BILLS!
LISTEN TA ME, YOU HUNK OF METAL!
AH WILL NOT BE IGNORED!!
WOOPS.

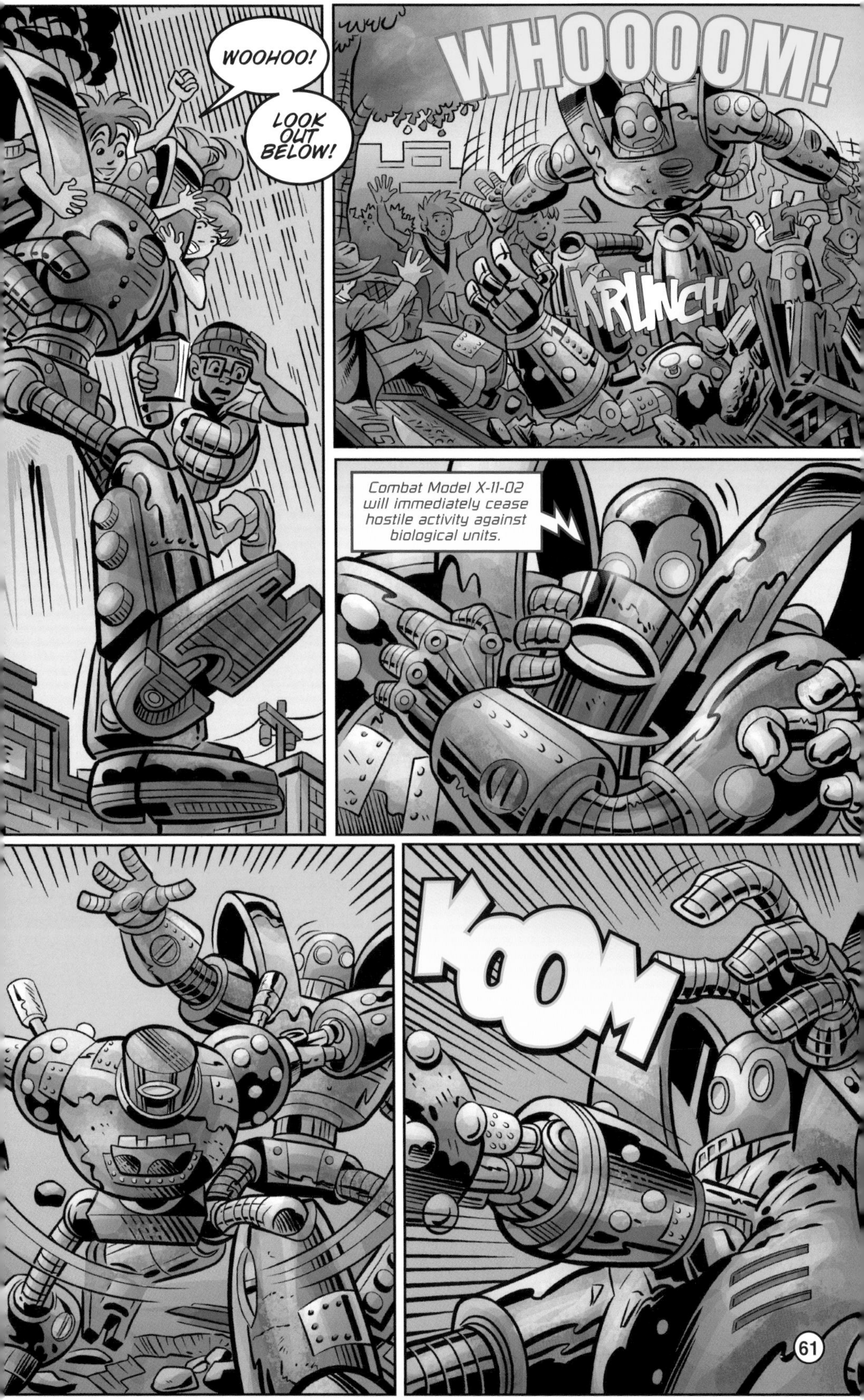
WOOHOO!
LOOK OUT BELOW!
WHOOOOOM!
KRUNCH
Combat Model X-11-02 will immediately cease hostile activity against biological units.
KOOM

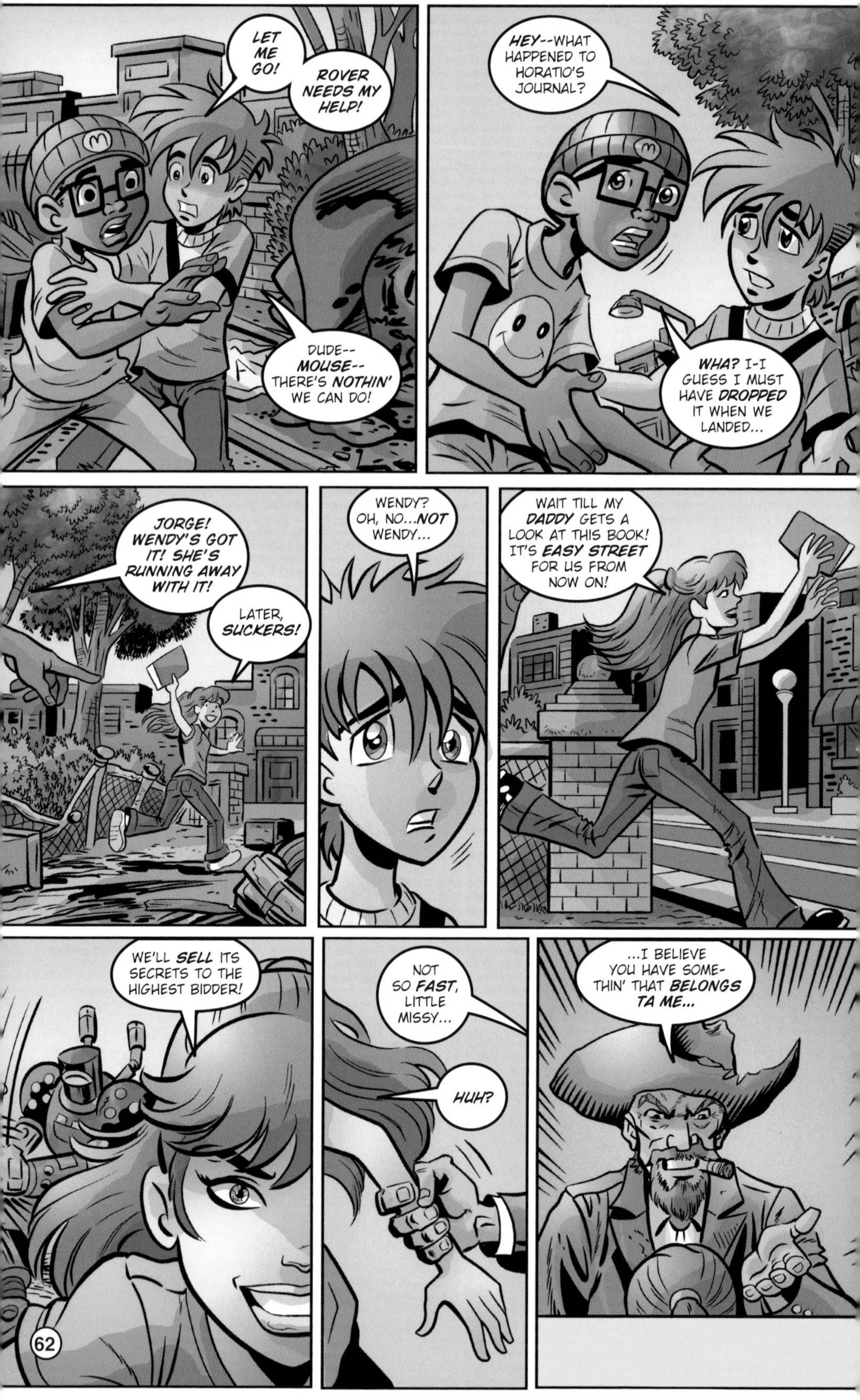
LET ME GO!
ROVER NEEDS MY HELP!
DUDE-- MOUSE-- THERE'S NOTHIN' WE CAN DO!
HEY--WHAT HAPPENED TO HORATIO'S JOURNAL?
WHA? I-I GUESS I MUST HAVE DROPPED IT WHEN WE LANDED...
JORGE! WENDY'S GOT IT! SHE'S RUNNING AWAY WITH IT!
LATER, SUCKERS!
WENDY? OH, NO...NOT WENDY...
WAIT TILL MY DADDY GETS A LOOK AT THIS BOOK! IT'S EASY STREET FOR US FROM NOW ON!
WE'LL SELL ITS SECRETS TO THE HIGHEST BIDDER!
NOT SO FAST, LITTLE MISSY...
HUH?
...I BELIEVE YOU HAVE SOME-THIN' THAT BELONGS TA ME...

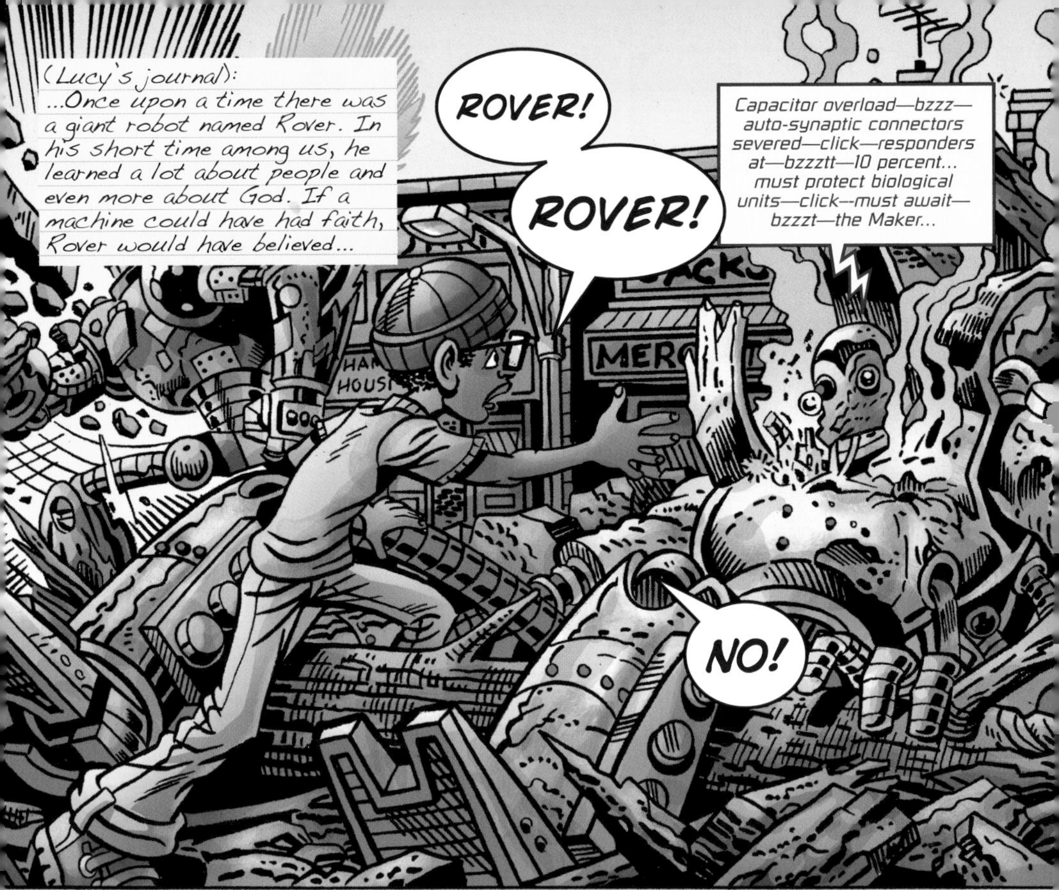
(Lucy's journal):
...Once upon a time there was a giant robot named Rover. In his short time among us, he learned a lot about people and even more about God. If a machine could have had faith, Rover would have believed...
ROVER!
ROVER!
Capacitor overload—bzzz—auto-synaptic connectors severed—click—responders at—bzzztt—10 percent... must protect biological units—click--must await—bzzzt—the Maker...
NO!

ALPHA & ΩMEGA!

STORY, COLORS, AND LETTERING: CRAIG W. SCHUTT
PENCIL BREAKDOWNS: STEVEN BUTLER • FINISHED ART: AL MILGROM
EDITING: SINDA S. ZINN • THANKS TO ONE AND ALL!

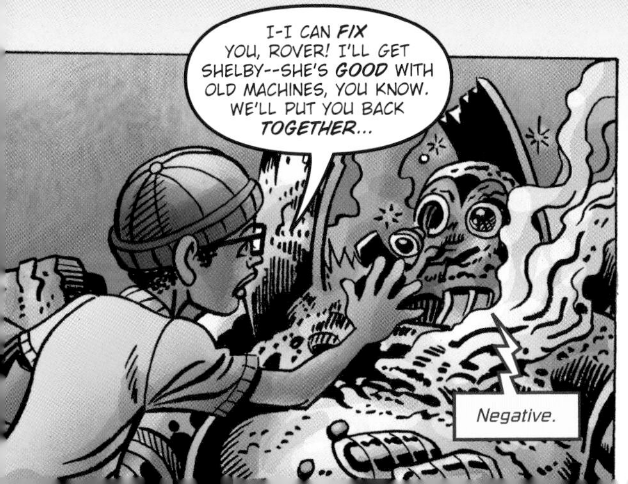
I-I CAN *FIX* YOU, ROVER! I'LL GET SHELBY--SHE'S *GOOD* WITH OLD MACHINES, YOU KNOW. WE'LL PUT YOU BACK *TOGETHER*...
Negative.

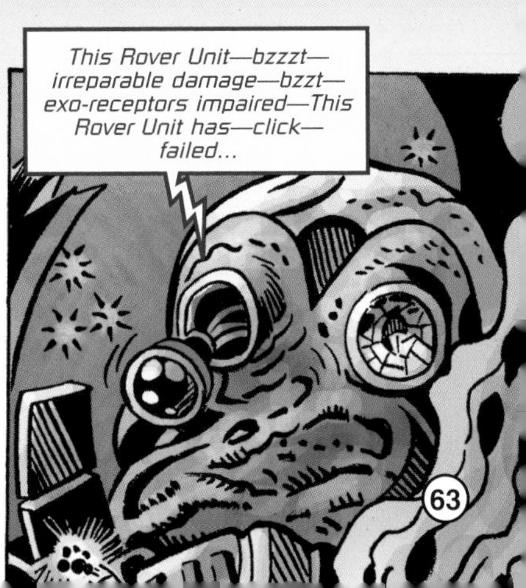
This Rover Unit—bzzzt—irreparable damage—bzzt—exo-receptors impaired—This Rover Unit has—click—failed...

YOU DIDN'T FAIL!

YOU **FOUGHT** THAT THING LONG ENOUGH TO LET EVERY-ONE GET AWAY! HORATIO HOLSOM--Y-YOUR **MAKER** --WOULD BE **PROUD** OF YOU!

I-I'M PROUD OF YOU...

Alert! Alert!

Power core breach! Bzzt—ethanol remnant—explosion imminent! Mouse unit—click-click-- in immediate danger!

WHA?

Estimated blast area—bzzt—thirty foot radius, plus—click—minus ten feet...

I-I CAN'T RUN THAT **FAR** THAT **FAST**!

HANG ON, KID!

OTTO EXPRESS COMIN' THROUGH!

WOWSERS!

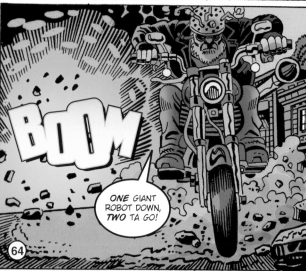

BOOM

ONE GIANT ROBOT DOWN, **TWO** TA GO!

64

M-MY F-FRIEND...

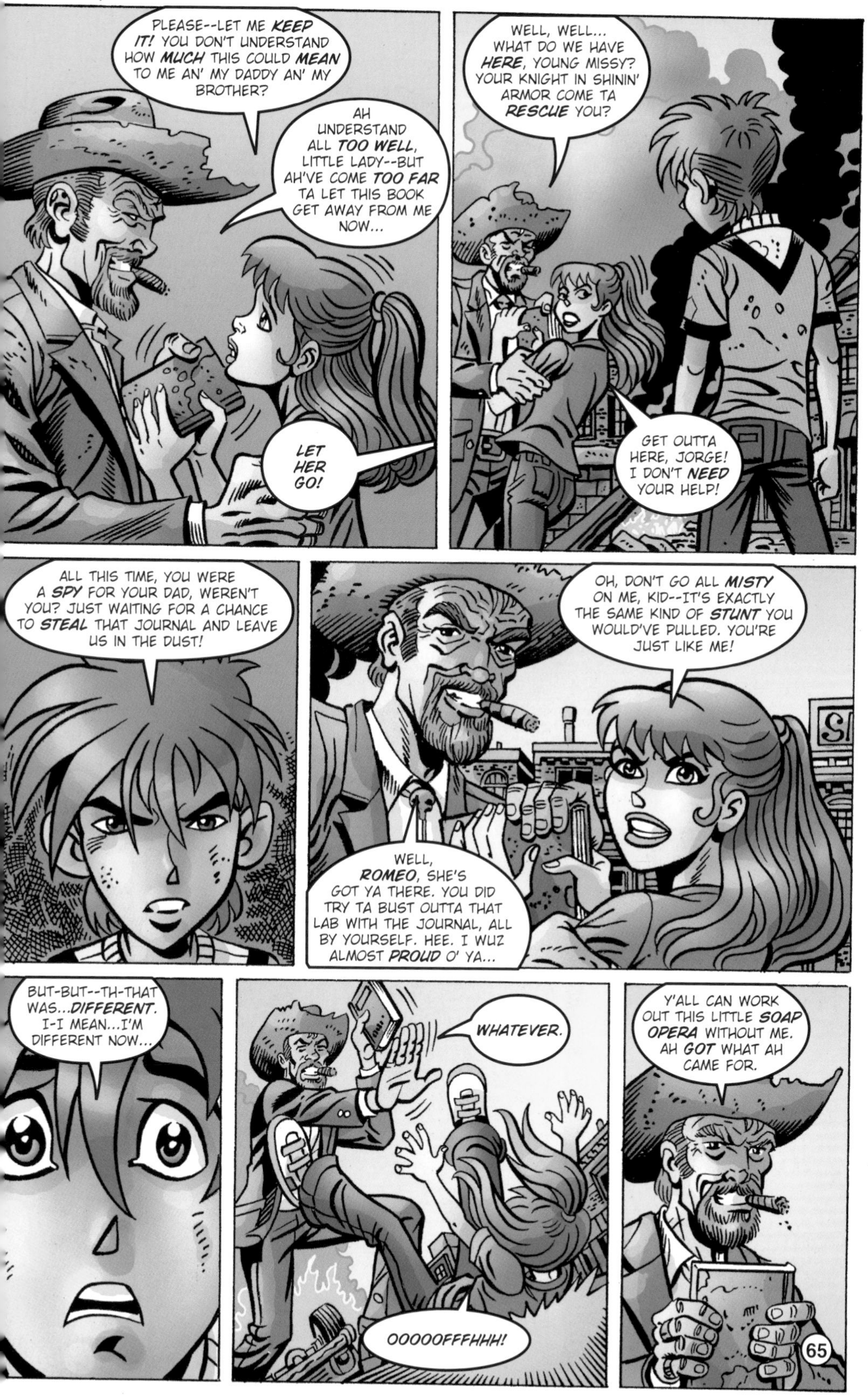
PLEASE--LET ME KEEP IT! YOU DON'T UNDERSTAND HOW MUCH THIS COULD MEAN TO ME AN' MY DADDY AN' MY BROTHER?
AH UNDERSTAND ALL TOO WELL, LITTLE LADY--BUT AH'VE COME TOO FAR TA LET THIS BOOK GET AWAY FROM ME NOW...
LET HER GO!
WELL, WELL... WHAT DO WE HAVE HERE, YOUNG MISSY? YOUR KNIGHT IN SHININ' ARMOR COME TA RESCUE YOU?
GET OUTTA HERE, JORGE! I DON'T NEED YOUR HELP!
ALL THIS TIME, YOU WERE A SPY FOR YOUR DAD, WEREN'T YOU? JUST WAITING FOR A CHANCE TO STEAL THAT JOURNAL AND LEAVE US IN THE DUST!
OH, DON'T GO ALL MISTY ON ME, KID--IT'S EXACTLY THE SAME KIND OF STUNT YOU WOULD'VE PULLED. YOU'RE JUST LIKE ME!
WELL, ROMEO, SHE'S GOT YA THERE. YOU DID TRY TA BUST OUTTA THAT LAB WITH THE JOURNAL, ALL BY YOURSELF. HEE. I WUZ ALMOST PROUD O' YA...
BUT-BUT--TH-THAT WAS...DIFFERENT. I-I MEAN...I'M DIFFERENT NOW...
WHATEVER.
OOOOOFFFHHH!
Y'ALL CAN WORK OUT THIS LITTLE SOAP OPERA WITHOUT ME. AH GOT WHAT AH CAME FOR.

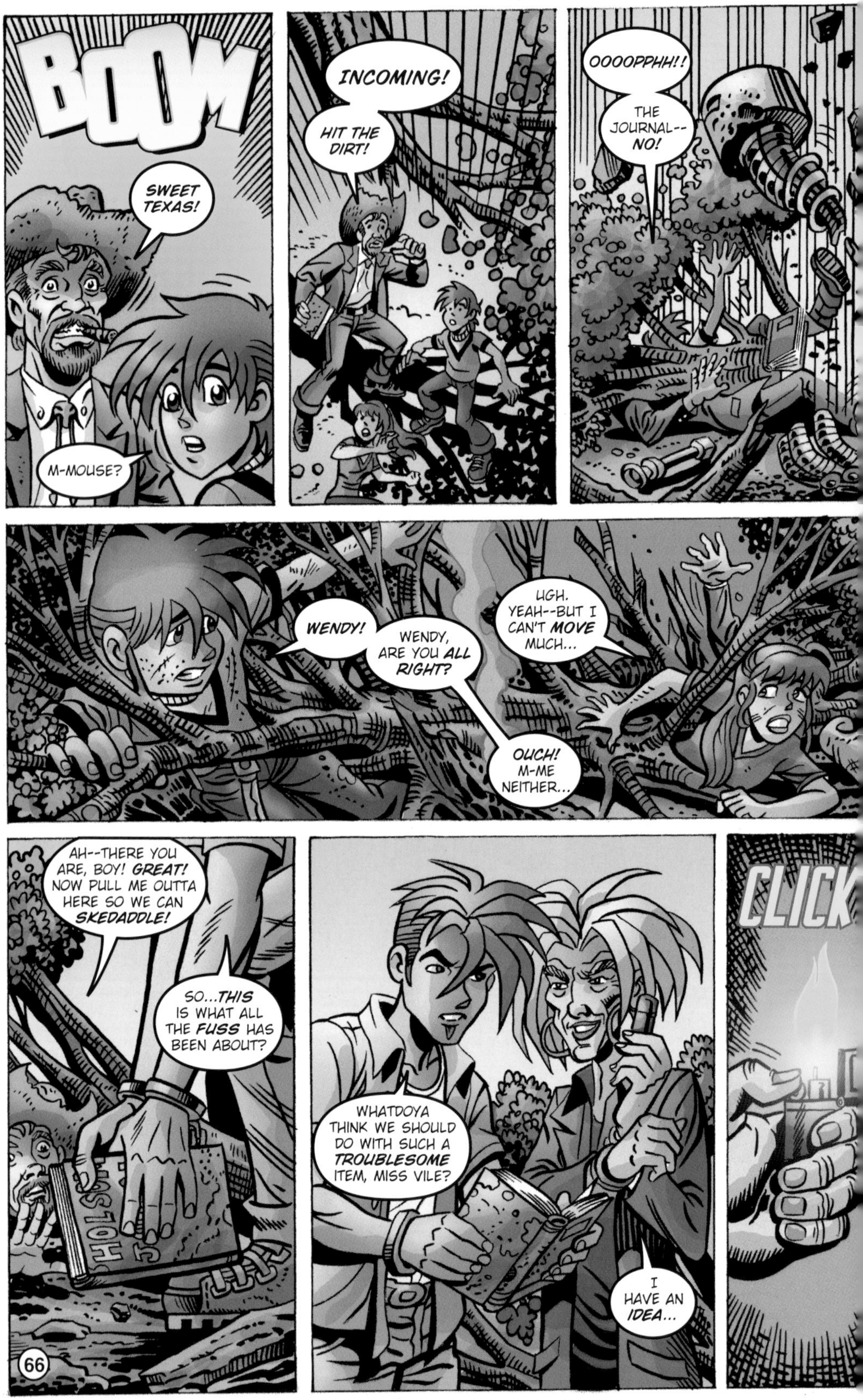

BOOM
SWEET TEXAS!
M-MOUSE?
INCOMING!
HIT THE DIRT!
OOOOPPHH!!
THE JOURNAL-- NO!
WENDY!
WENDY, ARE YOU ALL RIGHT?
UGH. YEAH--BUT I CAN'T MOVE MUCH...
OUCH! M-ME NEITHER...
AH--THERE YOU ARE, BOY! GREAT! NOW PULL ME OUTTA HERE SO WE CAN SKEDADDLE!
SO...THIS IS WHAT ALL THE FUSS HAS BEEN ABOUT?
WHATDOYA THINK WE SHOULD DO WITH SUCH A TROUBLESOME ITEM, MISS VILE?
I HAVE AN IDEA...
CLICK

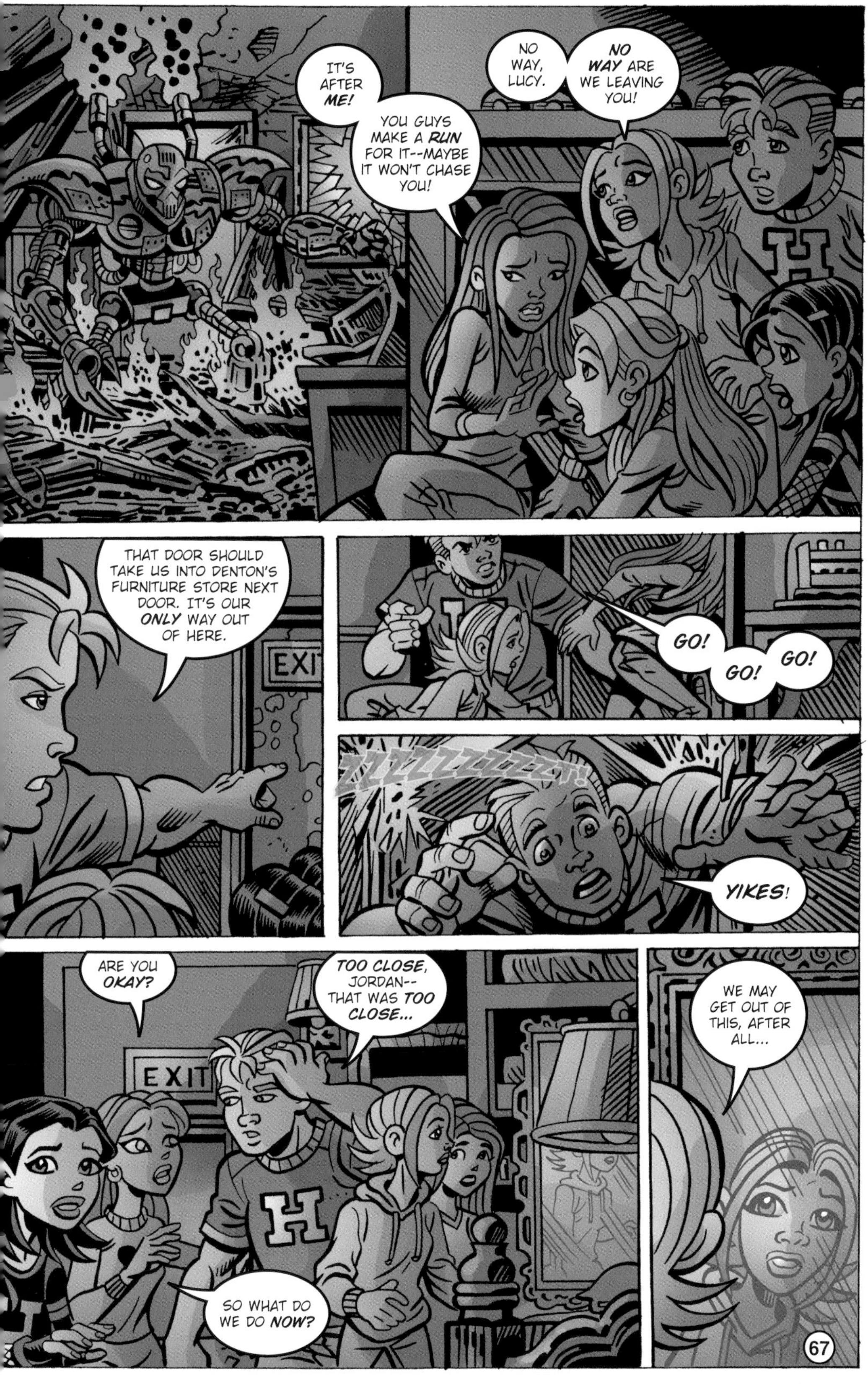
IT'S AFTER ME!
YOU GUYS MAKE A RUN FOR IT--MAYBE IT WON'T CHASE YOU!
NO WAY, LUCY.
NO WAY ARE WE LEAVING YOU!
THAT DOOR SHOULD TAKE US INTO DENTON'S FURNITURE STORE NEXT DOOR. IT'S OUR ONLY WAY OUT OF HERE.
EXIT
GO!
GO!
GO!
ZZZZZZZZZZT!
YIKES!
ARE YOU OKAY?
TOO CLOSE, JORDAN--THAT WAS TOO CLOSE...
EXIT
SO WHAT DO WE DO NOW?
WE MAY GET OUT OF THIS, AFTER ALL...

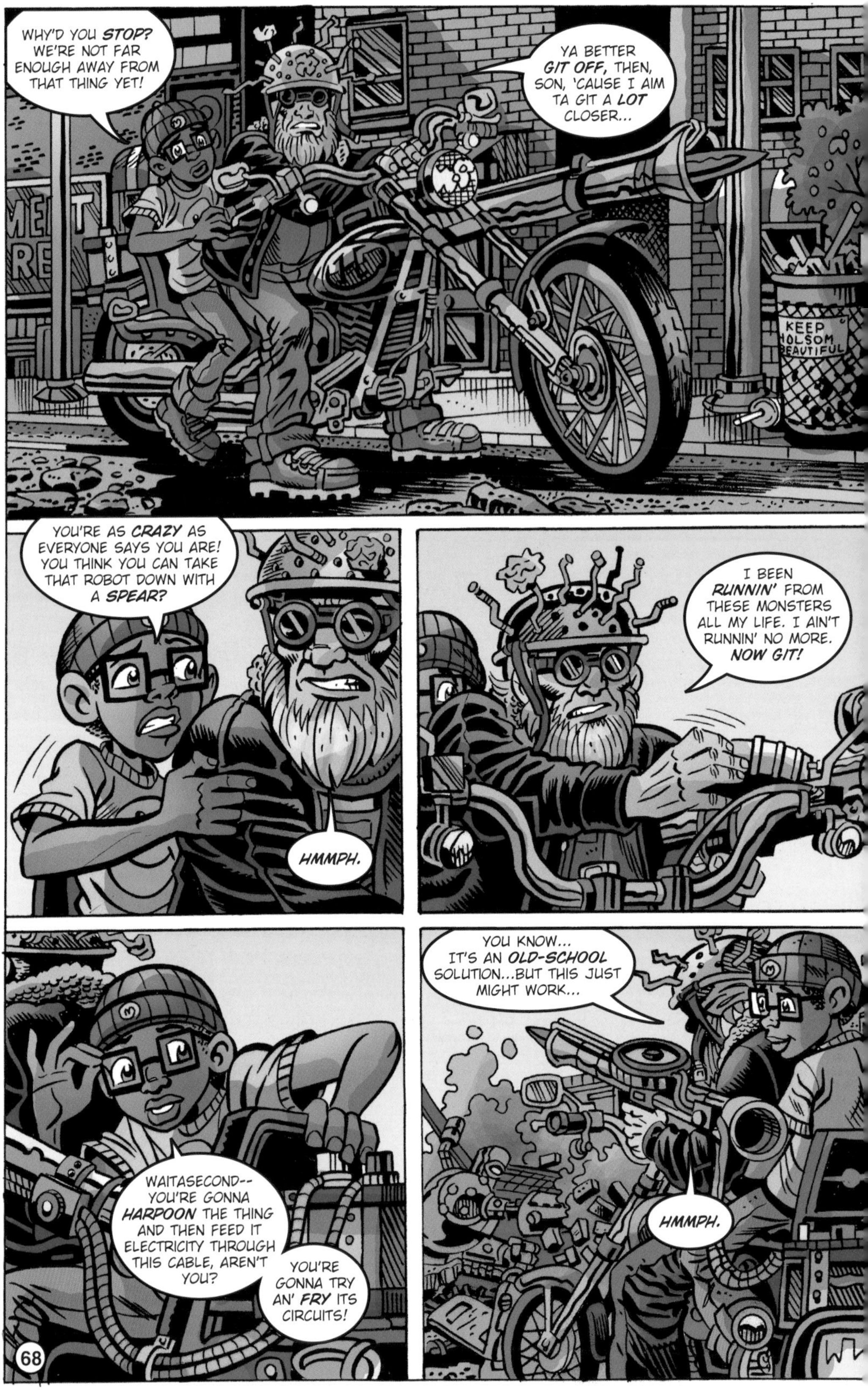
WHY'D YOU STOP? WE'RE NOT FAR ENOUGH AWAY FROM THAT THING YET!
YA BETTER GIT OFF, THEN, SON, 'CAUSE I AIM TA GIT A LOT CLOSER...
KEEP HOLSOM BEAUTIFUL
YOU'RE AS CRAZY AS EVERYONE SAYS YOU ARE! YOU THINK YOU CAN TAKE THAT ROBOT DOWN WITH A SPEAR?
HMMPH.
I BEEN RUNNIN' FROM THESE MONSTERS ALL MY LIFE. I AIN'T RUNNIN' NO MORE. NOW GIT!
WAITASECOND-- YOU'RE GONNA HARPOON THE THING AND THEN FEED IT ELECTRICITY THROUGH THIS CABLE, AREN'T YOU?
YOU'RE GONNA TRY AN' FRY ITS CIRCUITS!
YOU KNOW... IT'S AN OLD-SCHOOL SOLUTION...BUT THIS JUST MIGHT WORK...
HMMPH.

EXIT
HEY!
UGLY!
Y-YOU WANT ME? I-I'M OVER HERE!
R-REMEMBER ME? I-I GOT AWAY FROM YOU ONCE, YOU-YOU...BAD ROBOT, YOU.
BET THAT MADE YOU M-MAD, DIDN'T IT?
BRING IT ON!
OH NO OH NO...
ZZZZZZZAAAAATT!
KOOM

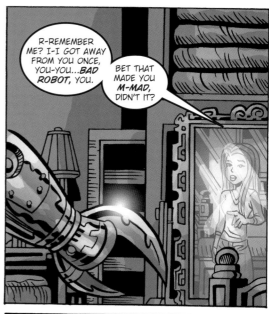

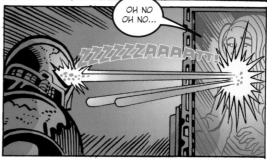

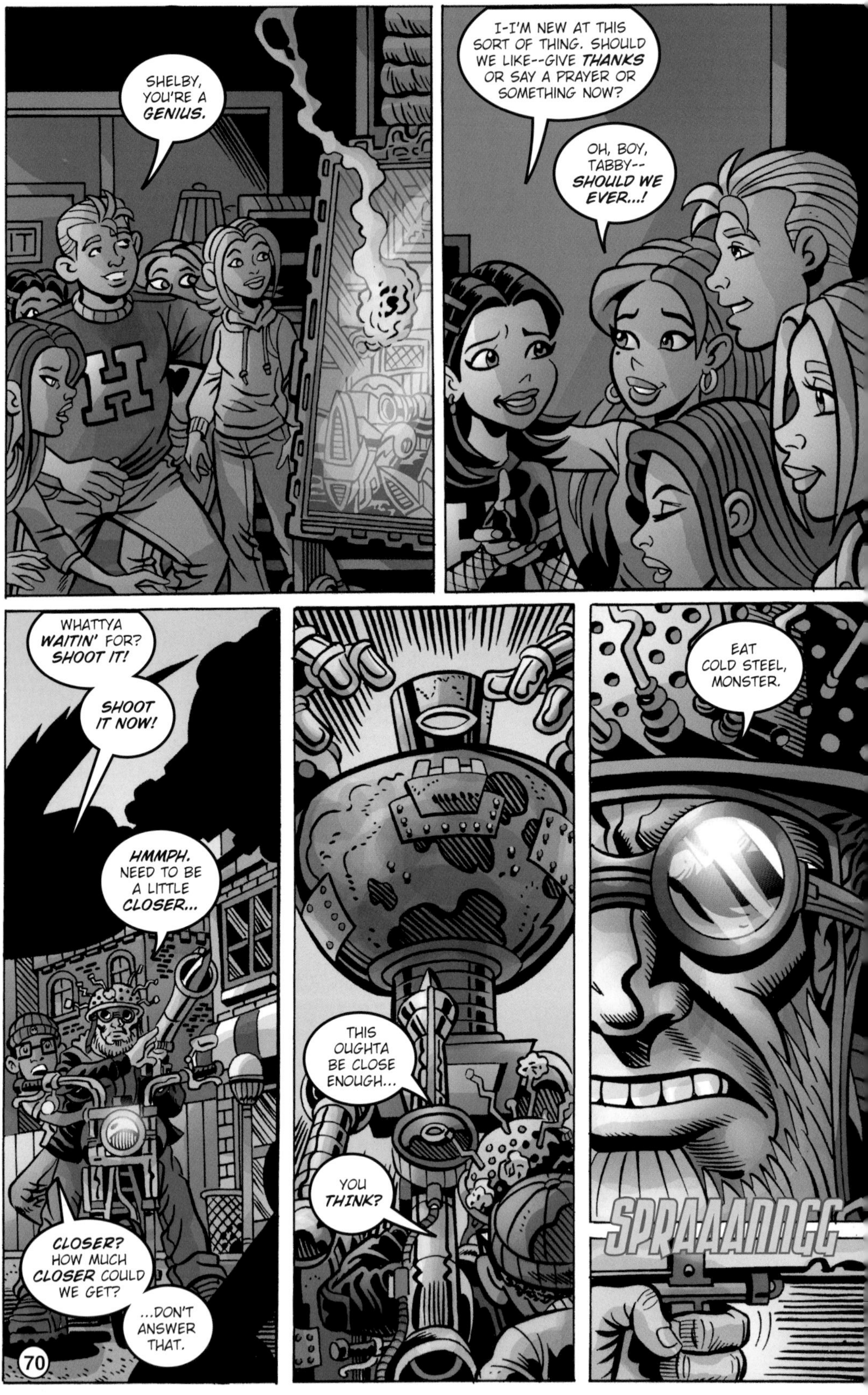

SHELBY, YOU'RE A GENIUS.
I-I'M NEW AT THIS SORT OF THING. SHOULD WE LIKE--GIVE THANKS OR SAY A PRAYER OR SOMETHING NOW?
OH, BOY, TABBY-- SHOULD WE EVER...!
WHATTYA WAITIN' FOR? SHOOT IT!
SHOOT IT NOW!
HMMPH. NEED TO BE A LITTLE CLOSER...
CLOSER? HOW MUCH CLOSER COULD WE GET?
...DON'T ANSWER THAT.
THIS OUGHTA BE CLOSE ENOUGH...
YOU THINK?
EAT COLD STEEL, MONSTER.
SPRAAAANNGG

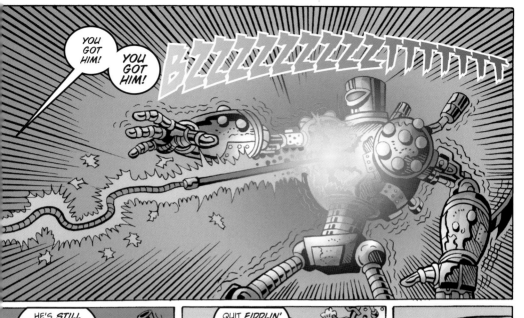

YOU GOT HIM! YOU GOT HIM!

BZZZZZZZZZZZZTTTTTTT

HE'S *STILL STANDIN'*! WE NEED *MORE JUICE*!

QUIT *FIDDLIN'* WITH MY BIKE, SON!

QUICK! PUT IT IN NEUTRAL AND HIT THE *GAS*--THAT SHOULD GIVE THE ROBOT ANOTHER *SHOCK!*

HMMPH. BOSSY KIDS THESE DAYS...

IT'S *WORKING!* IT'S *WORKING!*

KA-CHUK

DIDN'T WANT YOU BOYS TO HAVE *ALL* THE FUN, YOU KNOW?

HMMPH.

71

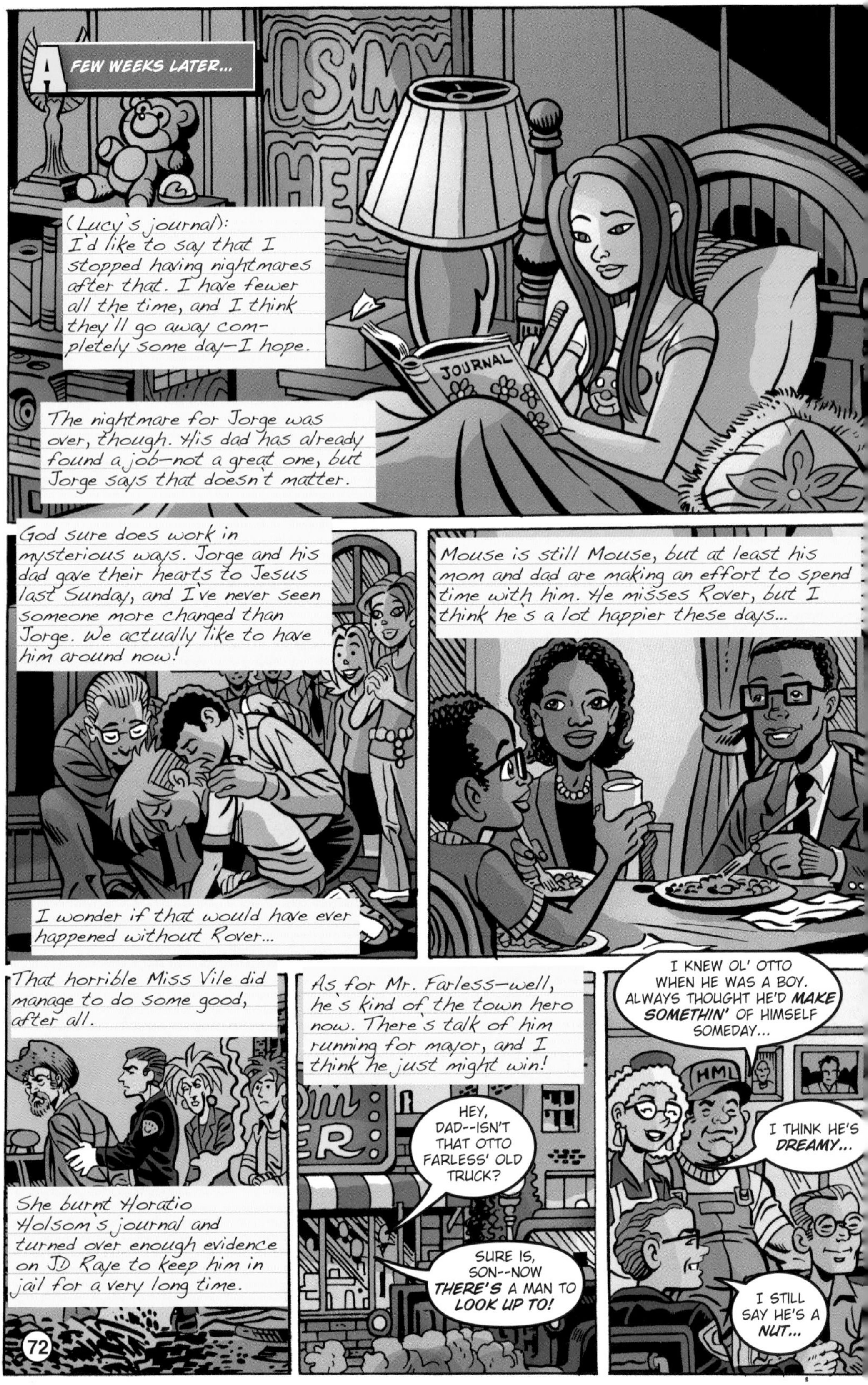
A FEW WEEKS LATER...
(Lucy's journal):
I'd like to say that I stopped having nightmares after that. I have fewer all the time, and I think they'll go away completely some day—I hope.
JOURNAL
The nightmare for Jorge was over, though. His dad has already found a job—not a great one, but Jorge says that doesn't matter.
God sure does work in mysterious ways. Jorge and his dad gave their hearts to Jesus last Sunday, and I've never seen someone more changed than Jorge. We actually like to have him around now!
I wonder if that would have ever happened without Rover...
Mouse is still Mouse, but at least his mom and dad are making an effort to spend time with him. He misses Rover, but I think he's a lot happier these days...
That horrible Miss Vile did manage to do some good, after all.
She burnt Horatio Holsom's journal and turned over enough evidence on JD Raye to keep him in jail for a very long time.
As for Mr. Farless—well, he's kind of the town hero now. There's talk of him running for mayor, and I think he just might win!
HEY, DAD--ISN'T THAT OTTO FARLESS' OLD TRUCK?
SURE IS, SON--NOW **THERE'S** A MAN TO **LOOK UP TO!**
I KNEW OL' OTTO WHEN HE WAS A BOY. ALWAYS THOUGHT HE'D **MAKE SOMETHIN'** OF HIMSELF SOMEDAY...
HML
I THINK HE'S **DREAMY...**
I STILL SAY HE'S A **NUT...**

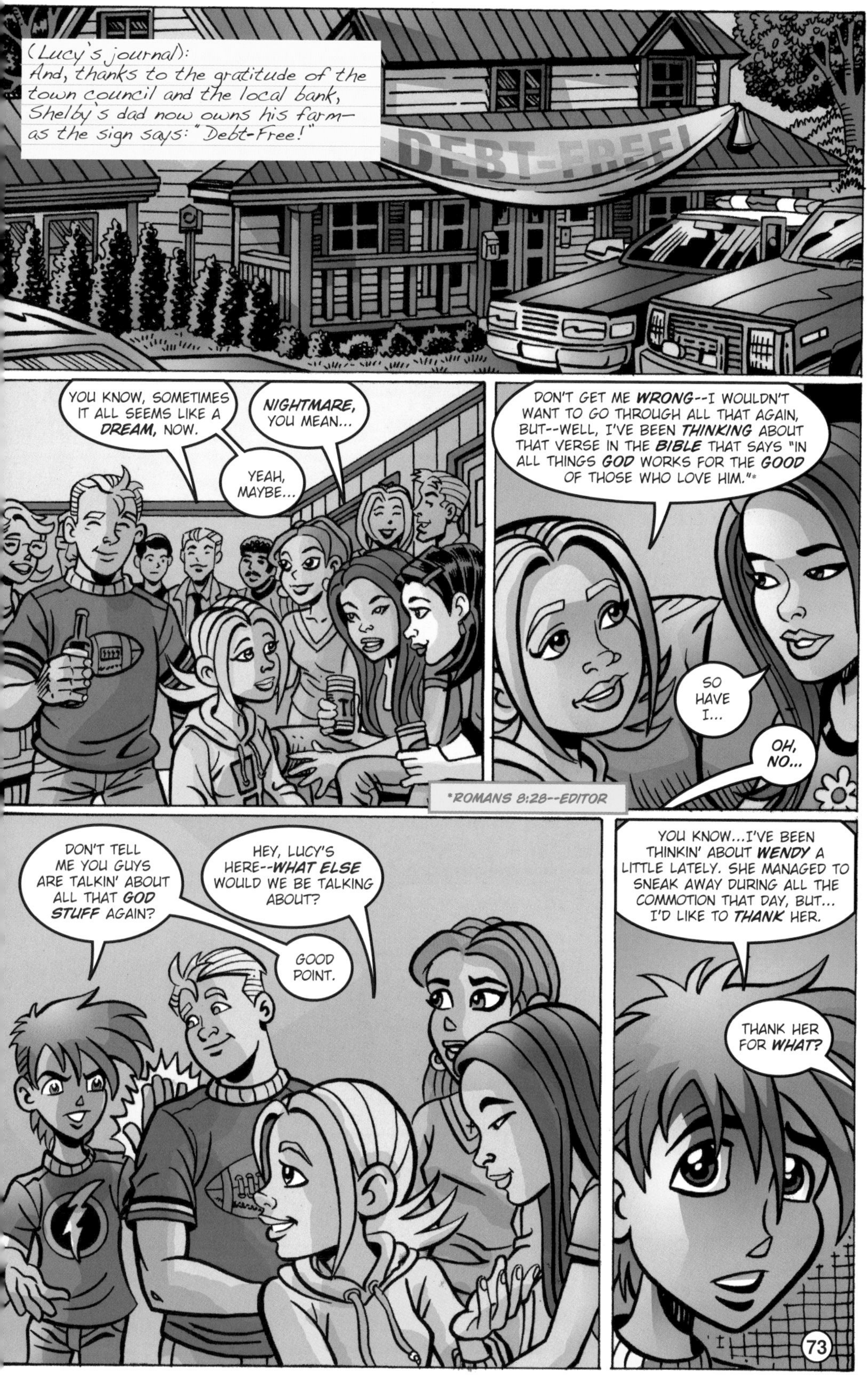
(Lucy's journal):
And, thanks to the gratitude of the town council and the local bank, Shelby's dad now owns his farm—as the sign says: "Debt-Free!"
DEBT-FREE!
YOU KNOW, SOMETIMES IT ALL SEEMS LIKE A DREAM, NOW.
NIGHTMARE, YOU MEAN...
YEAH, MAYBE...
DON'T GET ME WRONG--I WOULDN'T WANT TO GO THROUGH ALL THAT AGAIN, BUT--WELL, I'VE BEEN THINKING ABOUT THAT VERSE IN THE BIBLE THAT SAYS "IN ALL THINGS GOD WORKS FOR THE GOOD OF THOSE WHO LOVE HIM."*
SO HAVE I...
OH, NO...
*ROMANS 8:28--EDITOR
DON'T TELL ME YOU GUYS ARE TALKIN' ABOUT ALL THAT GOD STUFF AGAIN?
HEY, LUCY'S HERE--WHAT ELSE WOULD WE BE TALKING ABOUT?
GOOD POINT.
YOU KNOW...I'VE BEEN THINKIN' ABOUT WENDY A LITTLE LATELY. SHE MANAGED TO SNEAK AWAY DURING ALL THE COMMOTION THAT DAY, BUT... I'D LIKE TO THANK HER.
THANK HER FOR WHAT?

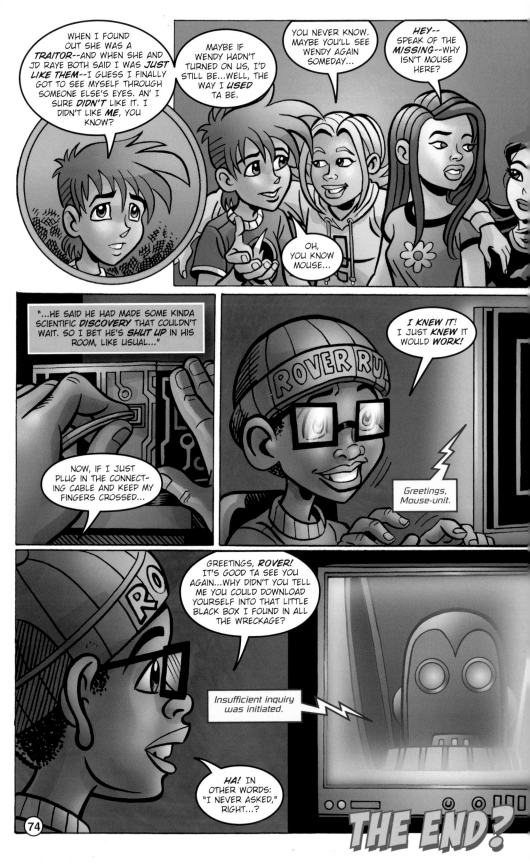

WHEN I FOUND OUT SHE WAS A *TRAITOR*--AND WHEN SHE AND JD RAYE BOTH SAID I WAS *JUST LIKE THEM*--I GUESS I FINALLY GOT TO SEE MYSELF THROUGH SOMEONE ELSE'S EYES. AN' I SURE *DIDN'T* LIKE IT. I DIDN'T LIKE *ME*, YOU KNOW?

MAYBE IF WENDY HADN'T TURNED ON US, I'D STILL BE...WELL, THE WAY I *USED* TA BE.

YOU NEVER KNOW. MAYBE YOU'LL SEE WENDY AGAIN SOMEDAY...

HEY-- SPEAK OF THE *MISSING*--WHY ISN'T MOUSE HERE?

OH, YOU KNOW MOUSE...

"...HE SAID HE HAD MADE SOME KINDA SCIENTIFIC *DISCOVERY* THAT COULDN'T WAIT. SO I BET HE'S *SHUT UP* IN HIS ROOM, LIKE USUAL..."

NOW, IF I JUST PLUG IN THE CONNECT- ING CABLE AND KEEP MY FINGERS CROSSED...

I KNEW IT! I JUST *KNEW* IT WOULD *WORK!*

Greetings, Mouse-unit.

GREETINGS, *ROVER!* IT'S GOOD TA SEE YOU AGAIN...WHY DIDN'T YOU TELL ME YOU COULD DOWNLOAD YOURSELF INTO THAT LITTLE BLACK BOX I FOUND IN ALL THE WRECKAGE?

Insufficient inquiry was initiated.

HA! IN OTHER WORDS: "I NEVER ASKED," RIGHT...?

74

THE END?

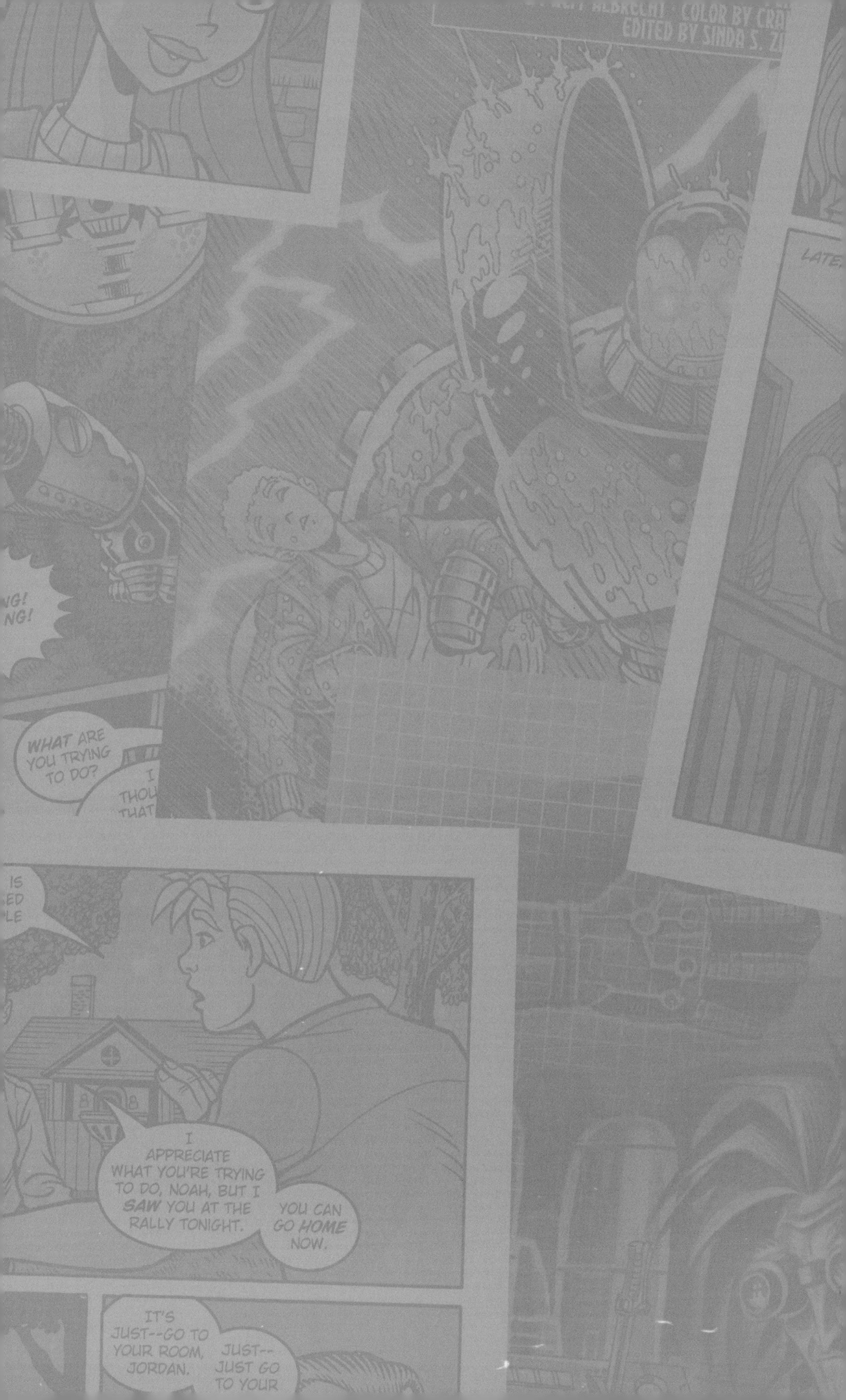
WHAT ARE YOU TRYING TO DO?
I APPRECIATE WHAT YOU'RE TRYING TO DO, NOAH, BUT I SAW YOU AT THE RALLY TONIGHT.
YOU CAN GO HOME NOW.
IT'S JUST--GO TO YOUR ROOM, JORDAN.
JUST-- JUST GO TO YOUR

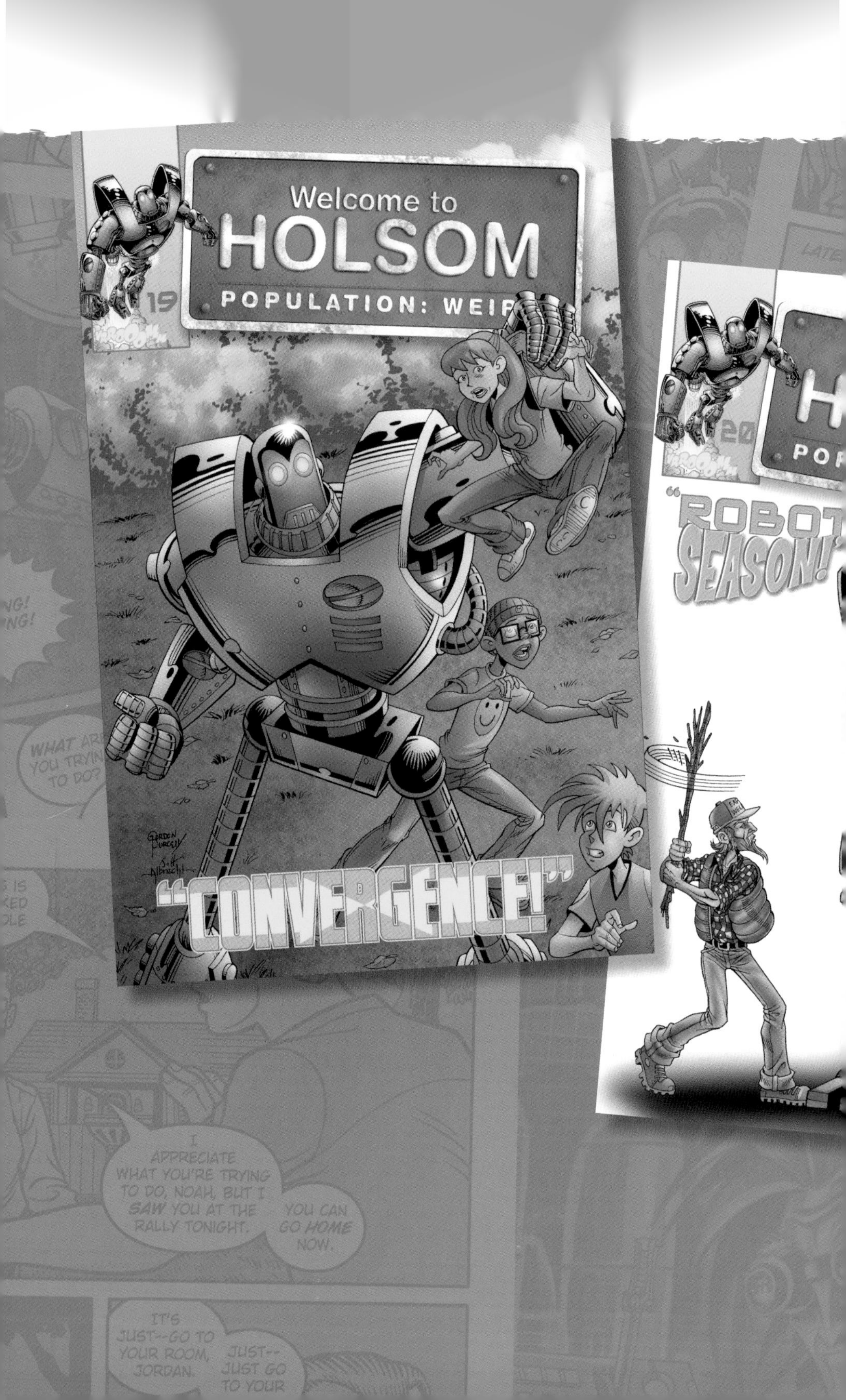
Welcome to
HOLSOM
POPULATION: WEIR
19
"CONVERGENCE!"
20
POP
"ROBOT
SEASON!"
WHAT ARE YOU TRYIN TO DO?
I APPRECIATE WHAT YOU'RE TRYING TO DO, NOAH, BUT I SAW YOU AT THE RALLY TONIGHT.
YOU CAN GO HOME NOW.
IT'S JUST--GO TO YOUR ROOM, JORDAN.
JUST-- JUST GO TO YOUR

COVER GALLERY

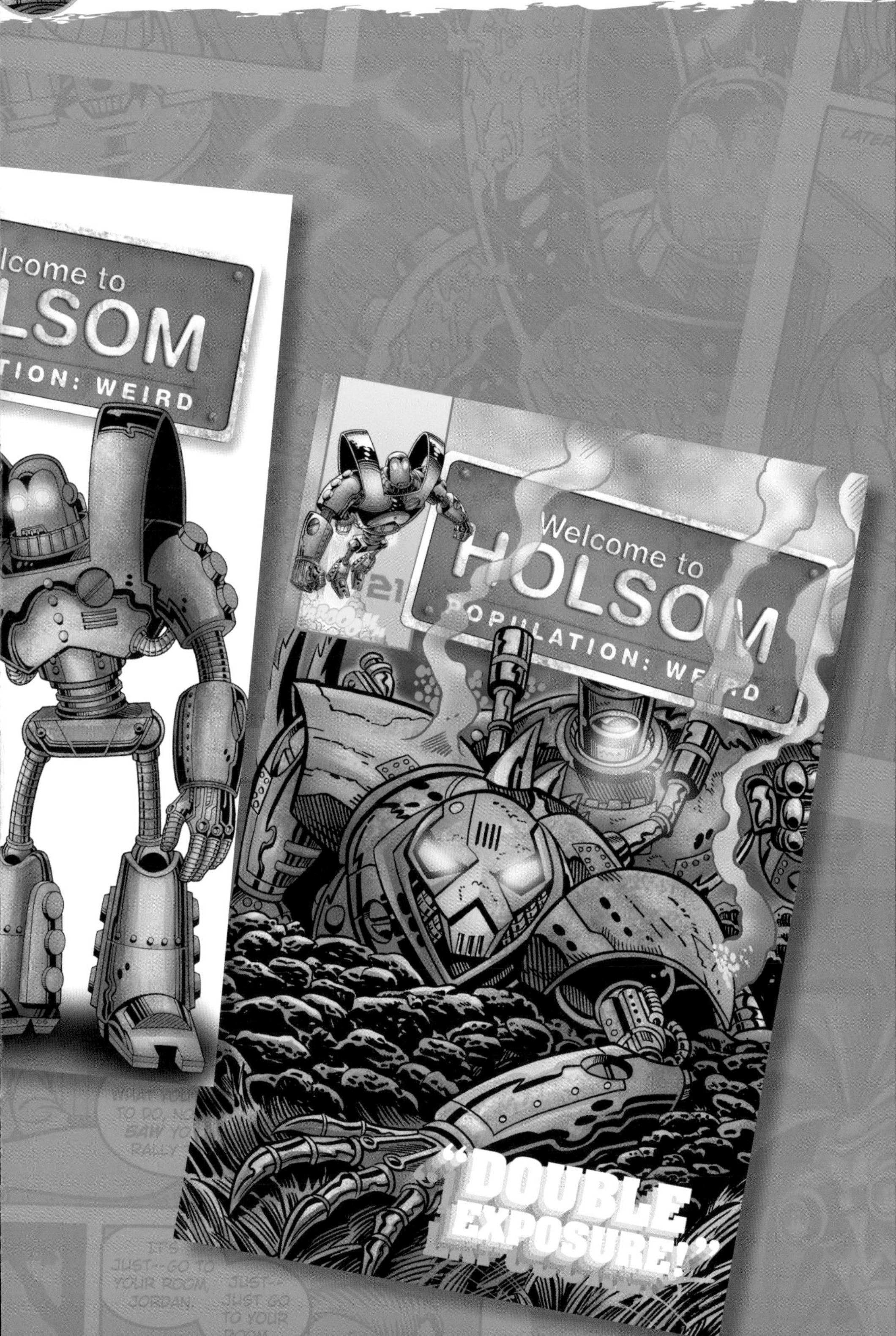

Welcome to
HOLSOM
POPULATION: WEIRD
"DOUBLE EXPOSURE!"
IT'S JUST--GO TO YOUR ROOM, JORDAN.

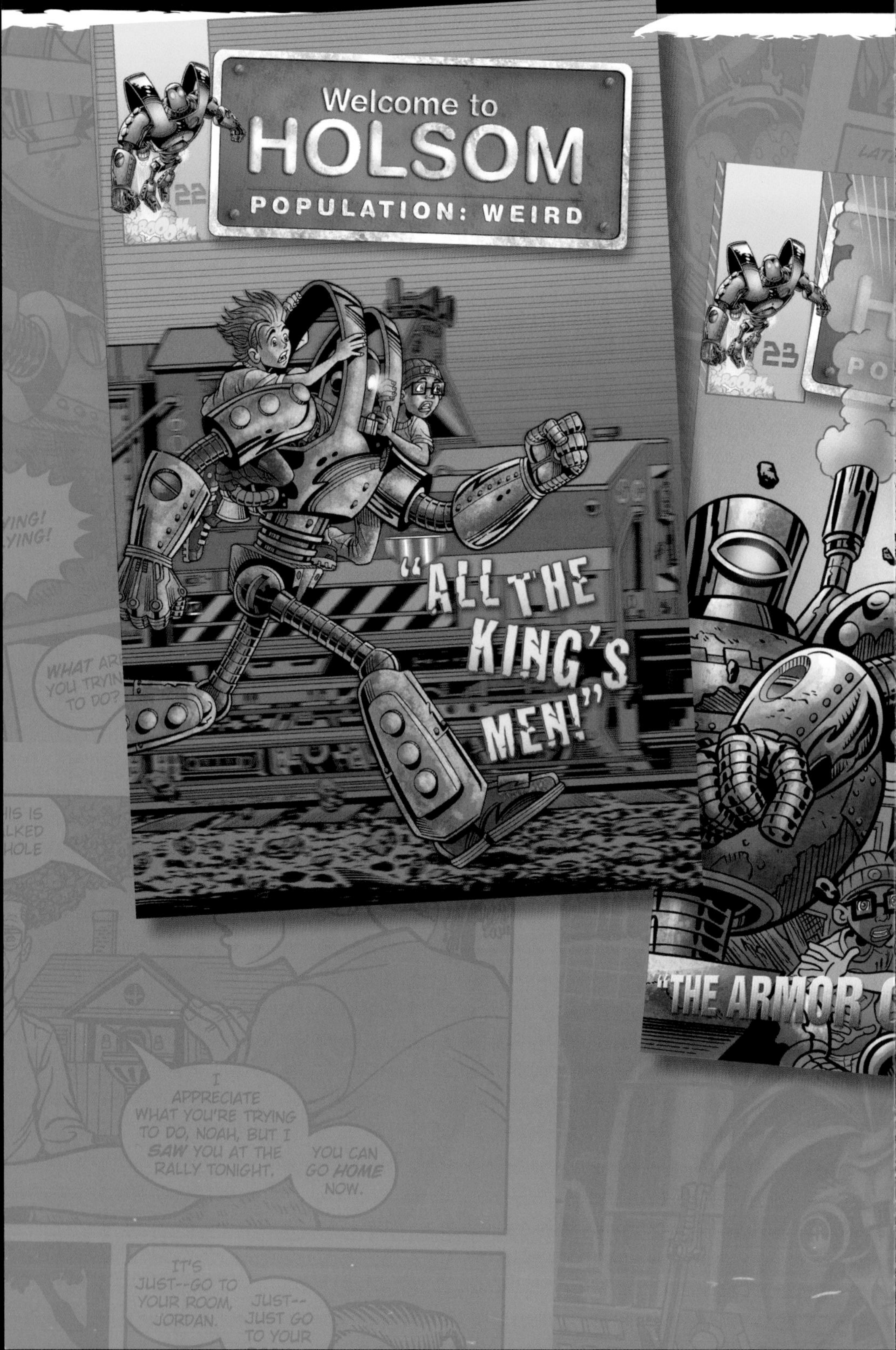
Welcome to HOLSOM
POPULATION: WEIRD
22
"ALL THE KING'S MEN!"
23
I APPRECIATE WHAT YOU'RE TRYING TO DO, NOAH, BUT I SAW YOU AT THE RALLY TONIGHT.
YOU CAN GO HOME NOW.
IT'S JUST--GO TO YOUR ROOM, JORDAN.
JUST-- JUST GO TO YOUR

COVER GALLERY

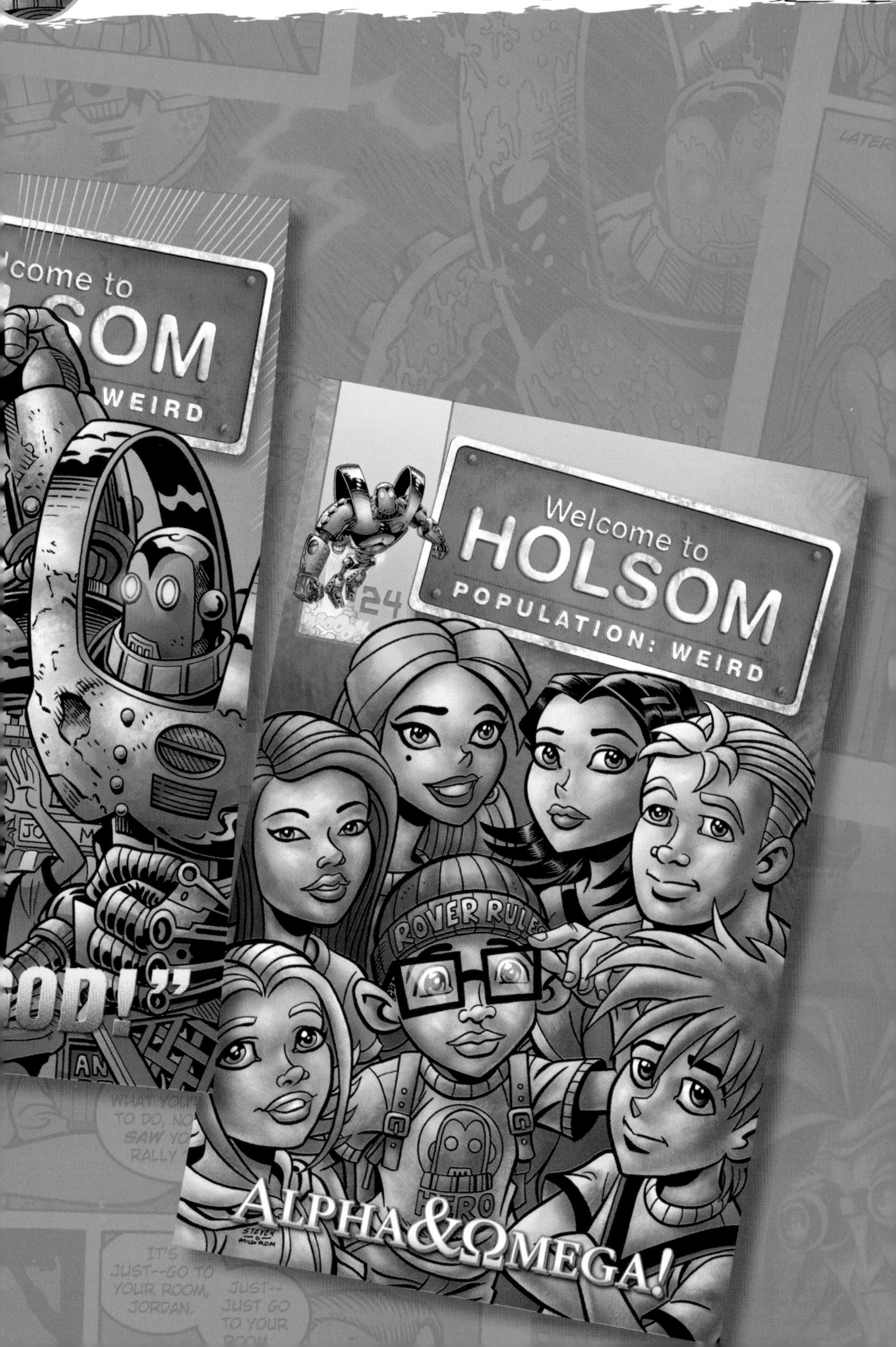

Welcome to
HOLSOM
POPULATION: WEIRD
ROVER RULES
HERO
ALPHA&ΩMEGA!
IT'S JUST--GO TO YOUR ROOM, JORDAN.
JUST-- JUST GO TO YOUR

WELCOME TO
HOLSOM

www.welcometoholsom.com